# VICTOR & ME IN PARIS

# VICTOR & ME IN PARIS

## An Imogene Durant Mystery

By Janice MacDonald

Victor & Me in Paris
© Janice MacDonald 2024

Published by Ravenstone, an imprint of Turnstone Press
Artspace Building, 206-100 Arthur Street
Winnipeg, MB. R3B 1H3 Canada
www.TurnstonePress.com

All rights reserved. No part of this book may be reproduced or transmitted in any form or by any means—graphic, electronic or mechanical—without the prior written permission of the publisher. Any request to photocopy any part of this book shall be directed in writing to Access Copyright, Toronto.

Turnstone Press gratefully acknowledges the assistance of the Canada Council for the Arts, the Manitoba Arts Council, the Government of Canada through the Canada Book Fund, and the Province of Manitoba through the Book Publishing Tax Credit and the Book Publisher Marketing Assistance Program.

This novel is a work of fiction. Names, characters, places and incidents are either the product of the author's imagination or are used fictitiously, and any resemblance to actual persons living or dead, events or locales, is entirely coincidental.

Printed and bound in Canada by Friesens.

Library and Archives Canada Cataloguing in Publication

Title: Victor & me in Paris : an Imogene Durant mystery / by Janice MacDonald.
Other titles: Victor and me in Paris
Names: MacDonald, Janice E. (Janice Elva), 1959- author
Description: Series statement: The Imogene Durant mysteries
Identifiers: Canadiana (print) 20240486048 | Canadiana (ebook) 20240486293 | ISBN 9780888017925 (softcover) | ISBN 9780888017932 (EPUB) | ISBN 9780888017949 (PDF)
Subjects: LCGFT: Detective and mystery fiction. | LCGFT: Novels.
Classification: LCC PS8575.D6325 V53 2024 | DDC C813/.54—dc23

*This one is for my mom,
who would have happily been along for the ride.*

# VICTOR & ME IN PARIS

# Mise en scène of the Crime

It had been a post-pandemic bureaucratic decision to get rid of the ice machines in hotels and motels because of sanitary issues. As with buffets, it was deemed a risk to have various people digging in the machines to fill their buckets and deposit their germs. Monsieur Passi had decided that the kitchen would fill orders for ice from the room service line, and so today it was Guy's task to turn off the pipes leading to the machines in the hall on each floor, dig out the ice from each machine into the deep plastic wheelbarrow purchased especially for the task, and dry out the machines in preparation for their removal.

He had completed the process on floors Two and Four, thankful that an earlier management had decreed there would be machines only on every second floor of the hotel. He wheeled the wheelbarrow back into the elevator, having just dumped another load of ice cubes onto the growing glacier in the back alley.

The shut-off valve on floor Six was a bit sticky but nothing a shot of WD40 and a few minutes couldn't solve. In the meantime, he began to shovel out the ice, careful to prop the door open with the shim he had fashioned from a broom handle after the door of the machine on Two had almost cost him a finger. Never trust old hydraulics. That would be something he would impart to his child, if he ever had one.

A couple two doors from the ice machine alcove came out into the hall, laughing, and headed to the elevator. He nodded as they passed and the woman smiled at him. It was nice to see faces again now that most people felt comfortable enough to go without a mask when they weren't actually coughing up a lung. Of course, tourists seemed to feel they could wander about with impunity anyhow, he had noticed, as if infecting people in a foreign country whom they'd never see again was no matter. Had people always felt that way? Maybe that was how the fear of strangers began, not with distrust first but a knowledge that strangers would never have your safety as a consideration.

He turned back to the job at hand. The valve should be ready to roll, and it was. What had Cousin Jacques once said? Everything could be solved with either duct tape or WD40. The machine fell silent as the water stopped seeping into the icemaking section at the top. Guy unplugged the electrical cord from the wall. By the time he had dug out the ice from the cooler section, the ice tray would have dripped down and could be opened and dried with a chamois. He got back to work with the plastic shovel he had picked up in the automotive section of the Castorama when he bought the wheelbarrow. He had one like it in the back of his car, for digging himself out of ruts. This one was bright pink because that was all that was left in stock. The one in his car was neon green.

Micheline, one of the housekeeping staff, stepped off the elevator, pulling the slotted tray holder, to pick up the room service trays left out in the hallway. Guy approved of housekeeping's system in the Grand. They cleared the halls early before check-out time, so that business people heading to their important meetings didn't have to skirt around sloppy trays of leftovers, and families checking out could pull their luggage cleanly down the halls. It helped out the maids pushing their massive cleaning carts, too, not to have to navigate around the detritus from the previous evening's meals.

"*Alors*, Guy, how's it going?"

"*Pas mal*. Not a job I'd want to do every day, but I'm getting into the swing of it. Should be done all of them by the end of tomorrow, I figure."

"You'll have a mountain of ice built up by then! It will be a good place to stand this afternoon when the temperature hits twenty-seven degrees, no? We'll all be thanking you for that." She smiled and lifted a tray to slot it into place before waving and pushing on down the corridor.

Micheline was one of the nicer people on staff, Guy thought. Maybe he should find her on his break and ask her out while they were standing and cooling by his ice-cube mountain. He watched her work down the hall to the bend, and then turned back to the job at hand.

Another two shovels' worth of ice went into the wheelbarrow. He faced the machine, keeping his elbows close to his body to keep from pulling a muscle, and pushed the pink shovel into the ice. It bit and went in several centimetres before stopping, meeting resistance. Guy had felt this happen with the machine on floor Four, where a block of ice had formed from older ice cubes, probably when a kid had left the door open too long. Or not a kid. An irresponsible adult could have just as easily been the culprit. He pushed a bit harder but still couldn't budge the blockage. He moved his shovel to the left of the block and pushed in, and took away a scoop. He did the same thing to the right. And once again on either side. Pulling on his suede work gloves, he reached in to the machine to dislodge the ice in front of the blockage. If he could manage it, he would lift out the ice block and then scoop out the rest of the ice cubes.

The ice in front slid easily away as he ruffled at the surface with his hands, leaving visible something entirely unexpected. Guy heard a guttural gasp, a sound from deep in the gut, and then realized it had come from him. He gulped and blinked, and then backed away from the ice machine and reached for his cell phone to call Monsieur Passi, the manager of the Grand.

In the centre of the ice, bluer than the centre of any of the cubes he had been shovelling, was a human foot, severed about fifteen centimetres above the ankle knobs. From where Guy was standing, he could make out the big toe, and while he waited for Monsieur Passi to answer, he noted that it was a left foot.

By the time all the ice machines had been taped off and emptied, several body parts had been discovered.

**Eh bien, what are we looking at?**

Toni's boss, Commander Leclaire, was texting her on the encrypted police channel. In deference to his age and seniority, she resisted any texting shorthand in response.

> Un coeur, one hand with what might be an engagement ring on the finger, two feet severed, possibly sawed, approximately fifteen centimetres above the ankle bones, a breast with what appears to be a partial tattoo near the nipple, and a finger.

**Are we looking at a young woman?**

> Sir?

She began to type, but Leclaire's new text overrode her. Just as if he was in the same room with her, she marvelled cynically.

> The body parts. You said there is a tattoo. What is the skin condition like? Taut? Wrinkled?

>> Frozen at the moment. Hard to say.

> But given the ring, the tattoo, would you estimate age at below fifty?

>> That wouldn't be for me to say, sir. I think we need to keep an open mind as we tackle Missing Persons for leads.

> Agreed. Is the scene secured?

>> Coroner has arrived. She's on the tenth floor at the moment. We've stopped excavation on the advice of Forensics, who are moving slower through the ice. I sent our folks down to the ice pile out back to revisit it, since there might be smaller pieces that weren't noticed already out there.

> Let me know the minute you think we can make the announcement to find the relatives of this woman.

>> Women.

> Pardon?

> People, in fact. This is more than one body, sir, and we cannot be certain yet that they are all women.

> How do we know it's more than one body, Lamothe?

> The feet, sir. They're both left feet.

There was some satisfaction in startling her boss, Toni had to admit. She had been a violent crimes investigator for going on ten years now, but due to her physical stature and probably her name, it took a lot of effort to hold her own in the testosterone-laden world of the Sûreté.

Detective Inspector Antoinette Lamothe had always wanted to be a police officer, even when all her friends were considering becoming astronauts or fashion designers. It stemmed from the satisfaction she got in finishing a puzzle, tying up the loose ends and following her hunches through a maze to the correct answer. She had admitted to herself long ago that her desire to keep the public safe and content came a low second to her impulse to solve a puzzling crime.

And this was a stumper for certain.

She did not want to be relegated to desk work on this case. She wanted to lead this investigation. And that wasn't going to happen if Commander Leclaire sent her away this soon. Taking a deep breath and squaring her shoulders, she typed another message into the textbox.

> May I suggest we continue here until Forensics are satisfied that all human remains have been discovered and accounted for? I can ask the hotel manager for a space to set up an onsite task force room.

> All right, Lamothe. However, let me stress to you that there is as yet no task force assigned.

> Yes sir.

Toni smiled. She had sown the seeds and it was all she could do. If there was a task force, she wanted to be the person calling the shots from the start. And Leclaire knew it. Everything in the Sûreté began with tacit understanding, and without that second-sense ability to read between the lines, an officer got nowhere. Toni didn't intend to get nowhere.

She clicked off the display of her phone and slid it into her pocket. It was time to find Monsieur Passi, the manager of this fine establishment, and set up a Murder Room. It occurred to her that somewhere in this hotel had already been a murder room, the cause of hers, to much different effect.

Monsieur Var Passi was a pleasant man who was obviously trying to keep the police presence to a minimum in his hotel. "We were told to remove the ice machines," he had explained. "It was an edict from the main office of the chain. Our sense was that they were not utilized that much in our hotel, probably not in the same manner as in the North American sister hotels. The idea of ice in every drink is a much more North American concept, I believe?"

Toni nodded. It was true, she didn't note a lot of ice being used in restaurants and bars. Usually the water brought to a table was bottled, either still or sparkling, and the bottle itself had been refrigerated, so no need for ice in the glass. And walking down a hall or even up a floor to get a bucket of ice filled seemed an oddly vulnerable thing to do, as well. Would guests walk in their sock feet? Would they forget to take their room keys? Would they worry about finding body parts in the mound of cubes?

A week later, the police presence in the hotel was becoming almost commonplace to the staff, who nodded politely as Toni and her team met them in the halls.

She had been right to ask for the conference room in the hotel for a command centre because there were enough electrical outlets for the equipment her team had hauled in. And the team allotted to her was almost everything she could have asked for. Of course, if she were thinking cynically, she might have thought her commander was giving her enough rope to hang herself with on a case that had no promotional value. But Toni refused to fall into that negative thinking.

This was going to be the way she proved herself to her superiors that she had what it took to rise within the ranks of Serious Crimes.

The coroner had returned the findings that there were remains of at least three people in their discovery. And that was just preliminary, based on blood type. They were still waiting for the DNA results, which could take months. After all, cold cases, and her body parts had been dead a while, didn't move to the front of the line, even if they denoted a possible serial killer. The coroner had underlined to Toni that it was entirely possible that one or more of the victims shared a blood type, meaning they had more than three victims.

Three would do for starters, though. Toni had one of her team combing the missing persons database for reports of people whose blood type had been listed and who had been gone more than three months, which was what the coroner believed the latest possible entry into the ice would have been. It had been Toni's idea to widen the search internationally, given that they might have been travellers staying in the hotel. It was just as likely that they were locals lured up to the killer's room, but for what reason beyond the actual purpose of dismemberment? It wasn't as if anyone was going to follow someone up to a hotel room with the promise of being chopped to pieces. There would have been some form of patter, some promise of delight, or profit.

"This is a very respectable hotel, Detective Inspector,"

Monsieur Passi was saying. He sat across from her at what had become a regular meeting every two days. His use of the word "respectable" brought Toni's thoughts abruptly to those of call girls being ordered up. Of course, call girls could look like one's maths teacher; they didn't all rig themselves out on the cheap. How would Monsieur Passi actually know who was using his hotel and for what purpose?

"How do visitors access guests here? If someone was coming to visit?" Toni asked.

"There is a telephone in the lobby for visitors to call up to a suite, but they have to know the suite number of the guest who is their friend. Then, if their friend wishes them to come up to the room, he or she can offer them a code for the elevator."

"And if they don't know their friend's room?"

"They would come to the front desk to ask for the person, and the concierge would call up to the room for them, without revealing the room number. If the guest wishes to speak to them, they are put through to the lobby phone. Otherwise, we take a message."

"But there is no way for a stranger to just get in the elevator and go up to a room?"

"Guests have to touch their keycard to the elevator pad or enter a code before pressing the floor buttons. It's very state of the art."

"And how often do you change the code?"

Monsieur Passi had the grace to blush a bit. "That is something I have been campaigning for, but it would require a more complex program and printing system for check-in. We haven't changed the code in the time we've had the system, which is, I believe, three years now."

Toni looked at him, and he shrugged in the way of all Frenchmen.

"We have had very little theft or harassment issues reported. I believe with this and our CCTV, we are a very secure building."

"And yet …"

"Yes, and yet."

# Planning Is Half the Fun

Imogene pulled the jeans out of her suitcase with bad grace. Diane had been horrified to hear she was thinking of taking denim at all to Paris.

"Imogene, you are going to be surrounded by women who would rather wear burlap than be seen in jeans. Paris is the nucleus of style and fashion. And denim is the flag of the blue-collar Monday and casual Friday."

"You don't need to rub it in. I am heading to a land where the women started smoking in kindergarten to achieve their parchment skin stretched over aquiline bone structure looks. And in I shall galumph, looming like some corn-fed Venus, unable to fit into any of their little black sleeveless mock turtlenecks and capri pants."

"You've been watching Claudine Longet movies again, haven't you? Why can't you just Duolingo your way into getting ready for your trip like an ordinary mortal?"

"Just let me know if you want me to turn down the Charles

Aznavour," Imogene nodded toward the stereo and laughed at her far more practical friend.

Diane was probably right. The way to prepare for a trip to a foreign country would be to ground yourself in at least the basics of the language, temperature, and mores of the populace. Instead, Imogene had rewatched a season of *Call My Agent,* added brie to her grocery basket, and ordered a copy of *Le Flâneur.*

Stepping into the unknown was both the appeal of the plan and the reason for her anxiety. Imogene had never been to France; she had rarely travelled internationally unless for a conference and she wasn't assured that the proper little-girl French from her childhood years in the convent school would see her through. Still, she had dreamed up the trip and told people about it, and set the wheels in motion; she couldn't back out now.

Actually, the dreaming up of the whole concept had been done by Mariel, her editor, who was still delighted with the sales of Imogene's first not-strictly academic book, and who was hoping for a second hit, or preferably a string of hits. "A female Bill Bryson with a literary twist" was how she'd put it. Imogene wasn't entirely sure she could pull off another *Fyodor & Me in Russia,* but she wasn't going to say no to a trip to Paris in the springtime. It would be a nice way to ring in the new age of retirement from university teaching Comparative Literature.

It was also, she thought, an exercise in being intentionally solitary, rather than being pushed into a solo existence through the will of someone else. It hadn't been her idea to end her thirty-year marriage. And for the first year, she had floundered a bit. She hadn't wanted to call too much attention to her situation, mostly because she didn't want the kids to worry about her, and partially because of the shame of it all. Of not being enough. Of having failed the assignment. Of realizing she'd never get the future she'd been paying into for so long, with every compromise and shift and adjustment she had silently made. No retirement walks down the beach hand in hand with her complementary greying partner, like in the old "freedom 55" advertisements.

Now, after a year of too many jigsaw puzzles and cooking too much for supper when she didn't opt for a bowl of cereal, she was waking up to the realization that her life was more than marginally better as a single woman. She had no monetary worries, since her needs were simple and she no longer had to worry about the far more boisterous spending patterns of her ex-husband. She had a list of "better nows" that her few visits to a terrifically grounded therapist had suggested creating, and it grew almost every day. The first one on the list was one she considered daily: she could dress with the light on and sit on the side of the bed to pull on her tights, instead of creeping out to the walk-in closet to dress balancing on one leg while he slept for another hour. She also no longer had to rise early on weekends to get her yoga and meditation in before he awoke and changed the patterns of the air to something less serene.

She loved her new apartment, with everything placed

where she wanted it and the sun streaming in windows that didn't need to be shuttered against rays that would fade the cushions or crack the leather. None of her furniture was worth much, besides her great-grandfather's rocking chair, and it had weathered more than a hundred years — it could handle a bit of sunshine.

Her plants would need watering the six weeks she was away. She was hoping her friend Lydia would take her keys and come over to do it, but if not, she could rely on Daniel, a former work colleague, or Marjorie, her daughter, to drop by at least once a week. Lydia, however, didn't have half the streaming services that Imogene indulged in. If she could help with offering an entertainment oasis and get her plants seen to at the same time, they'd both be happy.

Her luggage needed to be lightweight and minimal. She didn't want to be needing porters or losing track of multiple bags. One cross-body strap carry-on, one mid-sized checked suitcase, and her thin shoulder bag that fit inside her coat holding her cards, euros, passport, and the bank draft for the rent. She could manage a month on a micro-wardrobe, seeing as how nothing she wore would even come close to the effortless *chic* of Parisiennes. And it wasn't as if she were dressing for the office; she could wear the same outfit three days in a row and no one would notice. Black trousers, five T-shirts, a black cardigan, her oversized green sweater to wear on the plane and in case of a chilly spell, two wrinkle-resistant dresses, her flowery black blouse, a pencil skirt for dressier occasions, tights and underwear. She wasn't dressing to impress. More like dressing to blend into the background. She wanted to observe rather than be observed.

Her hairdresser was a little skeptical of her plan. "You are nearly six feet tall with giant red curly hair. You're going to be noticed, no matter what you wear."

She had to admit he was right. She would likely be noticed. So be it. She tossed the blue jeans back into the suitcase.

# Imogene in Paris

"Imogene Durant. That is a French name, no?"

"Canadian, but yes, of French descent."

"Ah, are you from Quebec?"

"*Non, je suis Franco-Albertaine,*" Imogene smiled and trotted out her best French, with the same strain that she always felt when having to explain that a very large, in fact the third largest, French-Canadian cluster was in none other than supposedly redneck, white-bread Alberta. Her assertion wasn't quite true either; she was a highly anglicized descendent of French Huguenots. But she wasn't entirely sure enough about how water had flowed under that particular bridge in France to be bringing that up.

The customs official smiled at her, stamped her passport, tucked her vaccination report into the back cover, and slid it all back to her. "*Bienvenue en France*, enjoy your visit."

She tucked her papers into the zippered pocket of the

leather purse hanging inside her coat, and smiled back at him. "*Merci beaucoup!*"

After a long hike and a tram ride to another part of the airport, retrieving her suitcase was a painless affair. She took a moment to sort out sliding her carry-on satchel onto the stretch handle of her suitcase, making it all of a piece. The way to the train was well marked, and Raymonde, her landlady, had told her exactly which train to look for and what station to aim for, even what the cost would be. She had purchased enough euros at home to have some immediate cash at hand, but Raymonde had also let her know her credit card would work without a hitch on most touchpads.

It had been a blessing to find a housing agent who was so sympathetic and personable, at least by email. She didn't want to impose, but it was daunting to consider all the things she didn't even know she didn't know about navigating Paris. Her stack of guidebooks were more the stuff of daydreams than practical advice, which she had optimistically taken to mean that Paris would be much like any large foreign city, and she had been in several of those: London, New York, Frankfurt, San Francisco, Guadalajara, Toronto, Reykjavik. And, of course, Saint Petersburg.

It would be different because she would be alone this time. In the past she had travelled with a husband, one or both of her now grown children, or with colleagues to a conference. This was going to be her maiden voyage alone, and more as a crone than a maiden. Not that she felt like a crone. She was certainly in better shape than she had been in years, thanks to the tidy little gym in her apartment building and her determination to walk whenever possible.

And here she was, propelled up out of the deep underground train station at Les Halles, searching for the signs Raymonde had told her to look out for. Sure enough, with minimal hesitation, she strode out the appropriate doorway and soon found the correct side street. Two short blocks, past interesting shops and several very inviting outdoor cafés with tables spilling around the corner, and she was there.

And there was a handsome older woman, wearing a navy jacket, a crisp white shirt, a scarf, and blue jeans. She would have to mention the jeans to Diane. It had to be Raymonde. She came toward her with an inquisitive smile.

"Imogene?"

"Raymonde? I hope I haven't kept you waiting too long. Your directions were perfection." Since they had been communicating previously entirely in English, Imogene took a chance at addressing her in English, which seemed fine with Raymonde. They shook hands and Raymonde insisted on taking hold of Imogene's suitcase. She obligingly pulled the carry-on off the handle and followed her landlady through the doorway of a seventeenth-century building that would probably still be standing when they'd pulled every structure in Edmonton down and rebuilt them seven more times.

"As I said in my email, there is no elevator, but there is no shame in resting a bit on each level," Raymonde smiled over her shoulder. "The fob will get you in the front door, and the key is for your door. We haven't bothered with a mailbox key, since I come by a couple of times a week to empty it, and will pop anything that may come for you under your door, if that's all right with you?"

By now they were three quarters of the way up the second level of the curving, almost circular staircase, and Imogene was wondering why she had worried about the climb. The rise of these stairs were perfect for her stride and she felt a soothing removal of worry. Her knees had never been good, and arthritis had begun to erode the cartilage early on, but she had aimed for strengthening the surrounding muscles, to avoid or at least delay the thought of knee replacement surgery. Her daughter had worried about the stairs and walking she was planning, and while Imogene had brushed it off, she had been secretly worried herself. Now she was more at ease. She could see herself popping downstairs for morning coffee at the nearby café and then reclimbing the stairs easily to get ready for her day.

There were doors every so often, one per every small, twisty level, and most of them showed some sign of individuality. The door where Raymonde eventually stopped and inserted the key had a welcome mat in front and a knocker on the door, right above a peephole. The number 6 was painted in calligraphy on the side of the door jamb. It seemed cleaner and more inviting than the door marked 5 they had just passed, which looked as if three centuries of marauders had attempted entry by scraping the paint and dinging the wood panels.

"The building is shaped like an L, with a sort of half level shift for each apartment. Yours faces south and west, while the ones below and above look north. Every suite is separately owned," Raymonde explained, "like your North American condominium concept. There are certain aspects to be maintained, but on the whole, the owner is able to do anything they want to the interior, within reason. Some of the owners have used the high ceilings, and built mezzanines with loft beds, but one must hunch over to utilize the space. I myself think it is better to work with the bones of the building to produce a harmonious effect, and this is what has been created here."

She waved her arm with a flourish, like a game show presenter or magician's assistant, and Imogene stopped inside the threshold to admire the effect she was describing.

It was a lovely apartment, eclipsing the photos she had been sent. The corner living room received light from windows on two sides, and the bedroom's gauzy curtains gave it a pinkish glow in the afternoon sun. The kitchen, open to the living area, was all golden tile and shiny appliances, and the bathroom looked very modern for such an old building. Raymonde explained that the pipes in the building had been upgraded to accommodate everything and rarely were troublesome, but if something were to happen, she was only a phone call away.

After demonstrating how the oven and washing machine worked and how to control the heated towel rack, Raymonde noted the list with the wifi password and various numbers of local businesses. She mentioned that the café below was a very pleasant place, and gave directions to the nearest grocery store and bakery. Imogene assured her that she had brought a map and several guidebooks, and intended to find every cheese shop in a radius of three kilometres.

"I do hope you will be comfortable here, Imogene. The people in the building are, for the most part, very sympathetic, and most are quiet and well-behaved. We even have a police detective in one suite." Raymonde smiled conspiratorially. "Perhaps that's why everyone is quiet. Allow me to give you a call in a few days? To check in?"

"That would be lovely, thank you. I think this is going to be just perfect."

"And call me anytime, if you should need anything."

Pretty soon Imogene was on her own, and she headed to the window to watch Raymonde leave the front door and turn down the street opposite to the way she had come. She wondered idly where the landlady lived.

The trick to travelling without jetlag, she had been told, was to change your watch the minute you settled onto the airplane and have a shower immediately upon arrival. She had decided to follow the shower advice, and after a surprisingly brisk blast of strong water pressure, she towelled off with the luxuriously thick towel folded on a glass shelf at the other end of the tub, and padded out to the bedroom to dress. Since Raymonde had stocked the fridge with milk, six eggs, and a baguette, she had no need to go out foraging just yet. There was coffee in the cupboard and tea bags in a glass canister on the counter. Imogene decided to get out her map and guidebook and plot her exploration for the next morning.

The first thing she needed to see would be the Seine. Perhaps it was because of the North Saskatchewan River being such a central focus of her own hometown, or because of a study book she'd been given in junior high about a barge trip down rivers in France, but the Seine held a magic for her even greater than the Eiffel Tower as a symbol of Paris. In orienting her, Raymonde had said, "There's south, toward the Seine. If you walk in that direction for ten minutes and your feet get wet, you've gone a bit too far."

To hell with waiting till morning. She was in Paris and it was irresistible. While she didn't intend to get her feet wet, she could manage an early evening stroll to the river. It would still be light out for another two or three hours, after all. She followed the directions and soon found herself on the Pont Neuf, or New Bridge, ironically the oldest bridge in the city. The Seine slid beneath, placid between its concrete and stone banks, a graceful grande dame of a river. Imogene broke into a grin of delight.

And there, off to the right, she caught sight of the Eiffel Tower, and realized that, as touristy and oversold as it was, it held a magic for her too. She stood by the rampart of the bridge and snapped a quick picture on her phone. As she slid it back into its pocket in her purse, she pinched her wrist lightly. "Oh my god, I'm in Paris!"

# First Impressions

Imogene wondered what someone fanciful would make of her as she strolled past, wrapped in her trench coat with her carefully tied scarf at her neck. She knew she didn't look like a local. They were bundled up in down coats, thinking this warm spring air too chilly. And she didn't look German, because they all seemed too healthy. Her hair wasn't manageable enough to be European or blow dried enough to be American. And she was too tall to be anything but Scandinavian, but her colouring was all wrong for that. She smiled. There were likely no people watching her at all. And that was part of the beauty of this trip.

It was a time out from life. There was no one here to question her actions, no one to make demands on her time, except, of course, her editor. There weren't even any people here who wanted to engage her in conversation, because while she could manage well enough in French to get places, buy things, and ask questions, she was nowhere near fluent enough to discuss politics or the weather. And besides, the French she had met so far didn't appear to be the sort to expend energy on strangers.

There was a bag in the window of one of the small shops she went by that said *Rive Droite Fille*, and she presumed there was also corresponding Rive Gauche merchandise for sale. Although she didn't buy the bag, she knew she had become a Right Bank girl, for sure. Just as she was at home, comfortably ensconced on the side of the river that held both the grittier neighbourhoods along with the city hall, museum, art gallery, government centre, and most of the best restaurants. Across the river sat the university, wealthier enclaves, and Imogene's past. Paris had the same demarcation, with the Left Bank espousing the university and cultural elite and hosting the more bourgeois neighbourhoods rather than the edgy Pigalle and bohemian Montmartre of the Right Bank.

Funny how those sorts of alignments and partisanships happened.

She had spent the early part of the afternoon in the wee park at the tip of the Île de la Cité, reading and drinking tea from the Thermos she'd found in one of the kitchen cupboards. There was something so satisfying about sitting on a park bench in a foreign city with a Thermos. It seemed to mark you as a local. No one packed a Thermos for a holiday abroad.

She wasn't fooling herself into thinking that Parisians would mistake her for one of them. But she was hoping she fooled the bus tour groups clogging the corners near Notre Dame, just for a moment. True, she was taller than most of the women she passed on the street, and many of the men, but she took care to blend in as much as possible so she didn't stand out as an outsider. That's what came of reading Camus at an impressionable age, she laughed to herself.

Her first week had flown by, though Imogene knew she'd remember every moment of the days. She had found the bakery Raymonde had recommended and had taken herself to a museum every second day, so as not to have everything run together in her mind. After trying three separate cafés, she had determined that the Café Benjamin, with its glorious mosaic floor and pleasant wait staff, was going to be her regular haunt.

She had got into the habit of texting her son, Robin, in the morning with a vague idea of the day's itinerary. It made her feel just that bit better to know that if she were to disappear, her eldest could tell someone that she had "last been known to be heading to the Jardin des Plantes." Not that she thought a lawyer in Hamilton, Ontario, could do much to save her from imminent danger, and besides, she had no intention of being murdered in Paris. It seemed like the safest city one could possibly be a single woman in. Her safety radar had pinged only slightly the closer she walked towards Montmartre beyond the Galeries Lafayette, but she decided not to head in that direction after dark, and that was that.

And what a walkable city! Aside from all those steps up to Sacré-Cœur, which admittedly was worth the view, the roads were relatively straight and the sidewalks even. She was grateful for the spongy soles of her slip-on walking shoes, as she manoeuvred the cobblestones in the older streets and marvelled at some of the young girls running along in high heels. They were in a minority, though. And no one on the early-morning metro trains who poured out of the Les Halles station was wearing stilettos. They all had sneakers on, likely with pretty work shoes tucked into their backpacks or shoulder bags.

Having looked across at the Louvre for several hours from the Île, she strolled along the rue du Louvre on her way back to her apartment. Impulsively, she bought a ticket to get into the art displays at la Bourse de commerce, the round building that had once been the corn exchange and now housed modern art. Most of the days she'd been by, there had been lineups by the door, but today it seemed as if she could just waltz in, so she did. The building itself was as artistically worth seeing as the exhibits, and she spent over an hour wandering the circular halls and marvelling at the double helix staircases. She was taken by the humour of several artists and the emotion that could be wrought by large installations.

At one point, she looked out the window and realized the Bourse was on a straight-line trajectory with the Pompidou Centre, with the undulating roofs of Les Halles mall in-between. It was an interesting vision of modernistic Paris, landed in the very midst of some of the narrowest streets and oldest buildings in the city.

As usual, she went through the gift shop looking for souvenirs that would be light and flat to pack. She found several postcards of cartoonish maps of Paris that focused on Les Halles and la Bourse and, as a result, also featured her apartment. Just as she was considering a silk scarf for Diane, she heard a sound and turned to see a small mouse sticking its head out of a hole that had been made in the base of the wall of the gift shop. She realized with a start that the mouse was animatronic; it began to speak in a high, childish voice. She looked around to find out if anyone else was noticing this phenomenon, but there was no one else at her end of the gift shop.

The mouse retreated, and it was only then that she noticed a card off to the left, on the wall. The work was entitled *I... I... I...* and had been created by a British artist named Ryan Gander. Imogene snapped a picture of the card so she could look up more about the artist later, and then walked toward the hole, under which drywall detritus was scattered on the floor. That must drive the custodians crazy, she thought, trying not to sweep up the fine art as they cleaned the floors of the gift shop.

On her way home, she decided to brave the escalators and twists and turns in the Forum des Halles to pick up some soup and cheese at the Monoprix. After managing her self-checkout and bagging, and scanning her receipt at the automatic gate, she headed for the last escalator up and out of the grocery department store. She eyed the fancy pastries on the way out but didn't want to stop for yet another self-checkout. She nodded to the security man at the door, then turned right and right again, dodging pedestrians walking all over the street. She found her street and building, almost bumping into a young woman in a smart navy pantsuit looking at her phone. They both mumbled an apology and Imogene headed on to her door, fumbling in her purse for her key fob.

"*Je vous en prie,*" she heard behind her. It was the young woman with the phone, this time dangling her own key fob toward Imogene.

"*Je m'excuse,*" Imogene nodded and let the young woman ahead of her, while continuing to search for her keys to prove she too belonged through the door. Holding them aloft, she smiled at the young woman, who smiled back.

"*Nous sommes voisins, je crois.* Neighbours. *Je m'appelle Imogene.*" Taking a calculated risk that this professional-looking woman spoke English, Imogene reverted from her schoolgirl French into her own tongue. "I am here for the next few weeks," she volunteered.

The young woman smiled at her and replied in perfect English without any seeming irritation. "Welcome to Paris. I am Antoinette Lamothe, but call me Toni. I live here just below you, in *numéro 5.*"

"Ah, but not directly below. This is such an interesting and winding staircase."

"No, that is true. My windows face north, and my apartment stretches that way from the stairwell. It is as if the floors take half-steps."

"Perhaps that is why the ceilings are so nice and high."

"Yes, I love the light." The young woman smiled, and it was as if she herself lit up from within. Imogene realized that Toni Lamothe was a very beautiful woman, doing her best to hide that fact with a stern haircut and plainly designed, if beautifully cut, clothing. That was odd for this city of style and panache.

"I hope your stay is a pleasant one."

"Thank you." Imogene rushed her next sentence before Toni Lamothe had a chance to close her battered door. "Toni? May I take you out for a drink some time? It would be neighbourly, and a way to make up for crashing into you on the street. I'd love to get your take on elements of the neighbourhood and the city I should pay attention to. I am sorry to be forward, but I don't know anyone here, and I've not spoken to anyone except the odd sales clerk in almost a week."

Toni laughed. "I understand. Yes, I would like that. How about later this evening? Say, eight o'clock?"

"That would be lovely!"

Imogene felt herself bounding up the remaining stairs to her own door. A neighbour. A friendly neighbour. Project Citizen of Paris was underway.

# Antoinette of the Staircase

Imogene stood in front of Toni's door at five minutes to the hour, and was just about to knock when she heard the deadbolt turn. She took two steps back on the narrow landing, as if it would be less of a shock to find someone a metre away from you rather than right on your threshold.

Toni, who looked far less conservative in a white blouse and blue jeans, was made of sterner stuff than Imogene had feared, because her eyes widened only slightly and she smiled immediately. "*Ah bon*! I was just going to come knock on your door. Ready? *Nous sommes prêtes? Allons-y!*" She motioned to the stairs with one hand, and turned to lock her door with the keys in the other.

Imogene obligingly headed down the stairs, hand carefully on the banister.

"It's good that you use the banister, Imogene. These stairs are sympathetic, but they are twisty, and every now and then a landing tile gets wiggly."

"What do you mean, *sympathetic*?"

"They were built for the ease of the people using them, not the architects designing the balance of the building, haven't you noticed? They are very easy to climb, compared with modern buildings. Even Monsieur Arsenault, who lives at the very top of the building, has no difficulty in climbing them without a pause, and he is well into his eighties now. At some point, engineers took over and decided that a stair step should be between nineteen to twenty centimetres high, whereas the most ideal height for comfortable walking would be eighteen centimetres. That was fine when all the stairs were curvy and winding, or the staircase was a huge feature of the building, but as they grew more modern, and people wanted bigger furniture able to head up the staircases, the need for a higher step and smaller overall footprint for a straighter staircase took over, and that is why everyone except teenagers get winded on the *troisième étage*."

Imogene laughed, as she was supposed to, but was genuinely impressed with Toni's ability to hold forth on staircases. Soon, they were down at street level, and the Frenchwoman wound them through an alleyway and down another lane to a small bar where they found a table for two amid what appeared to be off-duty construction workers and two tables of people entirely dressed in black leather, making Imogene wonder where they'd left their motorbikes.

In answer to her question about why Toni knew so much about staircases, it was revealed that Toni's brother was an architect who had very strong opinions about the integrity and value of older designs in buildings. "He loves our staircase, and has taken all sorts of photos of it. Your landlady, Raymonde, wants to modernize it, but the fellow who lives above you and I are holdouts. To me, all of the history of Paris can be found on the nicks and repairs of those wooden treads."

Passion of any sort was fascinating to Imogene, who had often had to examine it as a character element when lecturing on literature. On the whole, it was harder to find the sort of passion in Canadian characters that Toni could whip up for a discussion of a staircase. She must have been smiling because Toni looked at her quizzically. Score another point for international writing.

"I taught and write about Comparative Literature and I have spent time pondering how much easier it was to read novels from places where people care so passionately about things. In romance countries, for instance, it becomes easier to understand the underlying reasons for large gestures—like affairs or crimes."

Toni grimaced. "People always find a reason for doing the unspeakable, no matter where, I think."

"You are right. And no country has the monopoly on ugliness. But I have pulled us away from your thread of thought. Are you also an architect, or just interested in it because of your brother?"

"He got the head for a slide rule, not me," Toni laughed. "I barely made it through geometry. No, my profession is far more allied with your quest for passion, I believe. I am a police detective."

"Really? How fabulous. Maybe I can ply you with food and liquor in return for answers to silly questions I may have in connection to my writing project."

Toni looked interested, and Imogene had to admit to herself, a bit apprehensive.

"You are here to write? A mystery novel, perhaps? Are you working on something here in Paris?"

"Well, according to my publisher I am working. But I am not a mystery writer, I am supposed to be writing about a mystery writer. And not certain that I will get much work done on my project while I am here."

Imogene noted that while the leather-clad folk were still at their table, the workmen had paid up and left, and the back tables were now taken over by young businessmen in made to measure shirts and sharply creased trousers. There was no pigeonholing this bar's clientele.

"You never know, I could have a burst of crazy energy and get writing, but my main focus is to relax and decompress from a rather stressful couple of years, and read. Any pages I get written while here will be a glorious bonus."

Toni raised her glass. "Here's to decompressing in Paris. Didn't Sondheim say something about coming here to be cured after being on tour?"

"What a remarkable young woman you are, Toni. Or does the entire Sûreté quote musical theatre?"

"Not likely, and I'm not as young as I look."

Imogene looked more carefully at her companion. There were light crow's feet by her eyes, now that she looked for them, and a slightly stronger line to the right of her mouth that almost passed as a dimple. Antoinette was obviously accomplished with makeup, in that she appeared not to be wearing any, but likely was using a mineral-infused foundation and moisturizer to blur any wrinkles that might denote an age beyond thirty-five.

Toni laughed at Imogene's obvious calculations. "I'm thirty-nine. It's old to be where I am in the police force. I detoured through academe, mainly psychology and sociology, before settling into my career. I am trying to catch up, and while I have no qualms about admitting my age, I try not to broadcast it. The gentlemen above always like to feel they are offering a step up to the *gentille demoiselle*, rather than making room for the woman nearly their equal in age and experience."

"You're doing an amazing job of it. I'd have guessed on the outside, thirty-one."

"And you, Imogene? You have a youthful aspect to you, which I suspect makes people think you younger than you are too."

"You are correct. I am looking directly at sixty, and most people take me for about a decade younger. My whole family has that going for us. We look ageless till we hit eighty and then turn into apple grannies overnight."

"Apple grannies?"

"Little dolls carved out of apples and allowed to brown

up and wrinkle, then stuck on a peg and dressed in gingham. They were all the rage for decorating kitchens a few decades ago. Here, let me find one to show you." Imogene pulled her phone out of its pocket in her shoulder bag and typed "apple granny doll" into the search box. Up popped several examples of the dolls she'd been describing, and Toni laughed with delight.

"They are adorable, and I cannot imagine that happening to you."

"And that is why I am buying you another drink."

They determined that it would be much more economical to order a bottle of wine, and spent another agreeable two hours discovering shared enthusiasms. Imogene learned that Toni had bought her apartment twelve years earlier, when she had inherited a sum from her grandmother. The location had been a bit rougher then, before the newest incarnation of the Forum des Halles mall had been finished, so she could afford it. Toni was impressed with Imogene's description of her own apartment at home, comparing it with the size and layout of those in their building. Toni pulled up Imogene's name on the bookseller app she favoured and immediately purchased and downloaded *Fyodor & Me in Russia,* her book on Dostoevsky, endearing her to Imogene forever.

"I insist on paying," Imogene pushed Toni's hand back from the check. "This has been my best evening in Paris so far, and I want to celebrate that."

"Only if you allow me to reciprocate soon again," smiled

Toni. "This has been very pleasant. It is not often that someone so sympathetic arrives in the building."

The two women strolled home via a slightly different route from what they had taken to get to the restaurant, and Imogene feared she might never find the place again, should she go looking for it. A bright window on the right side of the lane caught her eye. There was a dance class happening, with women of all stripes attending to their position in the mirror. The studio looked like every dance studio Imogene had ever seen, with mirrors covering the full back wall and barres set up attached to the mirror, and another free-standing barre close to the window.

"Oh goodness, a studio!"

"Yes, it's a good one. I take a ballet stretch class there on Thursday evenings whenever I can. You should come! You'd meet some more people and if you've done ballet before, you'll have all the language you need."

"But I haven't brought along any exercise clothes. Is there somewhere nearby to purchase tights and leotard?"

"There are a couple of famous places down by the Opéra Garnier, but you don't want to get anything more than your slippers there. I think you can find cheaper exercise gear in the Forum or even at the Monoprix. Some of the women do the class in bike shorts. The *maîtresse* doesn't mind. It just has to be tight so she can see your form."

"Well, all right. I will try to get kitted out in time for Thursday, as long as you promise to be there and help me sort out registering."

"It's a deal. Even if the task force gets going full strength, there has to be time for exercise and rejuvenation."

"You have a task force going?"

"There is a situation that has happened, yes, and I am hoping that leading it helps my career. But it is early days and it is not what you would call a fresh crime, so the work timing is not so concentrated as it might be if we had a tighter window."

"I would love to hear about it if you can ever talk about it."

"Perhaps someday, if only in the abstract, of course. It might be of value to summarize it in essence."

"Of course. Well, it would be an honour to be of any assistance, at all."

"And here we are."

Imogene looked up and realized they were indeed right in front of their apartment door. She had been so engrossed in the discussion that the walk had been on autopilot. It was astonishing to feel so easy that she could just amble; s ince she had arrived, it had been a constant noting of where she was in accordance with her map, her destination, and her route home again. Tonight, her inner navigator had taken a break and she had felt as relaxed as she did at home.

She followed the younger woman up the stairs, noting that they did feel easier to climb than most stairs she recalled. At Toni's landing, after popping her key in the lock, Toni turned and clasped Imogene by the shoulders and kissed her on both cheeks, something her friend Lynn back home had warned her to be prepared for.

"It was a very nice evening. Thank you for your company."
"I enjoyed myself, too. I look forward to the next time."
*"Oui, á la prochaine! Bonne nuit, Imogene."*
*"Bonne nuit, Toni."*

# Settling in

The next day Imogene started out early, aiming once again for the Seine. She made a quick visit to Shakespeare and Company, the most famous English bookstore in Paris, to which she had made immediate pilgrimage on her second day in Paris. Although it wasn't in the original location it had been when the owner, Sylvia Beach, had taken in James Joyce and published *Ulysses*, which was being banned everywhere else, the store was a mecca for any English speaker in Paris and indeed any visitor. Imogene had planned to just pick up a couple of Georges Simenon's Maigret murder mysteries but had also succumbed to a copy of Victor Hugo's *Les Misérables* in a new and celebrated translation. She then had a wander down the Left Bank to poke around the *bouquinistes*, the little green boxes that opened up into street booths along the river, selling old books, postcards, and magazines, before heading back to the north side of the Seine. Clouds were rolling in, so she decided to join a quick-moving line to get into the Pompidou Centre.

The Pompidou had become her art gallery of choice, mostly because no one had extolled its delights to her beforehand. Discovering something you hadn't known existed was almost like having a magical trick played on you. Somehow, she had never connected the huge building with the pipes and tubes all over it with an art gallery, let alone one of the pre-eminent galleries of modern art in the world. The escalator ride gave you the best view of Paris she could think of, with the Eiffel Tower in one direction and the shining Sacré-Cœur atop Montmartre in the other. She could see the graffiti at the top of the building across the street from her apartment from this vantage too. The people wandering below on the gridded square formed artistic patterns of their own and she had several photos of them on her phone from various visits.

Imogene had wandered through the huge galleries on the fourth and fifth floors several times, revelling in the modern art to be found there. For every artist she recognized, she discovered two or three more completely new to her. The Chagalls and Mondrians and even the Christo room were all a delight, but the Robert Delaunay painting of the Eiffel Tower had made her swoon. There was something about the angle that humanized it at the same time as it acknowledged its grandeur. She had delighted in beginning her French with the sympathetic young saleswoman in the upper gift shop, by purchasing the *montre avec la Tour Eiffel* from her.

She hadn't intended to buy another watch, having brought two of her collection with her, but watches were lightweight and useful, and this one would forever remind her of her first days of her grand adventure.

Today, though, she hadn't bought a gallery ticket. She wanted to sit in the upper café and read her books. Meeting Toni had spurred on her creative juices, and it occurred to her that she needed to get cracking on the reason she was actually here in Paris.

When her editor had suggested this trip, Imogene had thought writing about a mystery novel set in Paris might be fun. After all, the first of what would be this series had been based on *Crime and Punishment* and her favourite class to teach had been the senior-level popular culture studies course. It occurred to her that finding out about how the Sûreté worked now while reading about it in Simenon's time might be the hook her publisher was hoping for. She hoped she could ask Toni to fill her in on the more current aspects of the French police force. Meeting and speaking with her was the brightest element of her trip to date. Perhaps she wasn't cut out to be as solitary as she had envisioned.

In the café, she purchased a café crème and wound through the tables to a cleared one near the south windows. She settled her purse on the chair next to her, and pulled out her reading glasses along with one of the Maigret books. Simenon had been a favourite of her mother's. She wondered if her mother had ever heard the scuttlebutt that the author had been rumoured to have slept with a thousand women and whether that would have affected her vision of him. Her mother had often surprised her, in terms of what she condoned and what was beyond the pale. It was mostly intellectual laziness that irritated her, and non-ethical behaviour. Moral turpitude, as defined by some hidebound women's institute, wasn't such a deal breaker. Imogene smiled to herself. She missed her mother's company. Still, she had a fine example of living a full, if solitary, life when she thought of her mother, who had been widowed very young and went on to raise her daughter with enough energy for three or four parents.

Imogene had watched the Rowan Atkinson *Maigret* television series with interest. He was such a fine serious actor, and while she appreciated his clowning characters, like Mr. Bean, she often couldn't watch the entire arc of the obvious trail of destruction that was being telegraphed. *Blackadder*, however, had been inspired lunacy, and she'd watched and rewatched those.

This Maigret novel was set on the Right Bank, in the area to the west of Imogene's apartment, north of the Louvre and south of the Opéra Garnier. Imogene recognized the reference to the little covered galleria across from the Palais-Royale. There was something delightful in being able to place one's self directly into a novel, even if it was a mystery dealing with grisly murders laid out with precise descriptive flair. That had been the thesis of her talk, which had turned into *Fyodor & Me in Russia,* and she and her publisher were hoping that lightning would strike twice.

She read for another three or four pages, and made a few notes about the ranks of the various gendarmerie. She would see if she could bribe Toni with a bottle of wine to help flesh out her knowledge. Maybe having that injection of real-life policework would spice up the dated material of the printed page. She tried to push through another chapter, with the same resolve she'd used to begin grading student papers.

Soon, though, her attention was drawn to the other people in the café. She had never understood how other writers could work in crowded places like cafés or libraries. She had always required silence and a lack of distractions to allow her mind to focus. Back in her own undergrad days, she had joined her friends in study times at the library, but she was there mostly for companionship of the coffee breaks and would have to play catch-up later back home in her tiny apartment.

She looked about the café, once again indulging in her secret passion of creating backstories for the people around her. Here, for instance, were they all tourists in this lovely airy café? Or were those three women locals who had themselves been to the library on the third floor and now were meeting for their regular rendezvous to discuss books and politics and the tribulations of their grown children? What about that couple leaning in and laughing quietly together? Were they a pair of new lovers, discovering each other's delightful secrets? Or perhaps they were childhood friends rekindling a connection long lost? Something in the way their heads tilted in harmony told her they had a depth to their relationship, whatever it was. The girl on her own, dressed in severe black trousers, sleeveless black shell, and white running shoes, breaking her croissant into tiny pinches before eating it, was likely a clerk from one of the trendier shops across the rue Renard, escaping the buskers and crowds in Le Marais. And what about that solitary older woman, with the scarf wrapped around her neck and glasses perched on her nose, raising her cup of coffee and surveying the room? With a snort of recognition, Imogene pulled her readers off; she had just spotted herself in the mirrored column near the edge of the café.

Enough woolgathering, as her mother would have said. If she were really going to write here, she would have to get serious about her daily timetables. If she set her alarm, she could fit in regular writing time before she got ready to go out and explore the city. After all, nothing seemed to open before ten a.m. She could certainly get back into work mode, rising at six and writing for two or three hours after bathing and eating breakfast.

Another thing she had to do was find the ballet shop that Toni had mentioned. The exercise class with Toni would be the perfect way to continue to develop a friendship with the busy detective. Therefore, it behooved her to get cracking and find some appropriate garb. With a flourish, she finished her coffee and dropped her book and glasses back in her bag. A quick look at her map showed that if she zigzagged westward on rue Rambuteau, then rue Étienne-Marcel and rue des Petits-Champs, past avenue de l'Opéra to rue de la Paix, she would find find Repetto, where the ballet dancers all went for their shoes.

She decided on a side trip back to the apartment to drop the book bag, since the Victor Hugo impulse purchase easily had to weigh two kilos. She felt quite jaunty climbing the stairs, placing her feet carefully on the step onto the third landing, where she noticed a tile was indeed loose, as Toni had warned. Inside her apartment, she tossed the book bag onto one of her kitchen chairs. She took the opportunity to gather her hair back into a plastic clasp, to appear slightly less bohemian. There, she was ready to meet the scrutiny of ballet shop clerks.

It was just as well she was spending the day outside the apartment, because someone higher up the staircase was doing some sort of renovations. The whine of the saw or drill or whatever it was would have driven her crazy had she been forced to be at her computer the whole day. The thought of what she was escaping gave her even more of a spring to her step as she headed off on her shopping adventure.

Along her way, she came upon a bronze statue of Louis XIV on a rearing horse in a circle called Place des Victoires. She really did need to delve more into the history of which Louis did what. The buildings surrounding the royal square were lovely, and Imogene was pretty sure some upscale shops were to be found behind the conservative fronts. That was a thing she had begun to notice about Paris. While it flaunted its eyeglass shops and fashion stores up to a certain price point, the truly luxe establishments were coy about their product. On rue du Faubourg Saint-Honoré, she had passed a brass doorbell with a small matching plaque above that said *Vivienne Westwood* and that was the only sign that she was passing a house of haute couture at all.

Finally, she found the street with the ballet supplies shop. As she feared, it was geared to the professional dancer and the aspiring ballet student over the dabbling exerciser, but Imogene had long passed the point of feeling insecure under the eye of pretentious salesclerks. She was no longer a teenager wandering into Le Chateau back home in a mall. She steeled herself from being distracted by the glorious street and character shoes near the front of the store. She walked to the back, past the racks of tutus and skimpy leotards, wooly crossover sweaters, and lurex leggings, to the wall of pink shoes bundled in clear bags. A middle-aged woman in pegleg trousers and a white blouse appeared to be in charge.

Pulling together her best schoolgirl French, Imogene inquired about ballet slippers for an adult size 42, for an adult barre class. The woman nodded her head in understanding and asked, "*Noir ou rose, Madame?*"

"*Rose, s'il vous plaît.*"

All her slippers as a child had been black, and while she had never persevered to toe work, or had a class where ribbons rather than elastics were to be sewn on their slippers, she had secretly longed for pink ballet slippers. Having since seen pictures of the painful-looking feet of dancers, she was now relieved that her dance teachers had pushed her from ballet to Highland, citing her obvious height as being inappropriate for the ballet. Times, of course, had changed since then, and there were some lovely tall dancers to be seen, especially in *Les Ballets Jazz de Montréal,* one of her favourite troupes. However, it was obvious that dancers who had to be lifted and tossed about would likely be smaller, or at least smaller boned, to be successful. At any rate, dance became something Imogene had done only on Friday nights at the pub through her university days, and in the kitchen with the kids to the radio. Her exercise of preference had become walking and hiking, with some yoga stretches in the morning to maintain agility.

It would be fun to be in a dance studio again, she thought, admiring the pink full-soled leather slippers, which came with broad elastics already sewn across the instep. She wiggled her toes happily and caught an indulgent look from the salesclerk.

*"Madame a-t-elle dansé étant enfant?"*

Imogene beamed at her understanding. Yes, she had danced as a child. "Oui, mais il y a plusieurs années."

*"C'est le meilleur exercice. Je vous souhaite bon succès."*

*"Merci."*

On her way to the till, Imogene spotted a rack along the wall of larger sized dancewear, probably brought in for the likes of her and ballet moms who took a barre class while their progeny were in the other studio. She impulsively decided to buy a three-quarter-sleeved black leotard and matching warm-up shorts, along with some pink tights. It would work with what she had seen people wearing through the academy window, and would save her the hassle of searching out bike shorts somewhere else. The salesclerk near the till, who seemed to have received by osmosis the indulgence of the shoe clerk, smiled brightly at Imogene and suggested one of the fabric hair scrunchies surrounding a bit of netting that made for approximating a bun. She held up a black and green patterned one.

"*Avec vos cheveux, c'est merveilleux!*"

Imogene laughed and agreed. Might as well go whole hog. It did look nice against her hair.

She strolled home via the rue du 4-Septembre just to see different sights, swinging her distinctive pink bag. Meeting Toni had been a very good thing; already she could feel her absorption of Paris becoming deeper. And the cost of the day's purchases could be justified two ways. She was going to be exercising and therefore becoming healthier. And she had experienced the world of the ballet from its birthplace. How much more culturally appropriate could she be? She was delighted to think she had processed the entire time in Repetto *en français*.

Now that she was thinking dance and exercise, she was noticing more than the eyeglass shops around. In fact, there were a lot of art and stationery stores as well, at least down this route home. Maybe once you lived in Paris for a while, you just naturally developed artistic tendencies in some shape or form. She hadn't yet seen any music shops, but surely somewhere there were troves of accordion and guitar stores.

Perhaps she should stop in and buy some sketching pencils. She paused to look at the display in the window of the art shop featuring small, shiny de Kooning balloon dogs in their display. A little sketchpad and some pencils in her bag would be a fine thing to have along when she stopped in a park. She reached for the door, but it opened suddenly and she was face to face with one of her neighbours from up the stairwell, a young man who had seemed so irritated with her slower progress on the stairs a few days previous.

"*Oh, pardonnez-moi,*" she said.

"*Je vous en prie,*" he replied, less surly than she had expected.

"*Vous êtes mon voisin, non?*"

"*Oui, Madame. Je m'appelle René Montpelier. Enchanté.*"

He didn't really sound enchanted to meet her, but Imogene suspected he had been raised to be a polite boy. Still, he didn't seem the type to happily switch to English for her, so she pushed on in French, stumbling a bit to find the appropriate vocabulary. "*Je m'appelle Imogene Durant. Je me suis du Canada,*" she told him, and asked, "*Est-ce que ceci est un bon magasin? Pas pour de l'art professionnel, mais pour le loisir, pour me divertir?*"

"*Le loisir c'est bien, et oui, c'est un bon magasin. Je vous souhaite bien du plaisir, Madame.*" And with the recommendation for the store and his good wishes, he held the door for Imogene before bowing slightly and heading down the road.

She was bemused by his politeness since he had seemed so surly previously, but the entrancing store soon pushed René from upstairs out of her mind. There was nothing quite as wonderful as an art store unless it was an art store that was also a stationery store. She wandered through the aisles of paints, tiny glass tiles, and stretched canvases in white, black, and gold. Her eye was caught by a small paintbox that turned into a standing easel, something Tom Thomson would have taken with him into the bush to paint. Maybe in another life she could think of something like that, but she doubted it. Her love of nature included screened-in porches and hot running water. She couldn't see herself traipsing out into the wilderness for a plein air session, even on the Île de la Grande Jatte, like one of her beloved Impressionists. She would settle for sketching in a city park or from one of the little benches set into the bridge.

Sternly giving herself a mental budget, Imogene spent another glorious half an hour choosing a sketchbook, pencils, a gum eraser, two or three coloured pens, and a box of brown ink cartridges for a silly pink fountain pen that might persuade her to write in her journal more.

Back on the street, carrying evidence of her dilettantism so clearly with both her art store and ballet store bags, Imogene hummed quietly, heading homeward. She couldn't recall the last time she had felt so good and alive inside her own skin.

Of course, she really ought to get to work on reading for the book she had promised Mariel, her editor.

# Switching to Victor

Her career as an author had begun when she had given the Bessai Lecture, which had the added cachet of being published after the fact, on her sensibilities of reading *Crime and Punishment* when visiting Saint Petersburg for an academic conference back in 2007. Her thesis had been that location informs one's perception of narrative, even when there is very little shrift given to descriptions of place and setting.

Mariel, representing the publishers of the lecture series, who was now her very enthusiastic editor, had been the first one to approach her afterward, pushing herself ahead of the dean of Arts and pumping Imogene's hand with gusto. She was burbling, "This will make a fantastic book," and, of course, she had been right. *Fyodor & Me in Russia* was still selling briskly and had gone into a third printing in its second year, which Mariel assured her was unheard of for non-celebrity non-fiction.

And that is why, now that she had retired from teaching

and was officially a professor emerita, a title she didn't like to share because it made her feel more ancient than venerable, she was back on the road at Mariel's instigation, to try to make lightning strike twice. "Georges & Me in Paris" had been planned as the second title.

Imogene's initial idea had been to examine the world of Simenon through the eyes of his detective Maigret, seeing where the biographical man meshed with his fictional character. Aside from tossing the odd Maigret into her popular culture courses, she had spent a summer in her teens reading her way through most of her mother's novels. They were on the short side, much the same length as the Agatha Christies her mother also hoarded, but somehow grittier and more exotic, in that France had always seemed more distant and unreachable than Miss Marple's St. Mary Mead, or wherever Poirot found himself residing.

Imogene wondered once again how Simenon had had the time to write, in-between supposedly making love to more than a thousand women. She tried to do the math on it, because did that mean one thousand separate sexual acts? Or relationships of a loving and intimate nature with one thousand separate women, sometimes lasting one night, sometimes more? The statement never seemed to be "had sex with" a thousand women, but "made love to," intimating more time was spent together. Or was that just the language of the times? Or the cachet of the French? At any rate, it worked out to three straight years of coitus, even if he'd taken Sundays off.

Mariel had loved the choice of Simenon, especially since the television had brought him to the surface once more. And Imogene had dutifully read her way through the three novels she'd brought with her and one of the two others she'd picked up at Shakespeare and Company.

She had endeavoured to engage with the morose detective, and spent time with her map, trying to sort out where the action was taking place in the books, but when she walked the routes, nothing sang to her like it had in Saint Petersburg those years ago at the conference.

The truth was, it was Victor Hugo who had really begun to inspire Imogene. She wondered if she could somehow find something of value to write about that hadn't already been said about him. She had just spent a morning in the Hugo Museum in the Place des Vosges, inspired by her purchase of the new translation of *Les Misérables*. And, according to one of the Paris history books she'd perused from Raymonde's shelf in the living room, she was living just a block away from where the student barricade, where the characters Gavroche and Éponine and Enjolras were killed, had been built. It would be remiss of her not to widen her net and see if she could utilize Hugo instead.

Back in her student days, she had read that Dickens was considered the originator of the police detective, with his Inspector Bucket in Bleak House. That novel was written only ten years prior to Hugo's masterpiece, and Hugo had already transformed Dickens's admiration for the police into a fear of their unmerciful tenacity in the form of Inspector

Javert. It was lucky for the thin blue line that people like Lawrence Block had later come along with his 25th Precinct books, or the entire realm of detective fiction would be too many clever private and amateur detectives running rings around buffoonish uniformed police plods.

Imogene had never enjoyed that trope in the detective novels she had studied and lectured on in her popular culture course in Comparative Literature. She preferred novels where the police were the ones to save the day, gamely aided by an astute observer and amateur sleuth.

She wondered if Toni read mystery novels. There was always the conceit in the literature that detectives were reading detective fiction, but she had an idea that was more of an homage to previous writers than a verifiable element of police behaviour. It could be true, though, in the same way that police officers eating doughnuts was true. Simple coffee shops were often the only things open for officers on evening patrols, so of course a sugar hit of a doughnut was in order. Maybe the ease of reading mysteries kept their puzzle-solving brains attuned, or the inanity of some complex fictions amused them more than mainstream fiction. Imogene had once been told, and could believe wholeheartedly, that criminals tended to be less clever than mystery writers gave them credit to be. The idea of getting an easy score was the way out for the lazy mind. Really clever people usually found themselves trying to solve big things, often sharing their musings with the world at large. Pulling off crimes in order to get away with something against society spoke to a pathology that was much less common than a perusing of the mystery shelves in a bookstore or library would have you believe.

Imogene thought about her old French copy of *Les Misérables* back at home, which had once belonged to her mother. She would have liked having it with her to compare it with the English translation she had purchased at Shakespeare and Company. She had read it back in middle school and her French was now rustier, and she wanted to check things against what she had been told was a very fine translation. Maybe she would try to find a cheap second-hand copy of the original while she was here. Or maybe she'd just believe the hype about this translation.

There had been something about seeing Hugo's writing desk, which he'd had specially made so that he could stand and write, and the glass case of his first drafts that had thrilled her. Perhaps there was something predestined about her veering toward Hugo. After all, she was thinking about him as if he were a handsome man she was finding herself smitten by. It was so odd to think that until her second week in Paris, she had been certain that her next focus would be Simenon.

Today, it was past noon by the time Imogene pulled her head out of her books. She had covered five or six pages in handwritten notes, and managed to sort through the first couple of hundred pages of Hugo's classic to determine where he introduced Jean Valjean (57), Fantine (117), Cosette (140) and Javert (157). Hugo's epic had been bowdlerized for her initial read, she realized. This masterpiece was 1,300 pages of political polemic, romance, philosophical musings, and history. It was also intensely witty and acerbic. No wonder Victor Hugo was considered the most important writer of his time and one of the top of any time.

She shook her head and looked around her at the apartment she was still astonished she had landed. This building had existed for at least a century before Hugo had written of the student rebellion down the street. She wondered idly what sewer entrance Jean Valjean had used to get Marius to safety.

She knew herself well enough to realize when her mind had been made up. She sat at the small escritoire to send an email to Mariel.

```
I've broken up with Simenon and am rereading
Les Misérables. I believe it's going to be
'Victor & Me in Paris,' if that's all right
with you.

Xo Imogene.

P.S. eating a pain au chocolat for you right
this minute
```

The thought of the pastry she'd just made up for Mariel made her stomach grumble and she knew there was very little in her small fridge. She could head to the Monoprix for some spring pea and broccoli soup or to the bakery in the other direction for one of their ready-made sandwiches. She decided on the latter. She could walk to the

Palais Royal gardens and have herself a picnic in the sunshine.

The woman at the bakery was laughing with a customer ahead of Imogene, reminding her of a friend back home who she realized was also of Parisian extraction on her mother's side. How funny to think that laughter could be quantified as an ethnic marker. Imogene had chosen the fanciest of the sandwich selections, Camembert and pickle, and the woman smiled at her choice, or perhaps at the price point. Imogene nodded and dropped the sandwich and a bottle of lemonade into her shoulder bag. It would be a fifteen-minute walk to the gardens for lunch.

She had walked by necessity at home, trying to save her eleven-year-old car for long trips or bulky loads. Walking to work and back built in just enough exercise for her to allow herself the milk she enjoyed in her coffee and tea at breaks. But here in Paris, Imogene was determined to walk every inch of its fascinating streets. So far, she had been down only one entirely nondescript street, and even it had had a plaque to commemorate the site of the Théâtre des Soirées Fantastiques that had been founded by Jean Eugène Robert-Houdin, who she assumed Houdini had paid homage to with his stage name. Paris was a walker's dream city, which is no doubt why it was Paris where the whole concept of the *flâneur*, or non-deliberate stroller, gained its start. To walk without purpose, for the joy of walking and discovering new streets and vistas, was what Paris was built for. Imogene would have to confirm it with Toni, but she was pretty sure that even *pure laine* Parisians enjoyed flaneuring in their own city, when not walking crisply to their places of work.

Thinking of Toni put her back in mind of her neighbour's role as a police detective. She wondered what case it was that had her so wrapped up. Perhaps she could winkle some details out of her after their ballet barre class that evening. She hoped Toni would be of the mind to stop for a drink afterward, and if not in one of the restaurants on their street, then maybe up in Imogene's apartment. She had two or three decent bottles of wine and some cheese and crackers on hand.

She found herself at the covered galleria that would deposit her at the corner of the Palais Royal at the other end. She barely glanced in the Louboutin windows, having already ogled their wares when she had discovered this route. The luthier's windows were a bit more enticing, as was the tiny shop devoted to gloves, which never seemed to be open any time Imogene was there. It was cool in the galleria, but she felt the heat of the outdoors as she arrived at the end of the passage. Maybe sitting in a garden for lunch wasn't her best idea. She was going to end up as freckled as she had been as a teenager after this much sunshine. Somehow, being away from her regular routine, the sun exposure didn't bother her as much. She had made sure there was an adequate amount of SPF in her moisturizer, and that was all she was going to bother with.

Apparently, Parisian women were more concerned than she with sun damage, because Imogene found an empty sunny bench close to the westerly fountain and settled happily down to eat her sandwich and drink her lemonade. She pulled the enormous copy of *Les Misérables* out of her bag, along with one of the paper napkins the bakery lady had offered her. Munching away on her glorious sandwich, she settled in to read about the dismal Thénardiers and their terrible treatment of Cosette. She liked that Hugo had given Cosette the characteristic of lying to save herself, rather than making her an unbelievably holy and good child in the face of her awful situation. You could actually root for a child who was working to keep herself safe, or as safe as could be. Imogene wondered why it was that none of the lodgers in the inn ever noted how ill-used Cosette was. Surely someone would have made note of how badly she was treated. It's not like she was being chained up to a radiator in the basement, though, like one poor child Imogene had read about in a news report about present-day human trafficking.

Her friend Lynn had slid a Literary Map of Paris into the magazines she had brought over for her plane ride. Imogene had laughed, but it was coming in handy for her curious wanderings. She didn't want to deal with Orwell or Hemingway in Paris; that had been done too often already and mostly by men anxious to prove their semiotic virility. Imogene was far more interested in Colette, George Sand, Baudelaire, Balzac, Flaubert, Molière, Voltaire, Proust, de Beauvoir, Alexander Dumas, and, of course, Victor Hugo. She was fascinated by what was included on the map and what had been missed. Hugo's house in Place des Vosges wasn't listed, but the church two blocks away from her, Saint-Eustache, was there, because it was where Molière had been baptized but was refused burial there due to his connections to the theatre.

Imogene had taken a phone photo of the map, for reference on her walks, but there was nothing connected to the Palais Royal that she could find on the map. She knew that Audrey Hepburn had run through the gardens in the movie *Charade*, and she and Cary Grant had eaten in the all-hours restaurant Au Pied du Cochon, just down the street from Saint-Eustache. That restaurant, where Imogene had stopped by once for breakfast, was featured in a variety of books and restaurants, likely because it was open twenty-four hours, longer than anything else nearby. It was probably not because of their pork-forward menu, though the brass pig trotter door handles were a hoot.

She realized that her sense of wonder about food was stronger in Paris than it had ever been anywhere else, which she supposed was a given, since Paris was considered to be such a gastronomic delight. The thing was, Imogene normally couldn't stand even thinking about food unless she was actually hungry. Recipe books and cooking shows had never appealed to her, because the thought of ingesting when she was not actually ravenous made her a bit queasy. So it surprised her to realize that she had been quite taken with food and the consideration of what she might eat next while she was here.

Lunch over, she folded the waxy paper from her sandwich

up into a squared-off packet and tightened the cap on her lemonade. With nothing to do till it was time to change for dance class, Imogene decided to head toward the Seine. She walked the length of the Louvre under the greening trees, watching several *Bateaux-Mouches* glide down the river. One of these days, she promised herself, she would take one of those little cruises. The entire river fascinated her, so powerful even captured in its human-constructed banks and edges. She crossed the street leading to the Pont Neuf, smiling at the sound of a little old man playing the accordion near one of the inset benches. All she needed was a mime and a garlic seller on a bicycle and she'd score a full line on a Clichés of France bingo card.

The *bouquinistes* along the Seine, weren't all open yet, only perhaps a third of them. Maybe later in the season they opened earlier, when more tourists would arrive in the city. And how did one purchase one of the stalls, anyhow? Or were they willed from father to son, down through the ages? They all seemed to have connected on selling a reusable cloth bag with a picture of the river stalls, but she was pretty sure that was as far as they went in collaborating, beyond possibly watching a neighbour's stall when he went off to use the toilet.

She paused to look through some postcards of old *Vogue* covers, most of them featuring a shadowy Eiffel Tower in the background with a Givenchy or Dior model front and centre. She broke down and bought five, four to frame and one to send to her friend Rita. The light was with her to cross the busy Quai de la Mégisserie and make her way back to Châtelet Les Halles. Once she was up the winding staircase to her apartment, she felt she deserved a rest from her walking.

She made a pot of tea and settled in to read more of Hugo's epic novel before it was time to get ready to go out with Toni to their ballet class. Imogene shoved the sofa cushions up one end and cuddled under the mohair throw. While it might not be everyone's idea of an ideal vacation, to be able to read in a warm flat, occasionally gazing out over the leaded rooftops of an immediately discernable Paris, gave Imogene great pleasure. It was the leisure to enjoy the place that she was most thrilled with. She was ensconced there, not just flitting across its surface like a dragonfly on a pond. And when she eventually went home, she'd be able to say that she had actually lived in Paris for a time.

# Everyone Is Beautiful at the Ballet

Imogene left a Post-it on Toni's apartment door: "Ready anytime. Text me." And was true to her word when she received a corresponding text from her detective neighbour.

They met in the stairwell and clattered down the stairs, not talking much, knowing how well the sound carried through the doors to every apartment. Once they were on the street, they were able to hug briefly and greet each other properly.

"I am sorry to be late; work is taking its toll," Toni said. "But I didn't want to let you down, and also it makes me keep time for myself to work out, otherwise the job would swallow me."

"I am really looking forward to this class," Imogene admitted, "so I am glad you could make it. I know what you mean about having to watch out about letting your job own your soul. I have been guilty of it from time to time, and have seen it happen to colleagues at the university. I can imagine how, in the police, that would be a big problem." She thought of Javert, Hugo's driven policeman, and made a mental note to ask Toni more about her job over their next bottle of wine.

The studio was not far at all, but Imogene admitted she wouldn't have found it again on her own.

"There is something about sitting and pulling on ballet shoes in a dance studio in the middle of Paris to make you think you are living in a dream." Imogene smiled over at Toni, who was putting on her own elastic-topped ballet slippers. Even if she pulled a hamstring and ached for days after this class, having this moment, in a leotard and tights, in her lovely pink shoes, sitting on a low bench close to the rosin box, in the anteroom to the dance studio, would have been totally worth it.

"I know, I know! I feel like I am twelve again every time I come to class," laughed the young woman who had just walked in and plunked herself down beside Toni.

"Ah, Ginette!" Toni said. "Meet my friend Imogene, who is visiting Paris for a month and staying in an apartment in my building. I persuaded her to come to ballet barre with us."

*"Ginette Morêt, enchantée!"*

Imogene nodded her head and smiled at the young woman, who looked a little more elegant but not quite as formal as Toni. Ginette pulled off her woollen jumper dress to reveal her tights and leotard, and Toni explained to Imogene that Ginette was the first person she had met when she had moved to Les Halles, and that she had actually lived in the building across the street from them before she got married and had children.

"Yes, now I live way out at the edge of Montparnasse, but I try to get back here for *la maîtresse's* workout whenever I can."

"That says a lot for the calibre of the class," replied Imogene.

"I think you will enjoy it, too. Imogene. Madame is very stern about us working only to our particular limits, not to push beyond endurance." Ginette winked as she intoned what was obviously a rote speech they'd heard many times before.

"Of course, they all say that!" Imogene rolled her eyes and Toni nodded ruefully.

"Well, we can lick our wounds over wine after class," Toni suggested.

Imogene looked at her. "And I thought this would be the highlight of the day!"

"Oh, I wish I could come too, but my monsters will tear the house apart if I'm not home by eight," moaned Ginette, sounding not at all sorry to have to head back to them.

The class was composed of twenty-some women of all ages, though Imogene guessed she was likely the eldest. Madame had more wrinkles than she did, but then Madame was basically sinew and bone, so there was no spare flesh to smooth out her skin. Her hair was absolutely white and pulled back into a severe bun, but her eyebrows were black as pitch and her large eyes twinkled with spirit and mischief. She seemed very pleased to have *une Canadienne* joining the class, and made a point of placing Imogene near her at the barre, so she could keep track of her and *aider les positions*. Imogene wasn't so sure that was where she wanted to be on her first day of a barre class in over forty years, but neither her French nor her manners could help her out.

Something of her childhood kicked in as she placed her hand on the barre and turned perpendicular to it, in second position. It was as if she could hear Madame Emma, her first ballet teacher, whispering into her ear, "Float your hand down like a leaf on a zephyr." For the longest time she had thought a zephyr was something like a zeppelin and blamed that on why she had been placed in the back row at the recital.

Later, in a bar requiring less exertion, she and Toni were comparing aching anatomy.

"I think someday in hell, I will hear Madame saying '*Et répétez!*'" Imogene grimaced.

"Oh, I know, but it is a good sort of pain, non?" Toni replied, topping up Imogene's wineglass with the bottle of Côtes du Rhône they had ordered.

"It is that, and there is something amazing about doing ballet exercises in the city of ballet."

"Something the average visitor doesn't consider doing," smiled Toni.

"Thank you for calling me a visitor and not a tourist,"

Imogene said. "I want to settle in and feel how it is to belong, rather than skim the surface, if possible."

"Staying *chez* Raymonde's is a good start. It's not as if there are very many tourists wandering through the 1st. It's mostly date-night folks and residents in our few blocks."

"That was sheer luck on my part. I had tried two or three other agencies with apartments in other arrondissements, but they wouldn't book so far in advance, and I couldn't bring myself to buy a plane ticket without knowing I had a place to stay."

"Well, I am glad you are with us." Toni saluted her with her wineglass, and Imogene toasted her back and took a sip. Was every bottle of wine in Paris delicious?

"So how was your day? I've told you all about mine."

"It was satisfying but hard," Toni said. "I am in a new position, much more visible if I fail to produce results but also much more potential for proving my worth if I do get results."

"Can you talk about it at all?"

"It is, how you would say, almost a cold case, but we are not yet sure how cold, and whether it is an ongoing crime."

"Ongoing? As in over and over? As in murder? A serial killer?"

"I didn't say it was a murder case, did I?"

"No, but that whole 'cold case' aspect just led me there. I am an avid watcher of crime television. There is nothing but murder that would make you salivate over the possibility of promotion."

Toni shrugged and smiled. "As it happens, you are correct. It is a murder case, several murders. And while we may be uncovering the results of old murders of a criminal long gone, we may merely have interrupted him."

"Or her."

"Or her, though I think this is much more likely to be a male perpetrator, based on the requirements of strength and the bravado."

"And where did these murders take place?"

"I cannot tell you that, both for professional reasons and because we do not yet know. We have discovered only body parts, not yet the actual crime scene."

"Body parts?"

"I have said too much."

"Don't worry, I won't push you for details. But if you do ever need to talk things out, please know that I am your perfect choice. I am the soul of discretion, I barely speak French, and I don't know anyone to spill your secrets to!"

Toni laughed again. "Yes, the perfect sounding board! A popular writer!"

"I am not sure anyone would call non-fiction popular, or I suppose you would call it 'creative non-fiction.'"

"I looked you up, Madame Durant. You have a lot of ink on the Internet devoted to you and Raskolnikov. And deservedly so. I haven't read more than the first two chapters, but I very much like your style of writing."

Imogene blushed. Or perhaps it was the wine. It seemed like it had been a long time since someone had been interested in who she was enough to look her up and go out and buy her book. She stretched out her legs under the table and winced. Her hamstrings were already complaining. She made a mental note to have a long bath before bed.

It was as if Toni could read her mind. "I think perhaps we should call it an evening," she said, polishing off the last of the wine in her glass and making a high sign to the waiter who was standing conveniently nearby. He brought the bill and portable card reader, and before Imogene could pull out her wallet, Toni had paid the tab.

"I was hoping to get that," Imogene said. "You must let me take you out to dinner some time before our next ballet class."

"You don't have to do that."

"But it would be so nice for me to have your company, and to not eat alone. I can almost bear it at lunchtime, but I cannot bring myself to go into a restaurant alone at night unless I am staying in a conference hotel, and then there is usually always someone ready to pop by and share a table. You would be doing me a great favour, as there are several places I would like to try."

"Then it is a date, Imogene. How about Sunday evening? Fewer *amoureux* and the waiters will pay more attention to us, since they won't be getting tips from the men hoping to impress their dates."

"*Oh, bonne idée!*" laughed Imogene, and with a bit of a creak getting up out of her chair, she followed Toni out of the bar and down the street to their apartment building.

Later, as she was getting into bed, Imogene wondered about the crime that Toni couldn't tell her about. Were the lines she had spotted on Toni's face more pronounced because of the worry over this case that might be a ticket to more respect and a better position in the police force? If there was any way she could possibly help her new friend out, it would be churlish not to. It would be a favour returned, since Imogene had felt twenty times more connected to Paris since befriending Toni Lamothe.

And after all, as she had bragged to Toni, she did have some skills that could be brought to bear. What was a detective besides a professional reader of clues and signs and subtext? As in fiction, so it might be in truth.

# Meeting Cute *en français*

It felt like a relief for Imogene to transfer literary allegiance from Simenon to Victor Hugo, even if he didn't have the sense to get to Paris in his novel till page 389, if you didn't count the sad few pages preceding Fantine's downfall. That still left just under a thousand pages to read within the streets and venues of the novel, and she was doing her best to map out Jean Valjean's wanderings in order to be able to muse on them from appropriate benches and cafés. That would, of course, mostly be for colour. If this new book were to be anything like *Fyodor & Me in Russia,* it would be the reading of a story amid the layers of meaning the city delivered to people who visit or live there. Which was just as well, because, at 1,300 pages, it was going to be a challenge to get through *Les Misérables* once, let alone twice or three times while she was still staying in Paris.

Raymonde had told her that her flat was let to a baritone opera singer who would be moving in the day after she left, giving the housecleaning staff a day to tidy and reset things for the new resident. While that was still almost four weeks away, Imogene felt the time counting down in her head like a clock on a game show. She looked at the huge book sitting on the coffee table and sighed. It was a relatively grimy day outside, by Paris standards, but it wasn't actually raining. She would pop down to la rue Montorgueil and treat herself to some amazing cheese and perhaps a few ounces of Mariage Frères tea, and then come back home for the afternoon and settle in to read. When she was immersed in *Les Misérables*, the pages and time seemed to whip by, but bringing herself to jump back in was always a chore: she might get stuck in another hundred pages of dry history like the battle of Waterloo section.

There was no one on the staircase as she trundled down. She hadn't seen Toni for a couple of days and wondered what sort of hours her friend was keeping at her office away from the office. What was it the police called it when they set up shop near a crime scene? Maybe she should be reading more Maigret novels instead of Hugo, as if that would help Toni at all.

The high-end market that was la rue Montorgueil never failed to cheer Imogene up. The chocolate shop that was so famous already had a line out the door. The fishmonger's on the other side of the street was clean and gloriously laid out, but there was still that whiff of fish that couldn't persuade Imogene to linger. She moved toward the next block and the cheese shop she favoured due mainly to the charming young people behind the counter, who allowed her to speak French throughout her entire transactions while constantly plying her with smidgens of cheeses she'd never before tried.

Pointing at the block of Roquefort, she asked for twenty milligrams, which she knew was too much for her to consume in one day but would be delicious.

"*Madame devrait essayer ce fromage avec quelques truffes au chocolat, pour le contraste,*" said a voice behind her. Imogene turned to face an astonishingly handsome man with dark twinkly eyes that creased his temples into laugh lines and a full head of black hair smattered with threads of grey. He was what her students would have called a "silver fox," and Imogene found herself startled into an inability to speak, though she could understand him perfectly.

"*Si vous me le permettez, je vous inviterais à me rejoindre là-bas pour un café et une truffe, pour prouver mon point de vue.*" He pointed across the street to a cafe, where apparently he wanted her to join him for coffee so he could prove his point about the cheese pairing well with chocolate truffles. His glorious audacity stunned her into silence.

Imogene was saved from standing forever, staring at the stranger, by the cheesemonger, who wanted to be paid. "*Madame, ça fera quatre euros cinquante.*"

She rummaged for her charge card, aware of the handsome man just out of eyesight. "*Merci,*" she acknowledged, taking her cheese and once more turning around to the man still behind her.

"*Ah bien, au café,*" he said, and, taking her elbow, led her across the road to a café she hadn't had the nerve to enter solo. "*Deux cafés, et une plat des chocolats, s'il vous plaît.*" He spoke to a hovering waiter with panache, and held Imogene's chair for her before sitting across from her at the small table by the wall.

"*Je m'appelle Marcel Rocher, à votre service.*"

"*Je m'appelle Imogene Durant, et c'est un plaisir de vous rencontrer.*" It was indeed a pleasure to meet him.

"*Vous êtes americaine?*"

"*Canadienne, de l'Ouest.*"

"*Votre français est très bien pour l'Ouest,*" he said, complimenting her language skills.

Imogene wasn't sure whether it was the compliment or the electricity his twinkling eyes were creating, but whatever the case, she was coming close to the end of making sense in her relatively rusty French.

"*Vous connaissez bien l'Ouest du Canada?*"

"*Un peu.*" He said he had long ago been to Saskatoon as an exchange student and had travelled to Banff in the Rocky Mountains. "*C'était un endroit magnifique!*"

"*Oui, c'est tres beau, Banff, et les montagnes ne sont pas les Alpes, mais elles sont les plus belles montagnes de tout l'Amérique du Nord.*" She could hear herself speaking more slowly as she stretched to find words to knit together to laud the Rocky Mountains as being the most beautiful in North America. He was very articulate and easy to understand, but Imogene was beginning to panic. He asked where she lived and, when she said Edmonton, four hours from Banff, he said he had forgotten about how Canadians spoke of distance in terms of hours. "*C'est charmant,*" he said.

Just then the waiter returned with two huge bowls of café au lait and a small plate of truffles on a doily.

"*Enchanté,*" said Marcel. He turned to Imogene. "*Et maintenant, votre fromage.*"

Imogene pulled out the Roquefort and unwrapped it from the plastic. Marcel brandished a coffee spoon and dug a small amount of cheese from the crumbly block. Imogene followed suit with her own coffee spoon. They each ate the cheese and then plucked a truffle from the plate in front of them. Marcel smiled broadly as Imogene's eyes widened in delight.

"Oh my god, that is amazing!" Imogene's French deserted her.

"*Je suis tellement heureux que vous soyez d'accord.*"

Imogene thought he really did seem pleased that she agreed with him. "*Je ne me peux pas vous remercier assez de m'avoir appris ceci.*" Imogene's French was reaching its limits, as she stumbled in trying to tell him she was grateful for the new knowledge, and her sentence structure was getting simultaneously simpler and more formal as she went. She scrunched her face in annoyance.

Marcel smiled. "I have imposed my presence and my taste upon you, let us at least move into English to continue our conversation."

"It's that obvious, isn't it? I am so sorry. I feel as if I should be able to converse more easily in this lovely country in the appropriate tongue, and yet I manage so poorly the moment I veer off of discussing the weather or getting directions."

"I blame the language class phraseology they used when we were children. In an effort to give us a sense of the country as well as the language, each textbook was tied into some cultural aspect, as well. For instance, my understanding of Norwegian is predicated entirely on going cross-country skiing, which does me little good if I am covering the announcements of the Nobel prizes."

"Are you a journalist and do you also speak Norwegian?"

"Indeed I am, at any rate I was. And then a professor of journalism for a time. And your French is far superior to my Norwegian. And you, are you one of those psychics from the carnivals, who can sift through what people tell them to divine truths? Or a detective?"

Imogene shook her head. "I too am a professor, or, I should say, I was. I have just retired. I taught Comparative Literature."

"Ah, then you are indeed a detective of sorts. You read the text to discover its truths. But what is Comparative Literature?"

"You likely would call it World Literature. We study and teach international literature in translation, always cognisant of the translation adding to or obscuring the meaning, and taking into account the country of origin, the politics of the time, and the ways in which the canon of a country was developing in relation to other writers."

"As in would Molière have read Shakespeare in school?"

"Very much that."

"You are young to be retired, no?"

"Not really. But it is kind of you to say so."

"Ah, well, I have never understood the limits imposed on a career. I always believed I would work until I dropped, as they say, in the traces. But now, I freelance, that is all."

"I think we have been offered an ideal of retirement, as a carrot for those of us in a secular age. If we no longer believe in heaven, what will take us through the monotony of the middle of the journey without a vision of an idyllic time of rest?"

"And are you finding life idyllic now, Madame Imogene?"

"I am, actually, but you are right. I haven't actually stopped working."

She told him about the book series. Marcel waved a finger at the waiter, who was attentive without being obsequious, and soon they were sipping another bowl of café. She listened to his description of the articles he was researching on post-pandemic hobbies and pastimes.

"You should add ballet dancing to that list of new exercise regimes," she mentioned and he laughed in delight as she described her first class.

She wasn't sure which one of them looked at their wristwatch first, but it felt natural and sad to be pulling apart. Marcel reached for the bill and would not allow her to pay.

"You shared your precious cheese with me, it is the very least I can do."

She wrapped her scarf around her neck in what she had

decided was a totally French manner and pulled on her jacket. Marcel took her elbow as they left the café, with the waiter offering them a half-bow, making Imogene wonder if was because they were that attractive a couple or whether Marcel was a great tipper.

On the street again, Marcel turned to her and kissed her lightly on each cheek, in the Gallic style she was getting used to. "We must meet again, *chère* Imogene. Give me your telephone number, I beg of you."

French idiom translated verbatim sounded much more overwrought than when said in French itself, making Imogene laugh a bit giddily, but she willingly gave Marcel her number and he texted her immediately so she would have his number in her phone too.

"I will call you with ideas for outings that will assist your Victor Hugo readings. I shall be as useful as I am entertaining, I promise."

"This has been lovely, Marcel."

"It has indeed, Imogene. My day has been brightened."

And with a quick wave and a twinkle in his eye, he moved away into the crowd, leaving Imogene standing with a bemused look on her face and very little Roquefort left. She decided not to make up the deficit because she felt she'd blush under the gaze of the cheese seller. Instead, she walked down the block to the fancy tea store. The whole idea of reading at home that she had envisioned at the start of her day looked less appealing, but she couldn't help that. She had to get through the Hugo and into her actual response writing soon, or she'd have nothing to show for her trip.

Well, nothing but a friendship with a lovely police detective and a flirtation with a very handsome and clever man.

Just then, a street musician started playing Charles Aznavour's "*Non, je n'ai rien oublié,*" and Imogene wondered if things could get more perfect.

# Unofficial Consultant

Feeling rather schoolgirlish, Imogene had an urge to connect with Toni, her only possible confidante in town. She hoped the younger woman wouldn't find her too pushy and found herself writing and rewriting the message two or three times to achieve the right air of ease and spontaneity.

> I know I had promised you dinner one of these days, but I am heading to Place Victor Hugo today. Any chance of meeting you for lunch along the way?

Her phone buzzed back almost immediately, which made her smile.

> With pleasure! Shall we meet at Framboise for a crepe?

Imogene sent back a note that she could find the place easily and they agreed to meet in an hour's time.

Imogene was hovering outside Framboise when Toni arrived, and smiled broadly at her. "I thought I would just wait till you got here before heading inside. I am still not sure about reservation issues here in Paris and whether you had called ahead or not."

"I didn't, although I probably should have. We are eating unfashionably early, though, for most Parisians, so we will likely get a table. You don't mind heading deep inside, do you?"

"Oh no, I am as vaxxed as I can be, and I really don't mind anything except crowded elevators. And the Louvre."

Toni nodded in agreement. "Yes, I can understand the comparison." She conferred with the waiter at the door, and soon they were ensconced at a small table in the back alcove, just before the kitchen doors but protected by a small screen.

Imogene slid out of her jacket and let it hang backward on her chair. Toni unwound her massive scarf and folded it on top of her large purse on the floor beside her chair.

"I am so glad you had time for lunch," Imogene said. "I have been immersed in reading Victor Hugo and needed to get a sense of good and upright police detectives in my head again, instead of the Javerts of his world."

"Not a great role model for the Sûreté was he?"

"And yet the rationale that Hugo offers is always understandable. He is drawn as the antithesis of Thénardier, the innkeeper and crook, who seems to find his way through the world by presenting himself as what he is not, or what people seem to want to see, whether they know it or not. Javert, on the other hand, stands by the letter of the law, rather than succumbing to any understanding of moral decency or mercy that might bend a rule. I think it is a mistake to set Javert in relation to Valjean, which most of my colleagues seem to have done in their disseminations of the novel. It is how the world of Javert versus the world of Thénardier affects Jean Valjean. The ripples of righteousness versus the ripples of larceny and deceit."

Imogene winced at the look on Toni's face. "I've dropped into lecturer mode, haven't I? I am so sorry. I get carried away from time to time."

"It's not that so much, although I think you must have been a very popular professor. It's your speaking of the ripples of crime that caught me. I was just thinking a similar thought earlier this morning."

"On your case? I've been meaning to ask, can you talk about it at all, even in a general way? Because I did mean it. If you ever need a completely impartial sounding board, I am available. After all, reading a text for artistry and meaning, especially a text that has been given to you in translation, is detective work of a sort itself, no?"

"You have a point. Yes. I am not sure my superior would agree with my sharing my work with non-police personnel, but it would be good to lay things out before fresh eyes. Are you certain you have the desire to listen to what could be quite grisly elements?"

"If it could help you, I am more than willing. And of

course, wildly curious. I don't mean to paint myself as completely altruistic."

"Right, then. So, there is a hotel, I won't say exactly where, that we were called to, because their ice machines were being dismantled and removed. These machines were on every second floor of the building, though not on the top three floors because those suites are more given to long-term residents and have their own kitchen areas."

Toni continued to speak about frozen body parts that were found in the ice machines, with Imogene interrupting infrequently, just to clarify a point or other. Toni described their efforts to identify the body parts or murder sites and the overwhelming amount of forensic evidence they had retrieved from rooms that could have had a hundred different tenants occupying them since the murders. There still hadn't been a motherlode of blood residue or even bleach clean-up. The team had discovered traces of adhesive, similar to what would be left by duct tape, on a ceiling fixture, leading Toni to believe the killer might have cloaked the entire room in plastic to avoid blood stains. Then one of the forensic team pointed out it might have been left over from when the hotel had last painted the room, dashing Toni's faint hope that they'd uncovered a lead.

After twenty minutes or so, the younger woman sat back in her chair. "*Alors*, what do you make of all that?"

"Well, no wonder you look as if you've aged five years in the last three weeks. What a conundrum."

"If we don't find the kill site soon, even more evidence

will be washed away. Hotel cleaning staff are remarkably trained." Toni sighed and looked at her friend. "Does anything I've said give you any ideas about where the body parts were hacked apart?"

"Well, actually, yes. I don't think the murders happened in the hotel at all."

Toni looked quizzically at her.

"Think about it. Unless there are some things you're not telling me, and I suppose there are plenty, it seems to me that the body parts in question are all small enough to enter the hotel in a suitcase that wouldn't be too large. Nothing that would require a bellhop or seem extraordinary if the owner of the suitcase wouldn't relinquish it to a porter's cart. So I think you are likely looking at someone who is travelling in to the city and depositing parts, rather than someone using the hotel itself as an abattoir. I am not sure if it would be psychologically like marking one's territory to do something of this sort, but it does feel as if the killer is somehow playing with the hotel or the police or someone, by delivering bits and pieces, evidence of the crimes, to be stumbled on by other travellers. By people requiring ice in hotels, so maybe drinkers, maybe those people in the urban legends luring strangers up to hotels and then stealing their kidneys and leaving them in icy baths."

Imogene reacted to the horrified look on Toni's face. "God, didn't you ever hear those stories? Someone would wake up after being roofied in a hotel bar, in an ice bath with stitches in his stomach and a note saying 'We've taken one kidney and half your liver, so call the ambulance and get yourself to a hospital,' or better yet, 'Call us with money and we'll sell your organs back to you, otherwise they're going to the highest bidder.'"

"But that's not true, is it? These urban legends?"

"I think it is likely true that some poor people are set upon for body parts that can be sold on the black market, but I don't think it happens every weekend in Las Vegas."

"I like your idea of the travelling depositor. We have tried to go through the books of the hotel to match timing, and the CCTV footage of people using the ice machines, but our coroner cannot be exact on the timing, due to the freezing of the parts."

"And they could have been frozen beforehand, and transported months after being sawed off," Imogene added thoughtfully.

"True. And are you thinking we could have body parts in hotels all over Paris?"

"All over France, or Europe, even. I think it would be riskier to get on an airline with a foot in your suitcase because you never know when Customs is going to want you to open your bag, and they examine checked bags from time to time, usually leaving a note to say they have. Your murderer comes by train or car and doesn't stay long because he or she doesn't want to be around when the part is discovered."

"Why do you say that?"

"Because New Year's Eve never lives up to the anticipation

of New Year's Eve. It is always better to set something in motion and then imagine how it's all going to work out than to sit patiently and watch something fall flat. And in this case, not even be discovered by another traveller at all. It was the fellow dismantling the machines who found the first foot, correct?"

"Yes, he and a maid."

"It would be too dangerous and way too expensive to stay that long in the hotel at any given time too. Unless it was one of the long-time tenants."

"Wouldn't someone notice the bag ever?"

Imogene looked thoughtful as she chewed one more bite of her delicious crepe. She set her fork and knife down regretfully on the plate in an indication she was finished and looked at her friend.

"No one notices that Monsieur Madeleine has brought a bag with clothing for Cosette to the inn."

"I beg your pardon?"

"In *Les Misérables,* when Jean Valjean goes to find Fantine's daughter she'd left with the miserable innkeepers, he arrives looking like a tramp and gives no explanation of why he is there. The innkeepers, the Thénardiers, are defined as corrupt and venal, and they have been mistreating the child the whole time, while extracting money from her mother, who is now dead. As the mayor of the town where she died, and the owner of the factory she was fired from, Valjean, who at the time was known as Monsieur Madeleine, feels a great responsibility for the child. He had been jailed but has escaped from a prison ship and has come to find her."

"I don't recall this part of the story, but, of course, I've only read excerpts of the book. Our class studied *The Hunchback of Notre Dame*."

Imogene nodded, and tucked away the thought that French schoolchildren were fed Hugo the same way English-speaking children had Shakespeare doled out to them, one or two in the high school years, with the choice going to the teacher.

"So, Monsieur Madeleine arrives, and there are people drinking in the inn. They are all watching the stranger, and Madame Thénardier is deciding whether he belongs and can pay. He goes and buys an expensive doll for Cosette that he had passed in the market, and that causes a stir, but it's not until he has laid out all the money they demand that he takes out the clothing for her that he's brought, mourning clothes. And that's what I'm talking about."

She looked expectantly at Toni, who looked back at her quizzically.

"I am not sure what you are talking about, I am sorry."

"I am talking about expectations of certain places. You expect someone to have a shopping basket in the grocery store. You expect an adult to have a child with them at a children's movie. You assume someone will be wearing grubby clothes when doing a messy chore. So it's not unusual to have a novelist skip over that sort of description."

"And Hugo skips over a description?" Toni was beginning

to see what Imogene was talking about. Imogene nodded, glad to be making the connection.

"Yes! The man who devotes interminable digressions to descriptions of convents and sewers says nothing about whether the tramp has a bag. But he does! He must! He has brought a bag with clothes for Cosette in it. You can flip back twenty pages and not have a bag or a rucksack or a suitcase mentioned. It is just assumed that people will have a bag of some sort, so common that you don't even describe a traveller as having one."

"So common."

"There is even a trope about people arriving at a hotel without a suitcase, as if they are up to no good. They are assumed to be having an affair or, at best, have had some mishap in their travels—lost luggage, a missed connection, or having been just tossed out of a marriage. It is odder to appear without a bag. But to walk into a hotel with a suitcase, no matter how bulky? No one would bat an eye."

"It would have to be small enough to avoid the eye of the bellman. Whoever is walking in doesn't want to have someone offer to take that bag away from them."

"Do you not think so? It might delight them to walk behind and see some innocent person carrying evidence of their evil deeds."

Toni shook her head, smiling. "You could be a crime profiler, the way you are talking."

"I don't have the psychological skills for that, but I do have the training to understand plot and motivation in a well-crafted story. In order to be believable, elements of the story have to hold some truth to them, something the reader will believe as being a logical, even if unexpected, action or reaction."

"Yes, I can understand that. All right, then, we have a killer who wants to disperse the proof of his crimes where people will eventually find them, but he or she is not necessarily performing the crimes in the hotel."

"I would think there may be more deposit sites, although you might want to think about why the hotel you've discovered them in was chosen. It might give you insight into other places where body parts might be or insight into which victims get placed where."

"I am not sure I follow your thinking."

"Well, perhaps the limbs and such you've found in this one hotel belonged to the sort of people who would have stayed in a hotel of that calibre. Well-off, European, rather than North American, either older and long-term sorts of guests or business travellers. Or maybe the victims are the complete opposite of that sort of hotel guest, and they've been placed there because it's the only time they'd ever be able to set foot, as it were, in such an expensive place."

"You are suggesting we profile the typical hotel guest to determine the type of victim?"

"Or you determine what you can from the body parts. I suppose you can tell from the level of calcium in the bones or the texture of the skin or the muscle to fat ratio, or whatever, relative possibilities of the victims' ages and lifestyles.

At least that is what I've gleaned from reading crime novels over the years."

"Forensic specialists are unwilling to make suppositions the way you see on television or in books. The best I will get out of them is an age range and possibly a sense of manual activity from the hand. I might be given a sex from the femur, but they will caution me that there are many tall females and short males. We don't have a pelvis, which would give me a better indicator of sex, nor do we have stomach contents. But you are right, there are some elements that will be presented after they have studied the body parts. I will be grateful if they can give me even a set number of how many actual victims I am looking for."

Imogene took a sharp breath in. What had been for her a captivating intellectual discussion had just at that moment hit reality. She didn't know how Toni could manage day in, day out, to deal with such horror. They were talking about people who had been killed and cut up and dumped, no matter how interestingly as a puzzle to be solved. At some point they had been frightened out of their minds, blubbering and bargaining for their lives. Or drugged and insensible, not realizing that those moments were their last. Did they know their killer? Had they been lured into the killing site, or were they trapped and brought there against their will? Was anyone missing them, or were they chosen because they were dispensable people? Was the killing the most important element of this ritual, or was the placing of the trophies to be found and puzzled over? In a way, this deliberation of placement reminded Imogene of the mosaic street art all over the city, anonymous and stealthily left for passersby to be annoyed or delighted.

She shared that with Toni, who wrinkled her forehead at her. "I am not sure what you are saying."

"I think there is a similarity to the way in which public art appears in Paris. It appears to have been crafted elsewhere, like the mosaics or the intricate art that must be created as stencils and brought to be sprayed on the chosen surface. Those mosaics, even the cruder ones, have been produced carefully somewhere else, and the heights or public areas they're glued onto offer a level of intrigue to the experience of looking at them. How could they have appeared overnight, with no one the wiser? Someone must have seen it happening. What did they think was happening? Were they aware? Were they approving?"

"Our killer is an artist, placing his pieces so that they elicit an element of awe as well as the reaction of horror or fear."

"In the same way the street artist wants us to admire the audacity of the placement as well as the craftsmanship of the art itself."

"Oh Imogene, that is a very interesting line of thought. You have given me a lot to ponder."

"I am delighted to help. For one thing, it's fascinating and, also, I am really pleased if I can be of assistance. As well, it's great to actually talk. I am only now realizing how little I've spoken in the last few weeks."

Toni nodded, and signalled for the bill from the waiter.

"It might be the solitude," Imogene continued, "but combined with having to speak in my faltering second language with service people or neighbours, I haven't talked this much since, well, since we went out after ballet."

"I am glad that you are benefiting from this as well, Imogene. I am finding it very illuminating, and to a degree restful to be able to think about work without having to be so guarded. The sense of people just waiting for me to screw up is very strong."

"I'd like to see them try to make any better sense of this crime," Imogene grimaced.

Toni smiled. "And this lunch is my treat. Consider it payment for consulting services."

The women gathered their belongings and walked companionably out of the café. Toni pointed out the direction Imogene should take to get to Place Victor Hugo, with a couple of suggestions of ways to head home easily. They air-kissed cheeks. Imogene stopped suddenly.

"Would the ice maker company have a record of what hotels it provided machines to? Could a couple of officers discreetly visit those machines and root around, just to have a peek if there are other landing sites?"

"That is not a bad idea. I don't think ice machines are the most common element of Parisian hotels. They are mostly installed for North American visitors, who for some reason expect them. You know, already that creates a story for your idea of presentation. If these are all hotels catering to a non-European clientele, are these victims likewise from North America?"

"I don't envy you the responsibility, Toni, but your job is fascinating in terms of the puzzle aspect."

"Ah, it is so seldom puzzling. Most of the time, crimes are committed by very stupid people leaving very obvious trails."

"I had better let you get back to your puzzle, then. Thank you again for lunch. I look forward to seeing you for ballet next week."

"Yes, unless I catch you on the stairs, we'll meet for ballet! Goodbye, Imogene. Have a wonderful afternoon."

And Toni was off in a swirl of scarf and moto jacket, looking as effortlessly fashionable as all the women Imogene admired on the avenues in this magical city.

# The Bolt-Hole

He stood quietly in the doorway across the street till the women had gone their separate ways. It was interesting that they knew each other. He had thought the Canadian was a complete stranger to the city, with no ties. Ah well, it should make little difference to his plans. Once he was sure his movement wouldn't cause either of them to look his way, he continued down the street, away from both of them.

He could walk anywhere at will without anyone noticing him if he so desired. It was like a superpower. Perhaps the world really didn't notice people unless they made a fuss. He felt, though, that it was a skill he had learned from childhood, when he had discovered his secret place, a sanctuary that had shaped him and his vision of how he fit in the world.

It had been a haven when he was a small boy, a secret space in their home that his parents didn't know about. In fact, if his mother had known about it, she wouldn't have been on at him to clean his closet. She would have been in there with a mop and duster, cleaning out the cobwebs and the dust bunnies.

He had found it when he was nine. Two small grooves in the baseboard on the outer wall side of the closet, which slid when he pushed his fingers into them. Without the baseboard in place, a handle at the bottom of the wall was visible and, when pulled, allowed the closet wall to swing forward on hinges hidden by the chair rail board that held the hooks he was supposed to hang his play shirts and trousers on. Only a very thin adult, or a solid nine-year-old, could slide into the space that had opened up between the actual outer wall and this false wall, and sidle behind the closet into a space roughly three times its size with a roof that sloped. The roof made him realize he was under the attic staircase, which made sense in a way, but if he had ever considered it, he had assumed the attic staircase followed the lines of the stairs leading from the kitchen to the next floor, not over his closet. He felt turned around and discombobulated. He also felt powerful in that way that anyone with a good secret feels.

It was dim in the secret room, with the only light leeching through from his closet, which itself had no lighting. He decided to head back out the way he had come and close the secret room till he had cleaned up his closet enough to placate his mother and not have her coming in to find his new treasure. As he hung up his clothes, piled his toys on the shelf, and swept the floor, he considered all he would need to explore and best use the secret room.

A flashlight, batteries, a cushion to sit on since there was no way he could manoeuvre a chair through the tight opening, dust rags for sure, and a garbage bag should be the first items he'd need. His mother kept a utility flashlight in the drawer next to the stove, along with matches and candles. Her idea was that in a blackout it was often too dark to find the matches, so the flashlight would be useful to help find the candles in the first place. He couldn't recall the last time there had been a power outage, so he didn't think she would miss it. His allowance should be able to cover purchase of more batteries if the flashlight gave out. He didn't think his mother would approve of him lighting a candle in the walls of their house.

When he finally got back to his room, it was after dinner, bath, and bedtime. It occurred to him to place his pillows under his duvet to make it appear that he was fast asleep, just in case his parents poked their heads in when they were heading to bed. It also occurred to him that he shouldn't wear his pyjamas into the crevice, since his mother would notice grime smudged onto them. He really needed to dust in there before anything else.

He stripped down and hauled on the shirt and shorts he had been wearing earlier in the day, and, lighting the flashlight, in he went.

The first thing he realized was that someone had been there before him but not for a very long time. The cobwebs were thick and the dust on the floorboards was even and undisturbed. There was, however a small stool in the corner, one of those cunning little three-legged twisty pieces of furniture that closed up like an umbrella. That would have been easy to slide through the narrow opening, he realized. Anything else would have had to be assembled in the alcove itself, because the entrance was too narrow to allow furnishings through in one piece. He shone his light on the edge of the small pallet and noted that it was held together with dowels slid in holes in the four-by-four legs. No hammering, no noise. He knew instinctively that this place had been secret from the moment it was designed. And secrets are good only if no one knows them.

Tying a scarf around his face to fend off the dust and keep himself from sneezing, he had got to work, wiping down the surfaces of dust, hauling the larger cobwebs out of the rafters above him. He shook his cloth into the garbage bag, holding the opening around his hand to avoid too much backlash. Within an hour, he had achieved quite a bit more clarity. The floorboards were rough, but there was a braided rag rug in front of the pallet that had been coated in enough dust that he just lifted it off like a sheet and placed it in the garbage bag. The quilt that covered the pallet was also embedded with dust, but he couldn't risk shaking it out and causing any noise while his parents slept, so he had carefully folded it back and dusted the wooden shelf bed it had been covering. A few books were tucked at the end of the bed, and he laid these out to examine them more thoroughly.

They were schoolbooks, as far as he could tell. One was a reader with short stories and novel excerpts from all sorts of writers, aimed at a middle or high school audience. Another was a catechism that looked vaguely familiar, similar to one he'd had when studying for first communion. And the third was a dry science text on the history of the potato.

Over the years he brought his own books into the secret space, and a battery-operated lantern that was much more effective than the kitchen flashlight. He had managed to pull the quilt and the rug out and shake them out the bedroom window on days when his mother was off visiting her sister, and had filched the odd cushion from time to time, making it a quite comfortable nest when he crawled in to get away from the world. It was very comforting, this little womb in the wall. Eventually, when the apartment had become all his, he entered the sanctuary less and less, as his projects took over his mother's cherished dining room table and piled up on the thin bed he'd left in his childhood bedroom. He had made the larger space his own, marvelling at times that there had once been three of them living in this place. His equipment covered all the surfaces his mother had once polished every second morning with lemon oil. He invited no one home.

He supposed his secret space had been a bolt-hole in the war, hiding Jews or Resistance fighters. Or maybe it dated from before then when there were other inquisitions from which to hide. There had been plenty of disputes and sides and factions over the course of history. The need for hidey-holes was not a new phenomenon.

In this age of technology, the ability to hide away from

being tracked was almost impossible. But here in the apartment he felt as safe as he had in the bolt-hole growing up, as if the whole house held him secure. He had a mobile telephone, of course he did. He would stand out as an odder duck than he already was if he didn't have that. But he kept the landline telephone his parents had used, hanging from the wall in the kitchen nook, and most often didn't have his mobile turned on.

It was just as well he walked everywhere, maintaining a slender build all his life, or he'd likely not fit through the entry to the secret room when he did seek perfect sanctuary. It was a calming place and the place where he felt the most creative. First the calm would come and then the visions. He wondered if the others before him who had been hiding had felt the same way.

Of course, they had been hiding for their lives, from zealots or political factions or Nazis. His was a different sanctuary sought. He wasn't really hiding from anyone.

He was hiding from everyone.

# Maybe a Date

Having made her way to Place Victor Hugo, toured the fountain, and checked out another lovely café, Imogene wandered home along the Seine, as Toni had suggested. Her delight in the river walk was undiminished by thoughts of murderous butchers. She cut across the Place de la Concorde and headed through the chalky garden walk, pausing by the carousel in the Tuileries to watch the children and their mothers or nannies enjoying the afternoon warmth.

She smiled as she spotted the neon sign for a famous detective agency across the street from the east end of the Louvre. Here she was in Paris, feeling like a detective herself. She should try to get a picture of herself under the *Duluc* sign sometime.

Passing the small bakery near a Mexican restaurant she made a mental note to try, Imogene decided to pop in and purchase a baguette to go with her soup for supper. She was exiting the bakery and turning down the street that would take her to the back of the Halles park closest to the Bourse, when she heard her name called.

It was Marcel, the lovely man who had bought her truffles and helped her eat her Roquefort. He must live nearby, but of course he would. It was just like Ginette admitting it was odd of her to go across town to the dance class: Imogene had noted from suggestions Toni and Raymonde had given her that Parisians didn't necessarily roam widely from home when going to the markets. After all, there were so many good markets dotted all over, they didn't need to go far, which was part of what made Paris such a walkable city. It made sense that Marcel would frequent the rue Montorgueil if he lived in the area, and they were barely two streets from there.

What must she look like? She had walked all over Right Bank neighbourhoods that afternoon. Then she wondered why she was worried about how she looked. Was she eyeing Marcel as a potential beau?

"I am so glad to run into you," he said when he caught up to her. "I have been feeling desolate about having eaten all your cheese yesterday. I was trying to think of a way to repay your kindness."

"Don't be silly. It was lovely and I was happy to share my cheese and enjoy the chocolates. It is nice to see you again too."

"Are you hungry? May I take you for an early supper? There is a wonderful restaurant not too far away that I would love to share with you."

Imogene found herself thinking Marcel was likely very good at his job of getting people to open up and talk to him, because she was bemused at how easily she found herself ensconced at a table in the corner of a charming restaurant, quietly cataloguing the face of her handsome companion as he ordered for them. He had a strong jaw and full lips, and one of his eyebrows had a slightly higher arch than the other, making him look a tiny bit piratical, even in his very respectable tweedy jacket and linen shirt. The wrinkles in his face were likely a combination of weather and laughter, Imogene surmised, because he didn't present as being older than her.

The waiter poured still water into their tumblers and set the bottle of water on the table between them, then took the menus and departed. Marcel twinkled at her.

"I have ordered us an appetizer of their snails, because of course you have to be able to say you ate escargots while in Paris. And frogs' legs. Have you had your requisite meal of frogs' legs yet?"

"Oh goodness, I wasn't aware that it was a requirement. I was focusing on cheese and bread mostly."

"And thank goodness you were or we'd have never met!"

The waiter returned with a carafe of wine and two large goblets and poured them each a generous amount. Marcel raised his glass. "To cheese and beautiful Canadians."

"To chocolate truffles and charming Frenchmen."

They clinked their glasses and Imogene marvelled at yet another delicious vintage.

"*Eh bien,* tell me what you have discovered today about our marvellous Monsieur Hugo. I am all ears."

Imogene told him she had just come from Place Victor Hugo, but that her great delight had been the standing desk he'd had custom-built that she had seen in the Hugo Museum. "Of course," she said, "now everyone is demanding a standing desk, but his was one of the first. I love that thought, that he was an innovator. And really, he was. There is so much of the narrative style that was new and innovative when one considers the time of his writing."

"How do you mean?"

"The novel as an art form was still pretty fluid when Hugo was writing. We'd moved into a sophistication of sorts for the reader, in that the writer didn't have to pretend they'd stumbled upon a diary or a passle of letters and create the reality in that way. But there was still a bit of the intrusive narrator to be found in *Les Misérables,* not as much as, say, Henry Fielding brought into his books like *Tom Jones*, but enough to make you feel you're being told a story by a master storyteller, rather than just sinking into a fictional world, as we do today in mainstream fiction."

"And you see Hugo innovating how?"

"There is a mingling of styles and methods happening throughout the novel. He will go from a straightforward expository style of presenting a historical time frame and then suddenly take you to the bedside of a dying woman with such care and pathos that you can imagine yourself there. It's like he's playing with a zoom button on a movie camera, huge panoramic vistas, then tight close-ups, and then a whole screen of notecards."

Imogene caught a twitch of a smile, just an upturning of the left side of Marcel's mouth, and caught herself. "I've gone into lecture mode. I do that, I am sorry."

"Oh no, I find it all fascinating. It has been many years since I've had strenuous conversations in English and my mind is enjoying the workout."

"That is a very diplomatic way of expressing yourself."

"Ah, Imogene, you expressing yourself is a very wonderful thing to enjoy."

"I am enjoying myself too. It is very nice to find someone to speak with, really converse with. I anticipated there would be few interactions while I was here, and since I live alone at home, I didn't think it would be much of an issue, but I was wrong. It has been such a relief to meet you and make a connection with Toni."

"Tony?"

"Antoinette, Toni, is a neighbour of mine. A lovely young woman who has shared her exercise class with me."

"Ah. I am sure you make friends easily, though. It is in your nature to, how you say, lean forward?"

"'Lean in' is what I think you mean, but that tends to now be usurped by business speakers. I agree, I do like to connect with people. That's probably the latent teacher element, wanting to make the connection. But I am also quite at ease on my own, and to be truthful, I often prefer my own company to that of many others." Imogene raised her wineglass to the handsome man across the table. "Present company, of course, excepted."

"I am delighted to hear it, because I would like to see you again and again while you are here with us. Without becoming a bother, I would like to monopolize your free time. Is that too forward of me?"

"I think that can be arranged, and it's just the right amount of forward," she remarked, feeling herself blushing slightly.

Marcel walked her to her building and took her hand at the door. Looking straight into her eyes, he kissed her hand, and then turned it palm up and kissed the inside of her wrist.

"*À la prochaine, chère Imogene,*" with just a touch of huskiness to his voice, making Imogene's body twitch almost imperceptibly in response. The next time couldn't come too soon.

# Leaning in to Paris

Imogene washed her breakfast bowl and coffee cup and set them upside down in the draining rack. There was a dishwasher in the apartment, just to the left of the sink, but there was something so lonesome and sad about a solitary plate in the dishwasher that Imogene tended to avoid them unless a lot of prep bowls and plates had gone into the meal. While she had mostly regained her equilibrium after the divorce, there were still moments that bubbled up and brought with them a surge of melancholy or sorrow. But just as quickly they were gone, tamped down at first with sheer will power and eventually by disinterest.

And now, of course, there were dividends to having been pushed off her intended pathway of being partnered into her dotage. She could travel wherever she wished, without having to bargain and compromise. She could set her own hours. And she could dream about a beautiful man who seemed equally interested in her. What a revitalizing feeling it was to be found desirable.

That sensibility infused her ablutions and dressing. She dug in her makeup bag for her eyebrow pencil to add just a tad more definition and dabbed some eau de parfum on her wrists. The silk blouse with roses slid on like a caress and tucked into her black pleated trousers that made her feel like Katherine Hepburn about to wade into witty banter. Scrunching some mousse into her hair to keep it from getting overly unkempt, she nodded approval in the mirror. She could handle the sidewalks of Paris with aplomb. And if not with aplomb, then with a certain delight.

On her way down the stairs, she heard the lock turning in the door to her right and Toni popped out three steps above her.

"Imogene! How lovely to connect. Where are you off to?"

"I'm taking myself where my fancy leads, Toni. Are you off to work? Why don't I walk with you?"

"I am and, yes, that would be tremendous."

They got to the street level and Toni led them off to the right to go down rue Étienne-Marcel. Imogene grinned to herself at the name "Marcel." It had been three days since she'd had the early dinner with him, but he had texted her several times over the interim and they had made plans to meet the following day.

"*Eh bien*, what have you been up to since we last met up?" Toni asked as they headed westward. Imogene regaled her with meeting up once more with Marcel and had Toni clapping when she heard they'd be going out the next evening.

"Ooh, you can tell me all about it on Thursday when we go to ballet!" She grinned and waggled her eyebrows. "Or you can tell me some of it."

Imogene grinned. They didn't call it the City of Love for no reason. It seemed like romance and sex were never far off anyone's mind. "I will be sure to give you a full-ish report!"

They stopped at a traffic light and then Toni ushered them to the right up a street Imogene hadn't explored. She had a feeling that if she followed it continuously, she'd end up near the Galeries Lafayette, that palace of consumerism, which she was a little too nervous to stay in for more than ten minutes at a time. She asked Toni, who nodded.

"Yes, about four more blocks and then one short dogleg. You have got yourself a very good sense of the city already, Imogene. Well done. I know an officer who moved here from Lyon who still can't find his way to the Pantheon."

They had stopped in front of a relatively unassuming building, with a very shiny black lacquered set of doors. Imogene looked up curiously and saw a small brass sign, polished till it gleamed, announcing the place as the Grand. Although it didn't look like it, it seemed to be a hotel.

Toni confirmed it.

"Parisian hotels, aside from a few of the more opulent ones catering to Americans, who assume there will be much fanfare outside, tend to provide a modest air to the street and reserve their grandeur for the interior. That isn't to say a red carpet might not be rolled out and down the step if a duchess were happening to arrive, but on the whole, the street is not where the money is shown."

"All the streets are beautiful in Paris," Imogene half-sighed.

"Spoken like a woman in love," intoned Toni, and quickly added "with Paris" when Imogene looked up at her, startled. "Anyway, this is where I am working at present. We have a situation room in one of the smaller banquet rooms. Thank you for walking me to work. I hope I have steered you toward an interesting adventure today, and will hear about it on Thursday too!"

She leaned forward and gave Imogene the habitual kiss on each cheek and then waved as she stepped through one of the shiny black doors. Imogene waved back and then jaywalked quickly across the street to take a picture of the front of the Grand Hotel. She'd get her friends back home to guess what they thought the building was.

Pocketing her phone, she kept on down the street toward the shopping emporium. She might as well tour it. Perhaps at this hour of the morning it wouldn't be quite so crowded.

It probably wasn't crowded, but it seemed to Imogene that all the people in Paris were inside the Galeries Lafayette, and most of them seemed to be eating. There were various counters to purchase food downstairs and a dining area ringing the tiers all along, taking advantage of the view of the domed glass ceiling. Imogene wasn't hungry, but she did lean over an open space on the balcony to take a photo.

Then, trying to make herself narrow in order not to bump

into anyone, she wandered through some of the clothing boutiques, which seemed to run from one designer to the next, much like the Hudson's Bay stores back home were organized these days. She considered looking for something chic to wear on her date with Marcel, but then couldn't imagine being able to afford chic in this environment. In the few weeks she had been here, window shopping and strolling through shops, she had determined some levels of shopping wisdom.

If it said "frip" somewhere in the shop's name, it was a thrift or consignment store and the prices were very reasonable. If there was an assortment of styles and colours visible from the door, it might be affordable. If there were signs in the window of the prices of the clothes on the mannequins, it was likely not affordable to most of the window shoppers, and please don't bother coming in. If from the door or window you could see only seven or eight pieces of clothing, and they were all in the same colour palette, it was definitely not affordable. And if it was in the Galeries Lafayette and a salesperson swooped in on you as you lifted the sleeve of a black sweatshirt hanging on a wooden hanger, not before you had seen it was 600 euros because it said *Alexander* on it, everyone could tell you certainly couldn't afford it.

Of course, having been so practical as to not buy anything beyond her means at the grand palace of consumerism, Imogene found it very easy to pop into the Monoprix on her way home and purchase the navy blue silky dress she'd eyed the week before. After all, it was nowhere near the prices she had just escaped from. The question was whether to wear her Paris frock to her date or to keep it for swanning about at home. Here, every woman who bought her groceries in the Monoprix would probably recognize it, just like Canadian women recognizing prints from Joe Fresh. On the other hand, it made her feel pretty and part of the scene. And she had no need to pit herself against any fashion doyennes here. She was only going to be here another few weeks.

And she really had to get started on her notes for "Victor & Me in Paris," the reason she was here. Not to dally with a handsome Frenchman or play detective with a friendly police officer.

To underline her resolve, she marched herself home and up the stairs. It was almost two and the perfect time for tea and a bit of cheese. She took her cup and small plate to her desk, situated between the two long windows in the living area of her apartment. Within an hour she had hammered out the outlines of four of the five sections. Her conceit was to model her own book on Hugo's *Les Misérables*, which was set out in five sections, each named after a character. So far, Imogene had managed to name three of her sections: Imogene, Antoinette, and Marcel. She was toying with making the quiet young René upstairs one of the theme people but wasn't sure there would be enough meat from their meetings to warrant it. She had spoken with him only once or twice since their meeting by the art store, and he was either monstrously shy or utterly disinterested in becoming acquainted. She could hear him well enough, though, thumping about and often pacing at night. Maybe she would give him his own section, just based on his existing up there above her.

Having sorted that out, Imogene moved with her large copy of the novel into a corner of the blond leather sofa. She pulled the pillows all behind her and drew her feet up to wedge them between the base cushions, then flipped the book open to the middle and dove back into the story of many parts, searching her mind and occasionally a map for signifiers as to where Hugo's characters were wandering.

Noises from below on the street were growing, making her realize the time had moved into the early evening. People were gathering at the various restaurants below her windows, and the notion of restaurants made her own stomach grumble. She thought about Marius's student friends who scrabbled for money and yet always seemed to have enough to gather at a restaurant for wine and political discussions. They wouldn't be quite so capable these days with the prices the way they were. Of course, Imogene was assuming that students today would be just as penurious as those in Hugo's descriptions, but who knows whether loans and trust funds weren't making all university possible anymore, especially study abroad.

It would be interesting to know the demographics of university attendance in France with French nationals. Did everyone seem forced to acquire a degree in order to get ahead, the way it appeared to have become necessary in Canada? Imogene could recall, even in her own undergrad days, when university was but one stream people took out of high school. Trade schools, apprenticeships, interning, retail work, and family businesses and farms were all acceptable paths toward a satisfying and successful future.

Nowadays, though, if you didn't have a degree or two listed on your resume, you didn't even merit an interview, let alone a job offer. Imogene wondered if René upstairs had a degree. What the heck did he do for a living, anyway?

She dipped back into *Les Misérables*, flipping into the Marius section, and began making notes about the students. Hugo was such a master. He created broad brush strokes to show the ways in which people made assumptions: Javert assuming all those accused of crimes were base; the *Abbé* assuming all people were basically good; Marius and his father assuming Thénadier was a good man; even Valjean assuming for a time that he was doomed. It was Valjean's ability to see that people could change that made him stand out. He saw himself change even though at the end he could not completely accept it. He beheld the layers that Fantine showed as she begged for the care of her daughter.

Assumptions were dangerous. That was what Hugo seemed to be saying. Even self-assumptions. If you truly wanted to change, you could, no matter the circumstances. And if you weren't self-aware, no matter what good fortune was offered you, you would always sink to the lowest level.

What assumptions was she herself carrying, Imogene wondered, lying back on the pillows, staring out at the darkening sky and the slate roofs of the building across the street.

Lights were coming on in various windows, lives were being lived, love declared, hopes dashed, arguments silenced, dreams fulfilled, dreams deferred. Had she opened herself up to new possibilities with this trip? Was she shaking off old habits and thought patterns, or just carrying the same tapes with her, to hit replay?

Surely something was different. After all, she was more open to conversations with strangers, especially handsome ones like Marcel. She was stretching herself physically with all the walking, the stairs, and her ballet class with Toni. And she was being much more adventurous with her eating choices.

Once again her stomach grumbled, so she heaved herself off the sofa and ambled over to the kitchen area to see what might be in the fridge worth noshing on. That had been one bonus to retiring, actually getting back in touch with her own eating patterns. It had been years since her stomach had grumbled to let her know when she was hungry, since a rigorous schedule had demanded she eat before and between classes, or risk getting light-headed mid-lecture. Now, she could indulge in her interests and break only when her body actually demanded it.

She pulled some Camembert cheese and grapes out of the tiny fridge and filled the electric kettle with water before rummaging in the cupboard for the box of crackers she had purchased in the Monoprix the week before, feeling rather heathenish buying packaged crackers in this land of boulangerie breads. There was just something wonderful about a crunch that didn't end up in bread crumbs all over your décolletage, though. She should ask Toni if she ate crackers. Maybe it was all a ruse, this slow food beautiful presentation. Behind their closed apartment doors, perhaps Parisians were just as plebeian as she was.

Somehow she didn't think it could be true.

The way in which the people of this city held themselves to a higher standard showed in their posture, and how they dressed, in how they kept their streets and buildings presentable and maintained in a way she didn't see happening in some other major cities. There was a pride of place, a sense of their place in the world order, in the city of lights, the city of love, the city of art. What did it take to inspire a populace to take such pride in where they lived?

She poured herself a glass of Côtes du Rhône and took her plate and glass back into the living area. Pulling one set of curtains on the windows that looked directly across the narrow street, she left the window looking down the avenue open. The tops of the trees hid her from the passersby below, and the angle of the apartments on either side gave her a sense of security that no one was looking directly in at her.

Not that she was up to anything worth watching.

Yet.

# The Plot Expands

Imogene's joie de vivre was somewhat dampened by Marcel's cancelling of their dinner date. He was full of sadness in his text but regrettably had to be out of town for a day or two. He promised to call her as soon as he was back in Paris.

She shrugged an approximation of a Gallic shrug to herself in the bathroom mirror, like she had seen mastered by a phlegmatic shopkeeper dealing with an irksome customer across the street from her apartment. It wasn't as if she and Marcel had some sort of commitment to each other, and wasn't it good to have someone suggesting a rain check rather than just disappearing? A week ago, she had been revelling in her solitude; was she going to get sappy and sad now? No. Besides, she had work to do.

Mariel had been more than happy to have Imogene switch to Victor Hugo. "We'd have been fighting about that 's' on the end of Georges constantly if you'd stayed with Simenon," she said in their last chat. "And besides, everyone has seen *Les Mis* so this will bring them to the book with the idea that they're already sharing an element of your voyage."

Imogene wasn't so sure that people who had only seen the musical or even the filmed version of the musical would recognize the original musings of Victor Hugo, but she agreed that there would be a perceived familiarity that could attract readers who might be happily surprised. It would be wonderful to bring people to the words of Hugo, somewhere beyond the Broadway Valjean or the Disney Quasimodo.

Mariel's enthusiasm had boosted her spirits and Thursday's ballet class with Toni had got her heart pumping. Imogene was sorry that Ginette wasn't present, but Toni said she didn't see her every week because she was so tied up in her children's lessons and projects. Imogene could recall that chapter of her own life and wasn't sorry to be out the other end, as much fun as it had been.

Even with the pliés Imogene had been doing all week while brushing her teeth or waiting for kettles to boil, her muscles were feeling the exercises Madame had kept them at. Spending such care to make one's arms move gracefully through the air might cause the muscles to scream at you later, but there was a sensibility of serenity that carried them out of the studio and down the lanes to the bistro where they were presently drinking wine, their necks just a little more extended.

Toni looked drawn. Her work was demanding, of course, but Imogene hoped it wasn't affecting her health.

"How are things going at work? I know you can't say much, but do you find yourself any further along?"

Toni raised her shoulders toward her ears in an authentic Gallic shrug, and took a slug of wine. "I am not sure, Imogene. Every time I think we are getting somewhere, things just stall. It's as if no one cares that these people have gone missing. And now, another hotel is involved."

"Oh my god!" Imogene looked around but no one was close enough to hear them. Still, she leaned in toward her friend. "Do you think this is a new site, that you've chased him away from the hotel he started with? Or has he been seeding his kills all over the city?"

"That is exactly the question we are asking. The freezing of the parts has made it more difficult for forensics to determine an exact time of death. There are relatively no identifying marks, as if the killer has been very deliberate in making sure no tattoos or distinctive birthmarks would be available for identification. And no one seems to be missing these people, Imogene. That is the most terrible part of all of this. How can so many people be killed and no one is coming forward to cry out for them?"

Toni took a gulp of her wine, and wiped her mouth with the back of her hand. Imogene could see the investigation was taking its toll.

"Surely, though, the fact that you've found evidence at another site has shown your bosses that this is a major crime worthy of your initial impulse to create a team. That has to be a good thing."

"You would think so, but my direct superior has intimated that the Minister of Tourism is flexing his irritation that we are not moving quicker. Every day that we don't come up with a suspect, we move closer to this coming out in the press and losing tourist dollars to Paris."

"Well, I am here, and the streets and museums and restaurants aren't empty yet," Imogene observed.

"Ah, but you are not a tourist, Imogene. You are what we would call a temporary citizen, someone who comes to live as a Parisian. When June comes around, the city will burst at the seams with knots of people on every corner taking pictures. They say that businesses close in August so that people can get out of the city's heat for their *vacances*, but in truth it is to escape the hordes of tourists from other countries, especially the United States, who have their school vacations then. We love our city and are proud to show her off, but it often feels like an invasion when the tourists arrive."

"Like that column of ravening ants that came through a plantation in an Elizabeth Taylor movie I saw when I was a kid," Imogene nodded.

"Exactly!" Toni laughed. "So, while I appreciate that this would be bad for tourism, I am not sure I would be all that sorry if it leaked out."

"Are you sure anyone would buy it, Toni? I watch the true crime shows and believe me, one rarely sees any community changing their behaviour because they think there is a danger out there. Where I am from, the rangers have to maintain a regular patrol on trails where they've clearly set up warning signs of grizzly bear sightings."

"People never think something will happen to them, which is odd when you consider how egocentric most people are," Toni said as she swirled her wine in her glass the way Imogene had seen sommeliers do, though she thought the young woman was just preoccupied.

"True. But so much is perception. It's like Marius's father in *Les Misérables*. He thinks that Thénardier is combing the battlefield looking for survivors and envisions him as a hero thinking of others, not himself. Whereas Thénardier is actually robbing corpses."

"So if a villain can be seen as a hero, perhaps a hero can be seen as a villain?" asked Toni.

"Oh, I don't know what I am saying, Toni. I am just trying to be a useful sounding board for you."

"You are very kind and it is such a relief to be able to discuss bits of this with someone without worrying about appearing weak. I do hope you know how much I appreciate this. And I don't mean to make it sound as if I am using you, but there really is no one else I could talk to about this. Friends like Ginette wouldn't be discreet, and while I am sure the other officers discuss various things with their partners or wives, I'm alone on that front, as well. It really does help to sound it out to someone with a clear head who isn't right in the middle of it all."

Imogene reached across the small table to pat Toni's hand. "I am absolutely riveted with interest and glad to be of help. And I can't tell you how happy I am not to be staying in a hotel on this trip. Otherwise, I'd have never met you and I might have ended up with a severed toe in my drink! Did you know there is a bar in the Yukon, up in northern Canada, where that is actually a tourist attraction?"

# Cue Cards

Things were beginning to come together in Imogene's mind for the manuscript. She had gone back to the stationery and art supply shop where she had first spoken with her quiet neighbour René, and purchased several packets of cue cards in different colours. Her organizing principle was to follow through with her earlier idea of mirroring Hugo by giving each section a character's name, by giving each section of her own story a colour.

Her solitary walks in Hugo's or his characters' footsteps were noted on yellow cards. Readings of *Les Misérables* in the context of their place all went on the pale green cards. Time with Toni was in pink. The interludes with Marcel were in blue, which was perhaps a choice she was making a bit hopefully. She added her connections to all other people, like René and her bakery lady, to the violet cue cards. She still had a pile of orange cards, but she hadn't sorted out a category for them yet. She couldn't imagine meeting anyone else as important to her time here as Toni or Marcel, but it wasn't impossible, she supposed.

After a lifetime of academic writing, the intimacy of creative non-fiction, which she assumed her personal wrestling with the texts amounted to, was both remarkably freeing and at the same time terrifying. It was so much easier to hide behind the passive voice and make a statement about the author's intention. To actually set down on paper the emotions evoked from setting her factual foot on the same cobbles as the fictional Jean Valjean made her feel vulnerable in a way she hadn't felt even as a young student being critiqued for being too naïve a reader.

Imogene laughed out loud, startling both herself and the pigeon that had settled on the windowsill to the side of her desk. She was almost sixty, with a full life of family and duties behind her and a promising future of travel and delight ahead. Anyone picking up her books was expecting to find her musings and feelings there; that is why they were reading them.

She tapped the blue cards earmarked for Marcel with her pencil and wondered if she would have anything sensual to add to them. As if by magic, the free app on her phone buzzed. It was Marcel. She pressed the talk button and waited a beat to be sure they were connected. "*Bonjour?*"

"Imogene? This is Marcel."

"Hello, Marcel! It is good to hear from you."

"How is your research going?"

"It is coming along better than anticipated. I may have a

rough draft by the time my time here is over. Which is not something I really want to think about."

"*Eh bien, non.* But let us make the most of things. I was calling to see if I could take you out for dinner tomorrow evening?"

"That would be wonderful. What time?"

"Shall we say eight? I can come collect you at seven-thirty and we can walk from your apartment."

"That sounds delightful. Text me when you arrive and I will meet you downstairs."

"*Parfait. À bientôt,* Imogene."

"*À bientôt*, Marcel!"

Those blue cards were going to come in handy after all.

# A Blue Card Event

Imogene's foot slid along Marcel's calf and under his foot. He responded by sliding his foot under hers and pushing up on her arch. She ran her fingers through the thatch of curly hair on his chest and sighed. He was playing with a lock of her hair, his arm curled around her neck. The streetlight below diffused by the sheer curtains in Imogene's bedroom window cast just enough light, allowing her to see him but making her less self-conscious of her own bare skin. She found herself far more interested in Marcel's skin, which was mostly covered in alternating grey and black hair.

Their lovemaking had been exhilarating and exciting, each of them bringing a passion to their discovery of the other's body. Imogene had not been aware of her own capacity for shameless adventure. Perhaps it was being far away from anyone in another country, or perhaps it was her own response to an invitation away from solitude from this fascinating, handsome man, but she couldn't recall the last time she had ended up in bed with a man whose middle name she didn't know.

Or maybe coming out the other end of menopause gave one a renewed sense of lovemaking for the delight of it. Maybe that was what heading into the final innings was all about, regaining one's sense of adventure. She could still recall that first packet of birth control pills looking like a passport to wild abandon. Back then, all her friends had been hedonistic because there were no deadly diseases about to frighten them and they all still thought they were immortal. Now, as she rolled into her sixties, the thought that her last fifteen to twenty years could be endangered weighed less on the scale when put against the idea of those same years being enhanced.

Marcel snuffled a bit, and she realized he was dozing, which made her smile. He felt secure and at ease, which made her happy. She slid her arm across his chest and closed her own eyes. Skin on skin was something she had missed more than she had realized. Let him sleep. She would delight in the sensory.

The restaurant he had led her to through a warren of small streets in the neighbouring arrondissement, Le Marais, had been quirky and lovely, with attentive wait staff and beautifully presented delicious food.

Marcel seemed genuinely interested in her research on Hugo and where she intended to go with her writing. "I purchased your Russian book," he admitted with a smile. "On the e-reader, I am afraid. I hope you receive adequate royalties for that fashion of purchase."

"Oh yes, they're very equitable for those sales, I think to make up for not pursuing international sales so much. Thank you for buying it, that's very flattering."

"I confess that while I am quite taken with your writing and am already several chapters into it, I had originally purchased it completely as a courtship gesture."

Imogene laughed out loud. "Clever you. The way to a writer's heart, after all, is through her books."

"Yes, I wanted it to be a splendid gesture. But of course, it is turning out to be a gift to me." He had bowed his head in acknowledgement and Imogene had blushed.

They had shared a bottle of Chablis at the restaurant, and Marcel had popped into a small Carrefour Express for another bottle on their way home. It had been an unspoken look between them asked and answered that he would be coming upstairs when they got to Imogene's place.

More laughter and more fascinating discussion ensued as they toasted various shared favourite authors, and it wasn't till Imogene was pouring the last of the wine into his glass that he pushed it slightly to the side and leaned in to kiss her.

She responded eagerly, their bodies melding into the kiss, which went on languorously. Marcel's arms were around her, with one of his hands sliding up her neck into her hair and the other kneading the small of her back. She in turn slid her hands along his jaw and pulled his head toward her before wrapping her arms around his neck.

"Take me to your *chambre*, Imogene," Marcel whispered huskily into her ear.

"Oh yes," she whispered back, wondering who they were trying not to disturb. They rose from the sofa, and, taking his hand, she led him to her bedroom. There, without turning on the lights, he deftly unbuttoned three of the front buttons on her dress and then lifted it over her head. She unclasped her brassiere and slid out of her underwear as he quickly undressed and they met on the bed, gliding into each other with a familiarity that Imogene found magical.

Although she hadn't known a plethora of men, and had been married and out of action for quite a long time, she had never quite felt the ease of connection she was feeling with Marcel. It was as if they knew exactly where to touch to offer each other the most sensation, and his smile of pleasure as he brought her to a shuddering, gasping climax was as much of a delight as hearing his own giving way to *la petite mort*.

"Is it something in the water? No wonder they call Paris the city of love, that was amazing," Imogene spoke as Marcel opened his eyes and smiled.

"No, Imogene, that had nothing to do with Paris. That was all us. It would have been the same had we met in Timbuktu."

"You really are a smooth talker, Marcel."

"I am completely sincere. Totally." He stroked her hair and pulled it a tiny bit, to make his point.

"Oh, I believe you. I think you can be suave and sincere at the same time. At least I hope you can."

"You bring out the poet in me, Imogene."

"And you bring out the hedonist in me."

"A very good thing to be, in the bedroom."

"A chef in the kitchen, a scholar in the study, a hedonist in the bedroom."

"And a companion in the living room. Isn't that the combination everyone is looking for?"

"Sounds like the perfect person, indeed."

"The perfect person is one who brings all that out in you, and you do the same for them."

"We should write a self-help book on relationships."

"No, we keep these secrets to ourselves and enjoy life. Let others fend for themselves." They both laughed and Imogene burrowed into Marcel's shoulder, drawing a deep breath.

"You smell so good."

"And you smell of peonies and roses."

"That is something I read once in a self-help article, that we are drawn to the people we are attracted to by their smell. That even if someone has other attributes we think would be appealing, their smell is what makes or breaks it for us. And that can change, as the relationships change. People are asked if they like the smell of their long-time partner when deciding whether marriage counselling is worth doing, or whether the relationship is doomed."

"Memories come to us by scent as well," Marcel nodded slowly. "Whole scenarios from long ago can return to us with just one waft of cinnamon or wood smoke."

Imogene wondered silently what smell would bring this moment back to her in years to come, or if she would ever forget this time of being limb-entangled with a handsome, intelligent, *sympathetique* lover. It had not occurred to her that she would be anything but solitary as she moved into this phase of her life. Every moment of this was an exquisite gift.

"What are you thinking?" Marcel whispered to her.

"Just that this is turning into a very good chapter of my life." She moved to see him better, and ran her foot down his calf as she moulded herself along his side. "What are you thinking?"

"I am hoping you will ask me to spend the night. There is nowhere I would rather be, and I have nowhere I need to be till tomorrow afternoon."

"Oh yes, please do."

"In that case, shall we get under the covers?"

# Morning after Blue

Just like in the movies, Imogene woke to Marcel ringing to be let back in after popping out for croissants and coffee. Thankful for the four flights of stairs he would need to navigate, she raced to the washroom, ran her fingers through her hair, and slid the washcloth under her eyes to catch any smudged mascara from the night before, and then grabbed her robe. She was just cinching the tie as he knocked at the apartment door.

She let him in and was closing it when she saw Toni below, coming out of her door. Her friend gave her a quizzical smile and she grinned at her and waved, and then closed the door and followed Marcel into the living room.

"I thought about taking your keys but that might be misconstrued as overly familiar, so I was hoping very much that you would wake up when the buzzer sounded," he said.

"Yes, we mustn't be overly familiar," Imogene teased. "Not when we've spent the night together."

Marcel smiled back at her and ran a finger down her arm, making her nerves shiver in delight. The coffee smelled delicious, but she could just as easily drag this man back to bed.

He must have been having the same thoughts because he shook himself and said, "We really should have our coffee and behave ourselves. I have a lecture to attend early this afternoon, and it wouldn't do to arrive there in my assignation clothes."

Imogene snickered at the term. "And what do you normally wear to a lecture?"

"The same thing you saw me wearing the first time we met, I suppose. A jacket and a scarf, and ordinary trousers, not the silky ones." He touched his leg, and Imogene noted the black trousers with a slight sheen and a sharp crease down the front. Even with all their acrobatics the evening before, he looked impeccable. She suddenly wondered where her Monoprix dress had ended up, but Raymonde had an iron and ironing board slotted into the closet for just such needs. She crossed her legs, making sure her robe didn't gape awkwardly, and took a slurp of coffee, which was strong and hot.

Marcel caught her bare foot and held it in his warm hand, massaging her arch with his thumb. The intimacy of his action made her catch her breath.

"When can I see you again, Imogene?"

It was just like the movies, and yet better, since the characters were of an age to be able to be candid with their feelings and generous with their time. Imogene leaned forward and kissed him gently. "Any time but Thursday, Marcel. My schedule is very flexible."

He laughed. "Why not Thursdays, out of curiosity?"

"Ah, that is when I go to my ballet class with my friend."

"Ballet! Yes, I had forgotten."

"I suppose I should be referring to it as an exercise class, but I prefer to think of it as a dance class, and I think so do the rest of the women. We all took dance as children and find it both invigorating and nostalgic, I think. At any rate, I am finding it so, and I enjoy my neighbour's company, so it's a bonus."

"How wonderful. You are the perfect visitor to Paris, aren't you? You come to celebrate the literature and immerse yourself in the daily rituals and become part of your community."

"How about I get you to write the preamble to my book? My editor would love it hear that I was such an admirable character."

"Ah, but you have no idea. Too many people come to Paris just to tick off an item on their list of things to do, with no sense of why they've come or what it offers. They go up the Tour Eiffel, they stand in line to go through the Louvre, they buy a baguette and a beret, and then they move on, leaving some litter and tour bus exhaust in their wake."

"Isn't that the way with all tourists, though? Even in my home city, I try to walk visitors through the river valley and across campus, which is quite beautiful, but then eventually I always drive them out to the huge shopping mall we're famous for. Apparently, it is the largest parking lot in the world. How is that for a tourist attraction?"

"You have the huge parking lot and we have the famous traffic circle," Marcel laughed.

"Paris has everything," Imogene sighed. "It is to me the most beautiful city in the world, not that I've seen them all, of course."

"Is that your goal? To see all the great cities and read within them?"

Imogene laughed. "Well, it seems to be my editor's goal, certainly. I am not so sure, myself. If this project is anything to go by, I keep flitting from author to author, and I'm not getting as much written as I would like to."

"I will do my best to help you achieve your goals. Why do we not say that while I am gone today, you will write until perhaps five o'clock? And then you will get ready for me to take you out and you can tell me how many pages or words you have achieved or whatever your measurement is for progress?"

"Out? Out where?"

"That isn't what you need to worry about. You need only concentrate on writing."

Imogene leaned toward Marcel, who kissed her slowly, lingering lip on lip. She felt her entire being straining up into her own lips, making the connection. At last, he pulled back slowly, and smiled.

"Do we have a deal?"

"I work till five and then get ready to see you again. What should I wear?"

"If it is pleasant, we will sit outside, so probably a sweater or light coat. And that is all I will say. Till this evening, Imogene."

Marcel stood, making it look as if getting up out of the slouchy sofa was easy, and held out a hand to her, as if she were Venus rising on her seashell. She closed her silky wrap together with one hand and walked with him down the short hallway. Marcel drew her into his arms and kissed her, then squeezed her with a vigour that felt like a flourishing coda.

"Beautiful," he whispered and smiled with his eyes crinkling. Then he turned and opened the apartment door and was gone.

Imogene stood in the hallway, naked under a thin, silky robe, four floors up in an ancient building in a foreign city, having just seen a lover off for the day with a promise of more to come that evening. Had anything at all like this been part of her expectations when planning this trip?

She moved into the bedroom and looked longingly at the tousled bed, but she needed to stay awake if she was going to produce any pages at all that day in order to have bragging rights with Marcel that evening. She pulled the upper sheet straight, fluffed the duvet, and tossed the pillows upright at the head of the bed, then got into the shower.

# Evening in Paris

Marcel rang at six-thirty.

Imogene pressed the speaker button and told him she would be right down. She took one more look at herself in the hallway mirror, affirmed that her preparations were as good as she could manage, given her micro-wardrobe, and walked to the sympathetic stairs, which is how she thought of them ever since her first conversation with Toni. She couldn't wait to discuss Marcel with Toni. There was something so delightfully unexpected about her liaison that she felt like talking about in a way she had never considered discussing a boyfriend in the past.

And there he was, comfortable in his own skin, standing next to the fabric wall of the main floor restaurant's outdoor patio. He looked up from his phone as the door closed and gave her such a warm, open smile that she was glad she had made the extra effort to roll her hair into the chignon and put on her zircon earrings, which were much bigger and showier than the small real diamonds she'd left at home.

"Imogene, you are a vision," Marcel simultaneously reached for her hand and gave a small half bow, and Imogene wondered if European men were taught their manners or whether they all just watched Marcello Mastroianni movies from childhood and absorbed the moves that made women swoon.

"Thank you, kind sir. You look lovely yourself." And he did. He was once more wearing the silky black trousers, and a black shirt with a silver thread picking up an embossed paisley pattern. His jacket was dark tweed, and a silky grey and black scarf was draped around his neck, with one end tucked up over his shoulder, inside his coat. He projected an air of sensuous academic, as if Cary Grant were playing a philosophy professor.

They walked down toward the Seine, past the cello player who set up near the entrance to Les Halles and some skateboarders doing tricks.

"Someone is going to get their pockets picked tonight," Marcel murmured, as they passed the tourists gathering around the boarders.

"You know, I chose the style of handbag I was going to bring, based on how to be safe in the streets, but since I got here, I've not really thought about street safety. Well, not any more than I think about it at home, at any rate."

"And that is another element that marks you as a citizen of Paris rather than a tourist, *ma chère* Imogene. If you were to be constantly on the lookout for those terrible Parisian gangs of pickpockets, you would be missing out on the joy of walking freely through this glorious city. The more you walk with purpose, the less likely you are to be a target."

"Speaking of targets, where are we going?"

"Ah, it is a surprise! I am glad to see you have good shoes on, because it's a little distance but worth the walk."

They walked down to the Pont au Change and continued across the Île de la Cité to the Left Bank. It was a beautiful evening, and they weren't the only couples strolling hand in hand up the boulevard Saint-Michel. Just past a huge fountain, Marcel indicated that they had arrived.

"Le Lutèce is one of my favourite restaurants and I wanted to share it with you," he said, ushering her inside.

"Monsieur Rocher!"

"*Bonsoir, Sébastien.* We are a little early, *avez vous un table pour nous?*"

"*Votre table vous attends,*" and with that the maître d' led them into the warmth, behind the sweeping staircase in the middle of the room. A table, with white cloth and silver and crystal set, awaited them. Sébastien pulled back Imogene's leather chair and then snapped her napkin and laid it carefully on her lap. Marcel twinkled at her face, which was likely broadcasting her surprise at the level of care being taken.

"This is a lovely place, Marcel. Do they have a speciality? What do you order here?"

"Have you had a cassoulet yet during your time here?"

"Cassoulet? No, what would that be?"

"I think you would see it a combination of a hunter's stew and perhaps chili, but with duck and lamb and sausage rather than the beef or pork you would consider as the viands. It is a wonderful meal, and we could order it for the two of us with a green salad to accompany it, if you would like?"

"That sounds fabulous. Let's do that."

"And, of course, a bottle of wine."

"I will let you choose the wine. I have a couple of friends who are very astute oenophiles back at home, but I tend to purchase reds with pretty labels or discounted prices."

"I cannot pretend to be very clever about wine, but I tend to aim for the middle of the pack and, of course, support French wine whenever possible."

"But of course!"

At any rate, the wine Marcel chose was smooth and rich, and supported the flavour of the amazing stew brought to the table in a steaming bowl with a matching ladle. Marcel did the honours, scooping helpings onto each of their plates. Sébastien seemed to be exactly where he needed to be to top up their wineglasses. Meanwhile, the conversation ranged all over the map, from the history lecture Marcel had attended, which was presented by a former colleague of his from his school days, to Imogene's connections in the history department at home, to the work Imogene had managed to get done that day.

"I normally don't discuss my writing much while I'm working on the first draft, just to keep it fresh in my mind. There is a feeling that I get after talking about it once or twice that perhaps it isn't very original after all, that it's been said before. Even though I know it was me who has been saying it."

"I shall not press you for details." Marcel outlined a cross on his heart, making Imogene laugh.

"It sounds much more cloak and dagger than it really is, and, of course, just wait till the first draft is done and I bore you with it from dusk till dawn!"

"Oh, I can think of other things to be saying during those hours," Marcel murmured, catching her hand and kissing her fingers.

Imogene felt herself blushing, as if the entire restaurant could tell at a glance what they'd been up to the night before and likely would be up to later on. Of course, this was Paris. Probably everyone in the restaurant would be heading off to make love as soon as they'd settled up the bill.

They walked back along the left bank of the Seine as far as the Pont Neuf, and Marcel led her into one of the rounded alcoves containing benches. Further down the bridge, a street musician was playing "La vie en rose" on an accordion. Marcel leaned toward her, kissed her, and then whispered, "Look, Imogene."

She turned her head to the west and saw the Eiffel Tower, all lit up gold, begin to pulse and twinkle, with a searchlight whirling through the dark sky. She felt she couldn't quite tell whether it was real or a product of the kiss. She looked back at Marcel, who was watching her, not the light display, and smiling.

"Every hour on the hour once the sun goes down," he explained, as if he could tell what she was wondering.

The lights, the music, the Seine, the handsome man at her side. It was all proving to be much more than she had bargained for.

# Le petit déjeuner

They had ended up back at her apartment, after strolling down the bank of the Seine, pausing to wave at people on a *Bateau-Mouche* and admiring the play of lights upon the water from the bridge lamps.

After making love, Marcel had padded out to the kitchen to get them glasses of water. He brought them back and crawled under the coverlet with Imogene. "The water of life, Madame," he smiled as he handed her a glass.

"The Celts would call that whisky, I think," she teased.

"And we French would call it wine, but sometimes it has to be water." Marcel touched the rim of his glass to hers and gulped half the glass.

Imogene sipped hers and then set it on the small side table next to the lamp, which she was not about to turn on. There was enough light from the street through the glass curtains to be able to see, and she suddenly felt self-conscious, naked under the sheets with a man she'd known less than a fortnight. Self-conscious about her middle-aged body and the saggy bits that had once been taut. Marcel turned to her after setting down his own glass and ran his fingers down the length of her arm, and Imogene forgot that she was self-conscious, or old, or even capable of speech. Skin on skin. The answer to everything that ailed you.

Eventually they slept. It wasn't until the garbage trucks were grinding their gears right under her window that Imogene awoke. Pushing the hair out of her eyes to see the time on the tiny alarm clock she'd been unable to set, she realized she'd slept through the night, without once being roused by sounds from the apartment above. Either her neighbour René had been away or she'd been so relaxed from lovemaking that nothing could have awoken her.

She turned to see Marcel beside her. Though he hadn't stirred, his eyes were open and looking at her. He smiled and reached for her, pulling her head to his, and kissing her languorously.

"Good morning, Imogene. My father once told me that in order to tell how beautiful a woman really was, you needed to see her as she awoke. No matter how rich she was or what age she was, the true look of beauty was a woman awakening."

"Oh lord, that would put the makeup industry out of business!"

"Ah, but he was correct. I knew you were a lovely woman, but now I can tell for certain how beautiful you are. The light of morning on your skin, and the clarity in your eyes, and the fullness of your lips. I am very fortunate to be with a woman such as you."

Imogene laughed with mixed pleasure and embarrassment. The French seemed to have no trouble stating their feelings, and it was somewhat shocking for her western Canadian middlebrow sensibilities to take.

Marcel took her laughter in stride. "So, Imogene, after we have showered and dressed and gone out to find some *petit déjeuner*, what will your day entail and when can I see you again?"

Not quite willing to think about leaving this nest, Imogene rolled on her side and slid her arm over Marcel's chest, her legs edging along his legs, and her toes finding his toes. "I will need to work on the shape of my book some more, and I think dive into the rough draft of the first section. Also, I was thinking of going out to the Père-Lachaise Cemetery for a wander."

"A wonderful outing. I will send you a map for your phone so you don't end up accosted by one of the self-appointed tour guides, who will try to say you have hired them to show you about."

"What about you? What is on your itinerary for today?"

"I am utterly free today. There is a break for the colleges, so there is no one available for me to interview. The story I am working on requires a strong academic slant, so that leaves me at a loss for the moment. I have some reading to do, but otherwise, it is a rejuvenation week for me, as well."

"That occurs for us in the depths of February, and is called

Reading Week," Imogene said. "It was originally installed to keep students from quitting or committing suicide after getting their mid-term grades, in the dark long winter days. Now most of them go skiing or to some southern resort and come back wind burnished or tanned, and we lecturers stare at them as if we've been invaded by gods."

Marcel laughed and then kissed her, hard. "It's time we got up. As a gentleman, I will allow you the first visit to the *salle de bain*."

Imogene slid out of bed. Her bedroom was so small, it really was mostly bed, with just enough room on either side to sidle out. She caught hold of her robe on the hook by the closet and crossed the hall to the washroom. Luckily her hair needed just a few squishes with wet hands to spring back to shape, so she was in and out of the shower within minutes. She dried off and slathered moisturizer on her cheeks and neck, and ran some mascara across her upper lashes. She brushed her teeth to be polite, and then wrapped her robe firmly around her and went back into the bedroom.

Marcel had folded his clothes into a neat pile and rose from the side of the bed and took his turn in the bathroom. Meanwhile, Imogene dressed, still feeling slightly clumsy and tingly from the night before. She pulled on black tights and her short black skirt, and tossed on her black blouse with the cabbage roses on it, without tucking it in. She pulled her hair back into her mock tortoiseshell clamp and checked herself in the mirror on the closet door. She looked presentable.

Out in the living room, she picked up the bits and bobs of clothing that had been tossed aside the night before. She drew the curtains back on a beautiful morning. Outside, below her windows, people were hurrying to work, but as yet no businesses had opened. She wondered where Marcel had in mind for them to go to breakfast.

He came up behind her and wrapped his arms around her waist, smelling of soap, her shampoo, and the warm musk that was his alone. He nibbled on the lobe of her ear. "Your shower is lovely and strong," he said.

"Isn't it? And the tub is a dream. My tub at home is so short that it never is quite the relaxing time I hope it will be. But here, I've had seven or eight baths already, and have been out to get bubble bath and bath salts, just to celebrate that length and depth."

"Mmm, that sounds decadent and enticing."

"I'm not saying it as an invitation, necessarily." Imogene laughed. "You are turning me into a nymphomaniac, Marcel, thinking about sex constantly."

"This is not a bad thing as long as you are thinking about sex with me, constantly."

"I think we should go for breakfast or we will never get the day started at all."

"Yes, *Madame la Canadienne puritaine*. Let us go. The place I am thinking of is only a five-minute walk from here." He kissed her once more on the side of the neck, and then they unwound themselves and got their coats.

"Be careful on the landings, there is a loose tile along here somewhere," Imogene remarked as she locked the door. Marcel nodded that he had heard her, and proceeded down. It must have been the serotonin coursing through her, making her steps as light as air, because she didn't notice the tile at all heading down behind him.

They ran into no one on the stairs, but Imogene considered that she'd really have something to share with Toni after ballet the next evening.

The bistro Marcel had chosen was indeed just a few blocks away, tucked into the rue Nicolas Flamel just down from the Tour Saint-Jacques that Imogene had been using as a landmark on her travels eastward. They sat just inside, with a large window view out onto the pedestrian-only street. Imogene noticed one of the little space alien mosaics up on the wall opposite them, much like the one on her building. She pointed it out to Marcel after they had ordered their omelettes.

"I've been seeing those little bits of street art all over the place. Is there some significance to them, do you know?"

"The space invaders? They are the work of an anonymous artist named Invader who has been creating and placing them since the end of the last century."

Marcel laughed at the look of incomprehension on Imogene's face.

"The 1990s, not 1890s. I also often forget that we are now completely into a new century. He has been written up quite a bit over the years in art magazines and city-style sections of the newspapers, and I believe he has works in other cities, as well. But he never reveals his identity, much like Banksy. What do you think of them?"

"I am rather charmed by them, and I've never been much for graffiti in the past. But there is such craftsmanship and effort taken, and I've noticed they are apparently themed to where he places his works. They seem to be the perfect sort of street art for Paris, which is so clean and proud of its splendour."

"You see us with such sympathetic eyes, Imogene." Marcel toasted her with his demitasse of dark coffee. "This is the vision of the visitor Paris deserves."

Imogene blushed. While she knew a lot of what Marcel was spouting was Gallic flattery, she hoped she was in a minor way deserving of it. She would hate to be thought of as one of those overloud tourists getting in the way of the trudging workmen trying to deliver something, or as one of the drunken ex-pats she had seen on various winter breaks to Mexico.

One had to be respectful when travelling and find ways to fit into the world one was experiencing. Thank goodness for Toni, and now Marcel, who were allowing her the joy of moving into what she felt was the real Paris.

She shivered with a recollection of physical sensation. Yes, indeed, thank goodness for Marcel.

Her shiver must have been visible because Marcel looked at her questioningly.

She grinned. "It is a good day to be happy in Paris."

# Projects

He had not expected the Canadian woman to be as pleasant as she was turning out to be. It really didn't do to get too close to people, but in this case it couldn't hurt.

He laid out his purchases on the dining room table that had been his mother's pride and which now had a few water rings on it, even though he did try to remember to put his coffee cup on a coaster. He also kept most of his wet work and his electrical tools over the kitchen counter where it made for easier cleanup. And although the place looked messier than it had when his mother had cleaned each day, he maintained a general level of cleanliness and kept things in working order, taking out the garbage regularly and staying neat and tidy himself. It wouldn't do to have people showing any sort of interest in him or his environment.

What would his mother and father make of all this? She'd likely look past all his work and fret about the water rings on the table. His father of course, would be another matter. What would company think? As if they'd ever had company.

She had washed the table lightly with lemon oil every second morning and waxed it once a month, polishing it till it shone and you could see the Sunday candles reflected in its surface as it held pride of place in their living room.

Now it was shoved up against the north-facing window, and piled with papers on the left and jars of pencils and pens across the back, since he had begun using it as his project desk. One hardy ivy spilled over its pot and down one table leg. He pretended to resent watering it but secretly admired the plant for its tenacity to life.

He was like that ivy, not getting much from life but flourishing anyway. Finding a way to make his mark.

# The Size of a Suitcase

"I think I am getting more limber," Imogene said, wiping her brow with a small hand towel before leaning over to pull off her pretty pink ballet shoes.

"And you are sure it's the ballet that is doing that for you? And not any other 'extra-curricular activities'?" Toni laughed at the blush Imogene immediately produced. "I saw the two of you heading off this morning. He looks lovely. Is that your chocolate truffle man?"

"You make him sound like a character in a Shaw play," Imogene replied, "but yes, that was Marcel. He is a journalist."

"A journalist?" A look of caution and possibly disgust showed itself on the police detective's face.

"A former professor of journalism, and don't worry, I have not said anything about you or your work. I have only referred to a nice neighbour I take a dance class with."

"Has he told you what he is writing about?"

Imogene shrugged. "Sort of. He is researching a story

dealing with post-pandemic interests at the Sorbonne. Well, I assume it is the Sorbonne. I suppose it could be any number of colleges or universities. How many are there in Paris?"

Toni shrugged in return. "There are a lot of language colleges set up for foreign nationals. And of course, the technical colleges. I would say, about forty-five?"

"That many? Whoa, perhaps I should ask him the next time I see him."

"Perhaps you should. Of course, perhaps it is more interesting to have mysteries about him? I don't know, that could be enticing, in a ships that pass in the night way."

"Your grasp of English idioms is startlingly good, Toni."

"I was very taken with American television for quite a while." Toni stood up. "Are you ready? I am in need of a great deal of wine and some good, solid conversation."

"*Allons-y!*"

They found their regular table, and Toni managed to communicate with hand signals to the waiter lounging by the bar. Soon they had a bottle of red open on the table, two large goblets in front of them, and a basket of *pomme frites* to share.

"There goes any ballet trimming of the midriff," groaned Imogene, dipping another fry into the spicy mayonnaise that came with them.

"So worth it, though," nodded Toni.

Looking across at Toni, Imogene could see the tension in her younger friend's shoulders, even after the intense workout they'd been through. "Has something gone wrong with your investigation?" she asked.

"Is it that obvious?" Toni asked. "They have taken away my base and sent us all back to the office. There are now too many angles to the case to warrant a situation room in the Grand. And yet I think we need to be in and among the hoteliers to understand the workings of this."

Toni told her that she had spent the day examining yet another catalogue of suitcases and carry-on luggage when her superior entered the office. She had been pulled back from the temporary workspace in the Grand Hotel two days earlier. Nothing had come of the task force except to realize that the crimes were not limited to the Grand. Four other hotels were now involved, though Toni cagily wouldn't offer more details than that, and, so far, the only outcome of the case was that the manufacturer of the ice machines was considering a lawsuit against the Sûreté for ruining his business.

"Meanwhile, my colleagues are giving me these distancing smiles, so they can ride the thin line between being on my side in case I bring this one in for a close but stand in scorn if I come short."

"Really? That's awful."

Toni shrugged. "Maybe I am reading too much into things, but it feels pretty cold at work these days, whatever the case."

"And all the other hotels have had the ice machines used, nothing else?"

"Nothing else. Where else would you think they might put a body part?"

"Well, the kitchen cold room, maybe."

"No."

"That has to mean something."

"I don't follow."

"Well, if the hotels have restaurants attached, there would be huge freezers in there where the killer could be hiding body parts. But if they are found only out where the patrons of the hotel can find them, and not the workers, then there is a plan, unless it would be too difficult to get in to the kitchen. So it's likely not a worker planting these trophies."

"Up to now, it's only been workers who have found them," Toni countered.

"But that is just luck, right? Because the machines were being dismantled? The killer wouldn't have known that. The most likely scenario would be that a visitor staying at the hotel would be digging for ice and come up with a hand or a toe. And then it would be all over the news, and the hotel would lose business."

"If this is an attack on hotels and not a means of dumping evidence of serial murders, and I'm not saying it can't be both, then what does the killer have against these particular hotels?"

"In all the detective novels I read, one is told to always *follow the money*. So, is someone trying to bankrupt those particular hotels? Maybe a rival hotel chain, to make them sell up to them cheap?"

"They aren't owned by the same chain; they are not all catering to the same markets of tourists. I cannot imagine a chain that would want hotels in both the embassy area and the Pigalle. They'd be targeting the Hôtel du Nord next."

"I take it that's not a great place?"

"It's famous for having been the setting of a film long ago. And for a famous line in that film: 'Atmosphere, Atmosphere, Do I have a mouthful of atmosphere?' I cannot tell you why but all you have to do is say 'Hôtel du Nord' to a film buff, and they will return with that 'atmosphere' line, complete in Arletty's cadence."

"So it's a famous hotel?"

Toni nodded. "Famous mostly for being somewhere you'd not want to stay. But, hey, 'atmosphere!'"

Imogene swirled her wine around, almost as if she knew something about wine. "Well, if it's not about the hotels themselves, maybe it's about ice machines."

Toni laughed. "Really? A serial killer who objects to cold drinks?"

"Oh, what do I know? You talk. I will be your springboard."

"Like a gymnast springboard?"

"Exactly, you bounce things off me and if your ideas meet a spark from me, you bounce into the next level of understanding."

"We are looking at the suitcases, which I have to admit comes from talking with you. Who brought in what sized suitcases, who may have been adamant about not receiving valet service, who walked out with much lighter suitcases."

"Oh, good thoughts! And?"

Toni sighed. "And nothing. It appears that people who work in hotels see so many suitcases that they don't tend to stand out, unless there are seven Gucci bags coming in all from the back of one Mercedes, and then the valets pay attention."

She took a long swig of her wine. "I have two people going through all the security camera footage, which goes back only thirty days and alternates floors, so there is no certainty that someone approaching the ice machine will be captured. Half of them don't even show the ice machines, because who thinks someone is going to steal free ice? One of my folks spotted a member of the city council coming out of a room with someone who wasn't her husband, but that is the most we have found so far."

"Ooh la la," said Imogene.

"Yes, I think that possibility is what has so few hotels really embracing the idea of CCTV here," said Toni, checking around the bar to see if anyone was within listening distance. Imogene looked too, but couldn't see anyone interested in the conversation of two casually dressed women.

"The City of Love," Imogene said.

Toni nodded ruefully. "One thing someone at the desk mentioned that I found interesting was that there are very few people travelling with large suitcases anymore. Even the wealthy tend to be travelling with carry-ons, and if they are here to shop, they ship their new clothes home straight from the shops."

"That is likely because the airlines are charging so much for checked bags and then losing them anyway."

"They have a ways to go before they can hire back up to the level of competence that they had before the pandemic shut things down."

"Yes, and I sense a fear that things could once more close up, so they are trying to get by on as skeleton a staff as possible."

"You could be right. There is also the idea that some people found that they preferred jobs where they could work from home, or work from anywhere around the world. Employers are scrambling all over to find people who want to come out to work." Toni made a sweeping gesture to encompass the purportedly missing Parisiennes who should be in offices.

"Ah," argued Imogene, "but there must be gregarious people who need human contact, like waiters and shopkeepers. And caring people who put themselves out for others, like police detectives."

Toni bowed her head in mock acknowledgment. "And of course, university professors emerita, who travel the world in search of adventure and love."

"Adventure, certainly. Adventure of a mild, amusing-anecdote-for-later form. Not necessarily a murder mystery. And love? No, one never searches for that, Toni. Not if one is sane."

"What, it just appears?"

"As if by magic, yes."

"*Alors*, tell me more about your magic."

"I really know less about Marcel than I do about you, but for some reason, being retired has given me a whole sense of abandon that I haven't felt since my early twenties. I mean, the sex is safer but the concept of consequences is about the same. You're right to compare it to a shipboard romance, I think. It's liberating to think it is ephemeral, something that might only last only while I am here in Paris. And, of course, it can't last beyond that. He has work and family hereabouts, and I have a plane ticket for the eleventh of next month."

"The world is so much smaller now, Imogene. People jet all over."

"Not so much anymore, though. And who knows what will happen if the price of travel increases with the price of energy? It feels somewhat flagrant to be flying places even for research. Just to visit? How does one justify that?"

"To a Frenchwoman, love is a better reason than work for burning up the ozone layer."

"Then here is a toast: to me becoming more of a Frenchwoman."

"To you."

Their glasses clinked and they laughed like schoolgirls.

Imogene dug into the depleted basket of fries, and then cocked her head thoughtfully. "You know, Toni. One wouldn't need a large suitcase or even a carry-on to transport most of the items you've found. A gym bag would suffice, right?"

Both women looked down at the gym bags at their feet.

"It could be someone coming into the hotel bar for a drink after a workout," sighed Toni.

Imogene nodded. "It could be anyone."

# "Who are you?"

It hadn't really occurred to Imogene till Toni had asked about Marcel's job that she really knew very little about the man she had invited into her bed. Twice. This wasn't at all like her. She wasn't sure whether it was some sort of response to the divorce, or Paris, or some sort of postmenopausal release, but she was acting with the recklessness of her youth in the early '80s, before death and distress cast a pall on the sexual revolution. It had been shortly after then that husband and children had occurred and put paid to her dalliances, but now it seemed the sense of dire risk somehow had left her once again. After all, she couldn't get pregnant, and even if she were to contract some sort of disease, most were curable, and even if they weren't, she was nearer the finish line now than she had been in her profligate youth.

Still, it seemed almost rude not to have asked Marcel more questions about himself. She knew he was divorced and had two grown sons, one of whom lived in Dubai. She knew he was a journalist doing research at a university but apparently she did not know which university. And she wasn't totally sure what his research was all about, because some things just didn't translate well. She wasn't quite sure whether it was the history of pastimes or traumatic release from post-pandemic pastimes that he had been speaking of, as he had bounced between languages and she had been more intent on the taste of chocolate and cheese together while he had been talking. And she had been more intent on other things when he hadn't been talking. She found herself blushing, the telltale heat behind her ears letting her know her cheeks were likely bright red. What a shameless hussy she had turned into while far away from home and judgmental eyes.

Maybe she wouldn't ask a thing about Marcel's work and background. Perhaps she should maintain the relationship as a glorious mystery, held in amber. After all, it wasn't as if it was going to continue as a long-distance romance. This was a pleasant *divertissement* for the both of them and would end with a bittersweet kiss on a train platform, if she were engineering it for maximum cinematic credibility.

And after all, what did he know about her?

Practically everything, really, at least about her present project. And her past career. Oh well, it wasn't as if it was against the law to bore someone with your old stories. And he hadn't appeared to be bored in her company.

She would make a point of asking more questions the next time she saw him. Meanwhile, she needed to get on with her writing. Now that she was set on reading Victor Hugo, she really had to get down to doing so. *Les Misérables* was 1,300 pages long and not for the faint of heart. No wonder so many versions she had seen previously were expurgated. Hugo tended to go on quite a bit into the social politics of why people were the way they were. And yet, the minute you saw the inherent villainy in the character, no matter what his name seemed to be, it was turning out to always be Thénardier in some sort of disguise. Equally, Monsieur la Madeleine had several names, and the reader was always aware long before the reveal that this was once more Jean Valjean.

Was there some ulterior motive to his use of names? Was it particularly French, or particularly Hugo? If, after all, the initial part of the book was Valjean being told by the priest that he was a friend and a good man, not a thief and a scoundrel, and then becoming that good man, was he not changing? Or had he always been a good man, even when stealing a loaf of bread, which had caused his sentencing in the first place? And that was what Hugo was trying to show? While prison had hardened Valjean, or so he believed, the priest had seen through to the goodness in his soul? Meanwhile, Javert, who had only the law to go by, could discern no shades of grey, only the concept that once one was designated a criminal, one was always a criminal.

And Marius's dilemma of having to change his mind about Thénardier, who, he was brought up to believe, had saved his father, while the reader knew from the beginning that he had been robbing him on the battlefield, wasn't that the ironic counterpoint to the concept that people never truly changed? Marius never was disabused of the notion that Thénardier had done one good thing in his life, for which he was beholden to him. As a result, though, the money Marius gave him at the end of the story provides the funds to head to the Americas to become a slave trader. Hugo was saying that you were born good or bad, and how society treated you had little to do with your actual character.

Imogene wondered if that were true. She had been rereading the section of the book where Marius was spying on the Thénardiers, who were making themselves even more miserable-looking in their garret to dupe Monsieur Leblanc out of more money. At that point, Thénardier is beginning to realize that Leblanc is Monsieur Madeleine, who he now thinks ripped him off by taking Cosette away. Thénardier's capacity to believe he is owed for his thievery is astonishing in its blatant greed. Marius's inability to switch gears quickly enough is irritating to the reader. Javert's inability to see the good in Valjean stretches the reader's patience. The only thing that moves with the reader is Valjean's ability to survive while offering the benefit of the doubt to begin with in his dealings with villains. He is the man we all wish to be, thought Imogene. Strong, stalwart, able to do good, able to perceive evil that must be vanquished. And yet always humble enough to realize he required the help of others. *Liberté, Égalité, Fraternité* indeed.

Imogene pushed herself back from her table to go get

another cup of tea. Her ideas were adding up and her copy of the book was beginning to bulge with the sticky notes she had wedged in-between the pages. It was time to begin her own writing, which was always the hardest part. There was something unnerving about a blank piece of paper or computer document. The cursor blinking; the screen dimming with inaction.

She looked at her cue cards. The pink cards for Toni were filling up more than the blue cards for Marcel or the yellow cards for Other People. Toni had definitely become part of her own narrative, and it was interesting to note how unlike Javert she was, given that she was a police detective in Paris. Her innate goodness shone through and she seemed able to see the good in others, even when Imogene could sense that, as a woman, she was having to push to be acknowledged in her profession. Imogene wondered if that ability or perhaps desire to find a connection with others would be what brought Toni success or what held her back in the police force.

In any case, she was glad to have found Toni as a friend here in Paris. Even more than the sensuous Marcel, Toni was making Imogene feel a part of the fabric of the place, more than a visitor, if not truly a citizen.

As if Toni were listening to Imogene's thoughts, the message app on her phone buzzed through a message from her. Her boss had given her tickets to a guitar concerto in Sainte-Chapelle that he couldn't use, and would Imogene like to join her that evening?

Imogene quickly texted back a yes, and then sorted out in her mind the time left to her that afternoon for work. If she could double down and get a couple of pages written, she would feel fine about breaking off slightly early to get ready for the concert. Just as in grad school, a deadline had a grand way of focusing her mind, and she was soon typing away furiously. Once the paper ceased to be blank, Imogene was of the same mind as the writer Anne Lamott, who espoused the value of "shitty first drafts." The idea was to get writing, and to edit and reshape things once you were finished laying it all out. The concept was a good one, because how could anyone possibly shape and hone something that wasn't already in existence?

Imogene had attended a lecture once by the late author Alistair MacLeod, who told the audience that his method of writing was to think of each sentence till it was perfect in his mind and then finally write it down and begin to think of the next sentence. There must have been an audible gasp that reached the podium, because he had smiled into the crowd and said, "Well, I'm sixty-four and I've only written one novel and a handful of stories. So I'm not suggesting this is the best way to work."

Imogene couldn't imagine working that way, but on the other hand, she couldn't deny the beauty of MacLeod's words. She herself was a believer in shaping the work once it was on the page. She rarely spoke about the work she was about to write, believing that first deliverance to have a power to it that was diminished by too much talk beforehand.

And now here she was, starting to set down her thoughts about reading Victor Hugo while situated in the locale he was writing about. According to Hugo's own precision of detailing location, she was actually living just down the street from where the students had set up their disastrous blockade on the rue de la Grande Truanderie. That was something she needed to sort out for herself. She riffled through her copy of the book to find the start of the blockade. Tomorrow, she would reread the section and then walk the route.

Maybe she should take the Paris sewer tour, to understand the route taken when Jean Valjean saved Marius. She shuddered at the thought. She had claustrophobia. Maybe she could leave some things entirely to the imagination.

# Concert in the Sacristy

"I kept thinking about lining up for the tour of this church, especially on sunny days because of the stained-glass windows, but the crowds just seemed to make me feel tired every time I walked past," Imogene said quietly to Toni as they settled into their seats. Rodrigo's *Concierto de Aranjuez* was going to be played with a chamber orchestra and a Swiss guitarist who was apparently very well known, especially to a crowd of young men sitting further toward the front of the sacristy where the orchestra was set.

"I know exactly what you mean," said Toni. "There are so many crowds even around Notre Dame, which hasn't been open since the fire. I think there should be something awe-inspiring about entering a place of worship, and to have to wait in line for that tends to diminish the effect."

"Yes, and ever since reading those novels by Ken Follett about cathedral building, I've been more impressed by cathedrals. The idea that the architect would not live to see the result of his imagination had never occurred to me."

Toni smiled. "There is a saying by Rajinder Tagore, about the one "who plants trees, knowing he will never sit in their shade, has at least started to understand the meaning of life."

"That's beautiful. How did you come to know that?"

"My brother the architect, again."

"The man with the staircase fascination?"

"One and the same! He had it as a poster on his bedroom wall."

"It's interesting. I suppose the builders of the pyramids must have been the same, but one doesn't tend to think of the time it took to put the pyramids together, in comparison with a cathedral."

"And there is some intrigue about whether a church will be designated a cathedral. Some begin as cathedrals-to-be, and others are granted cathedral status later in their existence."

"Was this always a cathedral?"

"Sainte-Chapelle? I don't think it is technically a cathedral, only Notre-Dame is designated as one, but it is tremendous, isn't it? Of course, so is Saint-Eustache, next to us. And then there are the basilicas, Saint-Denis and Sacré-Cœur. I think there are more than 190 churches in Paris alone."

"But only one can be a cathedral."

"The church of churches."

Imogene looked up at the long columns of coloured glass, the amazing windows of Sainte-Chapelle, for which it was famous. They glowed warmly in the lights, but she was sure the early-day sun cascading through the glass would be amazing. Surrounded as the church was by the walls of the palace, she wasn't sure how much sun the windows would ever see. She was about to ask Toni if she knew the best time to come for maximum sunlight, when the orchestra began its tuning noises that would lead to the beginning of the concert. Besides, she didn't know if she could make it up those tight little stairs without Toni along with her. It wouldn't do to have a claustrophobic panic attack in the middle of Paris on one's own.

They applauded politely as the conductor walked out to the dais, and then again, this time led by the more vigorous fanboys when the guitarist took the stage. He nodded solemnly, sat with his foot on a tiny step stool, and turned to the conductor to await his command. A magic descended on the crowd, with the mellow notes of the guitar bouncing off the glass and stone. Imogene could understand why the carol "Silent Night" had been such a miracle when Gruber's organ had failed; a guitar in an old church took on far more palpable tones than around a campfire or in a folk club. There was a life and warmth to the tone that couldn't be replicated outside of walls of stone. Perhaps that was what made the fado and flamenco of guitarists who recorded in caves so erotic. She startled herself by considering eroticism in the conclave of a church. What was happening to her, she who had once been considered the girl "most likely to become a headmistress" by some of her cattier high school friends?

After the concert, as they twisted their way down the

narrow staircase that had led up to the church, Imogene marvelled once more at the things she was experiencing thanks to the friendships she had made. She doubted she'd have tackled the twisty staircase on her own, but if you couldn't feel safe with a police officer, then what was the world coming to? She said as much to Toni as they exited the church and the official grounds.

"I don't think I'd even have ventured out at night on my own, let alone known about this, so thank you doubly for making this happen, Toni."

"Ah, it's all thanks to *mon capitaine*, but I understand you. It takes time for anyone to develop a sense of things to do, let alone when you are a woman alone and in a strange place."

"There would be a very good niche market for someone to create: cultural outings for solitary female tourists."

Toni laughed. "Can you imagine, though? Someone with a flag and a whistle, leading two rows of people dressed in denim shorts and anoraks into the theatre?"

Imogene wasn't about to point out the touch of snobbery in this very funny image. It would be hard to be a *pure laine* Parisienne, and constantly have tourists wandering through your city, gawking and slowing down the pace. It was nice to be considered worthy of inclusion, and she agreed wholeheartedly to stopping at the bar looking over at the Chatelet, across the river from where they'd just been.

"How do you handle the influx of tourists into your hometown?"

"What do you mean, Imogene?"

"Well, the crowds walking along with the tour guide with the flag, or the buses stopping to unload people at the Moulin Rouge, or the massive line-ups at the Eiffel Tower. Everywhere you go, you hear people speaking another language than French. Surely it must weigh on you at times? I don't think Marcel cares for it much."

Toni looked thoughtful. "I suppose, but when you are Parisienne, you know that you are a custodian of a great jewel, and it is obvious to you that people will want to come to see what you, by great good fortune, have been born to or, in my case, came to as a student and stayed." She shrugged. "So you grin and bear it, or sometimes you growl and bear it, but it is what it is. Besides, I am not sure I would have a job if it weren't for the number of people drawn to this city. Our force has grown in ratio to the populace, and the temporary population is also taken into consideration."

"And does your job get less stressful in the winter months when there are fewer tourists?"

"I have to admit," Toni said, "winter, when some of my old friends come back from their summer homes, is a more pleasant world. Not that I see anyone that often, with my schedule, but it doesn't help when the ones you want to see are all off in Aix or the Dolomites."

Imogene had been wondering about Toni's circle, given her obvious ability to extend friendship. It made sense that she was feeling a bit lonely left in town with friends who bounced between homes. Being a police officer couldn't be an easy life maintaining close friendships, anyhow. As she had intimated, it was impossible to talk about her job to people who lived alongside the things she was investigating. Maybe she, Imogene, was as much of a bonus to Toni as she, Toni, was to Imogene, alone in Paris. It would be nice to think so.

"So, fewer tourists and less sunshine but more friends."

Toni smirked. "Says the Canadian who arrives in the mid-season. Imogene, there are always tourists in Paris. People come for Christmas. They come all the time. Yes, things slow down a bit in the cooler weather, I suppose. But domestic issues still occur. Theft still occurs. And murder is rarely a tourism issue. Unless the body parts are left in hotels." She grimaced.

"Ah, so you've reached that conclusion for certain? That they are being brought into the hotels and dumped rather than 'created' in the hotels themselves?" Imogene leaned forward, both to keep her voice low and to express her interest.

Toni followed suit, lowering her own voice. "Yes, and the forensic team has discovered some anomalies in how long they think the various parts have been frozen. Some are relatively fresh while others have been frozen long enough for, for certain atoms, or maybe enzymes to break down? Something like that. Anyhow, there is a measurement they use to tell. And they're all up and down the ruler."

"Wow, where are all these people coming from and why isn't anyone reporting them missing?"

"That's the big question I keep asking myself. We have combed the missing persons lists, and we've reached out to our counterparts at Interpol to search their own countries' lists, and we're coming up empty. Also, no one has a record of a mass or serial murderer chopping up his or her victims in quite this manner. And as far as we've been told, no other hotels across Europe have been targeted." Toni took a gulp of wine. "Tell no one I told you any of this."

Imogene mimed her lips zippering shut. "I can barely order a sandwich in the *boulangerie* in this country without having to point. Your secrets are safe with me."

Toni smiled but her face looked strained. "I am sure all the other detectives and officers go home and discuss all manner of things with their wives and mothers, but they would make a huge case of my talking out of turn, being the only woman on the case. Because you know how we women love to gossip."

Imogene could tell there was an underswell of ugliness that Toni wasn't admitting to in her job, but it wasn't her place to prod. She sighed in solidarity and nodded.

"You get that in academe, as well. As if we're not allowed to discuss problem students with our friends or colleagues. Half of our male colleagues are thinking about sleeping with their students, but somehow it is morally repugnant for us to be talking about attitude and belligence issues in the classroom. It's really unfair, because even being able to just sound off about horrid little toads in the classroom enables you to paste on that professorial smile and go back into the lecture hall and give it your all, all over again."

"Yes, I can see that, and I do think discussing issues with

you has been very helpful to my way of thinking of the case. But I would never let my boss hear me say anything to that effect."

Imogene leaned over and poured the rest of the carafe of wine into their glasses. "Sometimes even just saying things out loud to another person helps to solidify ideas in your own mind." She proposed a toast: "Here's to productive gossip and chitchat and tittle-tattle and *il pettegolezzo* and *der klatsch* and, and what do you call it in French?"

Toni raised her glass. "*Les commérages, les potins.*"

"Yes, to *les potins,* those silly words only women are accused of, which mean so little and say so much."

"*Salut*, to gossip."

"And, for what it is worth, I feel very privileged to be chosen as your sounding board."

Toni nodded and smiled at her. "Thank you. The pleasure is mine."

# Return Engagement

It was two days before Imogene saw Marcel again, and in that time she had roughed out an outline and produced a solid opening two chapters. The first had been relatively easy to write, as it laid out the situation of the success of the first book and the premise of the narrative to follow. The second chapter dealt with her initial assumptions and how *Les Misérables* had won her over, even with the weight of it being akin to a kettlebell.

Now the heavy lifting, to continue the metaphor, was about to begin. She had to explain her connection to Hugo from before Paris and relate it to her understanding of Hugo from a Paris reading perspective. And in this case, which differed greatly from her sojourn in Saint Petersburg, her perspective had to do more with the people she had been meeting than with the buildings she was passing.

Marcel had texted her several times, mostly with cheery news or a photo of some part of Paris he was passing through.

They planned to connect for drinks after four, and Imogene was looking forward to telling him of her progress. She also was planning to ask him about himself and his work. The more she thought about how little she knew about him, the more embarrassed she was. How self-centred she must have appeared, conversing almost entirely in English and not seeming curious or interested in his background and past.

It hadn't felt that way when she was with him, of course. Their conversations had all seemed completely organic and flowed with a natural give and take. At the time, Imogene felt that Marcel was sharing the conversation equally. But now that she worked her way back through their times together, she could see that he was often asking questions more than answering any. Either that, or he was offering up historical tidbits about Paris, recipes and styles of cookery, literary allusions, and architectural analysis. She was starting to believe that there was nothing Marcel couldn't talk about at length, except perhaps his family background and personal work. He seemed to veer away from discussing his family with her, but that was understandable. They were having a moment, not building a relationship.

Marcel had secured a reservation at the little restaurant operating out of the embankment of the Seine just by the Pont Neuf. Imogene had pointed it out as a curiosity one day when they were walking, and it was a very thoughtful gesture on his part, she knew, because it was likely full of tourists and was not somewhere that Marcel would necessarily frequent.

Imogene based her entire outfit on the need to wear sunglasses at that time of the afternoon on the banks of the Seine. She decided to roll with the old-school movie-star concept. She pulled on her tight black jeans and a boat-necked, long-sleeved T-shirt in a marine blue, and tied her matching silk scarf into a broad hairband. With her dark shades and bright red lipstick, she thought she looked like she was headed off to ride a Vespa with someone named Giancarlo. It was exactly what she was aiming for. She tossed her keys and card wallet into her small cross-body bag and slipped into her black leather flats. They were considered walking shoes and she had bought them especially for this trip from the "good" shoe store back home, only to find out they were fine for a jaunt or two but not a full day of tromping about Paris. She had broken down after a few days and bought a pair of Skechers for her actual walking. But these shoes went with the role and would be fine for the few blocks' walk down to the river.

Along the way to her date, Imogene once again marvelled at her luck in finding such a good place to stay. In a different century, Les Halles might not have been quite so salubrious a place for a woman alone, but nowadays it was bright and well-populated and safe as anywhere. She thought about Éponine and her sisters being sent off alone on Paris streets, doing their father's nefarious bidding. And poor Fantine, finding herself pregnant and alone, having to skulk away to find a living for her and her daughter. Paris from Hugo's perspective was no place for a woman alone. Much like Dickens, he had a strong socialist vision of the world. But his vision seemed to hold that if a woman wasn't under a man's protection, she was likely as not to come to harm or be hardened in irredeemable ways.

Of course, there was the Esmeralda aspect to Hugo's women, too. In that case, the gypsy girl who was so adept at taking care of herself might go out of her way for one less capable. Therefore, there were three levels of women for Victor Hugo: the protected, like Cosette under Monsieur la Madeleine's care; the vulnerable and used, like Fantine; and the capable and streetwise, like Éponine and Esmeralda. Imogene wondered if she should reread *The Hunchback of Notre Dame* while she was in Paris. Not that she could get into the mid-restoration Notre Dame itself, but she might have an interesting gargoyle moment somewhere else.

She was walking along the side of the river, just passing under the bridge, when she spotted Marcel. He had managed to get them a table right along the river, across from the restaurant area itself. He looked up from the menu and caught her eye, and even at a distance, she could see the crinkle of a smile begin to emerge across his face.

He stood as she arrived at the table and embraced her, offering her the Gallic two kisses, before helping her into her chair. "You look perfect," he said. "As if you walked out of one of the black and white photos the man sells in his stall just above us."

Imogene acknowledged the compliment and admitted that was exactly what she was aiming for.

"My mother came to Paris before I was born," she said. "She lived a rather adventurous life for a few years before settling down and producing me, which I suppose for her was an adventure of another kind. At any rate, she had a photo album of pictures in which she looks like some sort of film star. I thought she was always a sort of less voluptuous Sophia Loren, but apparently she looked very much like a Swedish film star of the time named Märta Torén. Unfortunately, Torén died while Mom was in Europe, and it caused a bit of consternation for her, since it had been in the news and then people would turn around and see Mom and look really shocked. And I really don't know why I started that story." Suddenly self-conscious, Imogene looked down at the menu to avoid the bemusement in Marcel's eyes. This is why she knew nothing about him. She was obviously just nattering on about nothing at all any time she was in his orbit.

"I have heard of her," Marcel said. "She was in a Peter Lorre movie, *Casbah*, I think."

"It's amazing to me how many European film stars there were whom we North Americans never paid attention to. The Hollywood press and advertising were phenomenal. You couldn't go anywhere without recognizing the stars of the silver screen, but even with such famous filmmakers coming out of Italy and France and Sweden, there were precious few actors who would be household names—just Sophia Loren and Ingrid Bergman. I guess there still aren't. Let's see: Daniel Brühl, Isabella Rossellini, Cristoph Waltz,

Famke Janssen, the Skarsgård fellows. We're an awfully insular continent, when it comes down to it."

"Ah, but collectively only. Individually, there are still people like you who venture out beyond the boundaries of your conditioning. And *voilà*, here you are, a vision of the Paris we still aspire to."

Marcel turned to the waiter who had arrived at their table with a bottle of water and an attentive look. Marcel suggested they order three dishes from the tapas menu and a bottle of wine to share. Imogene was more than happy to let him order and settled in to watch the river and the people walking by.

"I am impressed by their menu," Marcel said after the waiter had left. "Everything is sourced locally and the chef has a philosophy of working in season and not wasting materials. In fact, that is why our crockery doesn't match. Everything is purchased at flea markets and reused."

"It's charming. Of course, you can get away with everything being sourced locally here. Back where I come from, unless we resort to some fancy hydroponic indoor growing conditions, we would be stuck with an entire season of eating rutabagas and rather wobbly potatoes."

"Rutabagas?"

"Large yellow turnips, really. Good either cooked or raw. They grow late into the season and keep well in cold cellars."

"We call those *les chou de Siam, je pense*. The English call them *swedes, non*?"

"Yes, swedes! I have heard that. Siamese cabbage? That is

unusual, but I am glad you know what I mean. Anyhow, what I mean to say is that our growing season is short, and we cannot grow much beyond apples and berries for sweet things."

"Is there any need for anything more than apples and berries, though?"

"Now that we have been so inured to refrigerated trucks, what would we do without our bananas and watermelons and star fruit and oranges year-round?"

"And that is the *tristesse*; we hate to give up what we have known to go back to what is sustainable. We think, ah, why should we bother? The world is about to disappear or shake us parasitical people off it; there won't be but another generation or two, and I won't be around to see the destruction and horror."

"True, and the accompanying thought of what can one person do that would make any difference at all?"

Marcel nodded.

"But we can," continued Imogene, realizing even as she spoke that she was getting on a hobby horse. "Our separate and individual actions can show others, and the companies who really need to change, that we are willing to make sacrifices for the greater good. We are able to move to collective action, and perhaps then something that would provide actual change could happen."

"I applaud your passion. But what would you do if the realization came that air travel had to be contained and you could no longer travel to destinations you desired, like, for instance, Paris?"

"Of course, I think about that sort of thing and even more since I am working on a book that espouses reading certain books in the very context in which they were written for a different and important cachet. Instead of using literature as a window to the world from the comfort of your own living room, I am advocating using books as a passport directly to the source. I have even discussed the idea of carbon offsets from the profits of the books, should we incur profits."

"And these profits would come from where?"

"Well, I have never had an agent, so I was thinking of using the ten per cent they would get from my royalties to plant trees, or purchase rainforest, or whatever the offset *du jour* would happen to be."

"That is admirable for you, but do you think it would cover all the people who will race off to read in Paris after reading your book?"

"I am actually unsure how many people will pick up and do that, for one thing. We never did see much of an uptake on trips to Saint Petersburg from the last book, but, then again, heading to Russia isn't all that easy or fun."

"Ah, but to come to Paris to read Victor Hugo. That is romantic and attainable."

"Do you think a lot of people showed up in Paris after having seen the musical?"

"No, but the musical wasn't saying, 'Come watch us sing with British accents about France *in* Paris,' now, was it?"

"Do you think my books will do harm, Marcel?"

"Harm is subjective." He pointed at one of the *Bateaux-*

*Mouches* passing them on the river, but Imogene was not to be distracted.

"Is it? I think we could quantify it. At least in terms of jet fuel, we could."

"Yes, but what about the ways in which the visitor approaches the city?" Marcel asked. "Instead of gawking and judging and remaining outside looking in, your fan would come, book in hand, and absorb the nature of the city. He or she would watch and listen, and find the rhythms, in order to read the book in their hands. And with luck, it would transfer from Hugo to Dumas, to Proust to Colette. You are opening the door to the tuned-in tourism of an ideal world. There is something good happening there."

"What makes that better than the tourists you already get, though?"

"Well, for one thing, there will be fewer of yours, just based on the fact that they would have to enjoy reading. I just read in the *New York Times* recently that, statistically speaking, thirty-three per cent of Americans never read a book after they graduate high school, and fifty-eight per cent who do read don't manage to finish one book a year."

"But that is Americans. I think Canadians are a bit different, statistically."

"You are also one tenth the size of the population of the United States. When we think tourists, we tend to think Americans."

"I hear a lot of Dutch and German being spoken as I walk about here."

"Yes, and they tend to be collectors of experiences, as I see them. It's as if they're still working on badges from their youth clubs. But they are somewhat more respectful, because they too get hordes of visitors to their small countries."

Imogene nodded. "I suspect that is true. We don't see too many tourists where I am from. Tourists landing in Ontario go to Niagara Falls and blanch when they find out the relative distance to anything else. Those who come my way are mostly from the East on their way to the Rocky Mountains, which get flooded with tour buses through the summer months. I tend to go to the mountains in May or September, just outside of the high months. And then, of course, ski season begins, and those of us who don't ski avoid the mountains entirely."

Their food had arrived and some manoeuvring had to be done to fit plates on the small table. Marcel set the wine bottle on the ground between his foot and the walled edge of the river. Imogene dug in and nearly swooned at the combination of tastes in the salad and the beef tongues. For a few minutes they didn't speak, except to mumble praise about the food.

Then Imogene sat back and sighed. "This is perfect. This is going to be one of my Proustian 'madeleine' meals, I just know it."

"And what will you recall, Imogene?"

"The chatter and laughter of people, the murmuring of the river, the sound of that police siren that makes me think of foreign films, the very handsome man across from me, and the taste of olives." She laughed. "And that will be enough to take me into my dotage right there."

Marcel smiled indulgently at her. "And I will recall a beautiful woman of keen intelligence who shared her moments in Paris with me."

"We are having some beautiful moments, aren't we?"

"Beautiful moments, and beautiful wine," Marcel pulled the bottle back up to fill their glasses. "Here is to our madeleine moments, Imogene, *chèrie.*"

Imogene clinked her glass to his, and realized that there was never going to be a good time to quiz Marcel on his background. As for his intentions, it was pretty obvious that he was indulging in a glorious temporary fling, and that was fine with her, given the timing of her stay. They would have this time together, and every time she raised a glass of French wine or ate some blue cheese with chocolate, she would recall Marcel, in the same way Proust remembered his childhood by eating a madeleine cookie. And that would be enough.

# More than Enough

Imogene ran into Toni on the staircase the next morning. While Imogene was dressed casually, just pulled together enough to make it to the bakery for a baguette and a croissant to go with her coffee, Toni was obviously heading off to work. They walked together toward the Metro entrance Toni was aiming for.

"How is it going?" Imogene asked.

"We have been officially turned into a mid-warm case, which means two weeks from becoming cold and off the roster. Nothing has happened since we discovered the 'parts' and nothing new has been found. There is nothing more to do except wait and see if something else occurs. This may just go down on the books as a weird mystery."

"But if it happens again? Maybe it's one of those cases where they go crazy every two months or once a year."

Toni shrugged. "Well, then we hope our notes and files are considered when they investigate those new occurrences."

"Oh, I am sorry. This sounds sad."

"Not really. It's the way of the job. Not everything gets, how do you say, tied up with a bow."

"Right."

"I really must go. But what are you doing this evening? Would you like to go to a movie at the Pompidou with me?"

"I'd love to!"

"Great. I will text you the details later. Have a good day, Imogene!"

And with a flourish of her hand, Toni descended into the Metro, leaving Imogene to head off down the street to her favourite boulangerie. There was a short line, and Imogene had enough time to decide to buy a sandwich for her midday meal later, as well as the baguette she had intended to buy. She wasn't sure why all these carbs weren't making her as large as a horse, but the reverse was true. She seemed to be toning up a bit and losing weight in Paris. It probably had something to do with having to tromp down and climb up interminable stairs in order to get to the carbs, she snickered to herself. The man behind the counter looked a little puzzled, as if he thought she had been laughing at him. Mortified, Imogene straightened up and gave her order in her best French.

Instead of taking the same route back she had earlier with Toni, she decided to walk the block behind their place and come out at the corner of the rue de la Grande Truanderie, where the student barricade made so famous in the musical of *Les Misérables* was supposed to have been formed. She could see that the building to her right between her and Saint-Eustache was new, all steel and glass offices. There must have been another older building in that place, possibly the tavern they commandeered. The building to her left was the same age as her apartment, which apparently dated into the 1600s. So were the buildings directly behind her, where the restaurants and their red awnings stretching into the pedestrianized street were already washing up to open for the coffee crowd. She moved closer to the building on the left, looking for a possible entrance to the sewer. There was something, near the base of the wall.

When she got even closer, she saw it was another bit of street art, a mosaic of a little rathole, with the head of a small plastic toy rat peering out. She thought it must have been modelled on the mouse in the Bourse de commerce she had seen the other day. She snapped a photo with her phone, bending over to get a straight-on shot of the little fellow. The tile work was beautifully managed, with blue and purple tiles alternating, making a three-dimensional effect for the rat's entrance.

Maybe this was a tip of the hat to Hugo's sewer entrance? Or maybe it was just another bit of Invader's work. Somehow, though, it seemed different from the little video game characters. There was more depth to the mosaic, and the addition of the rat head gave it an additional nuance. Perhaps this artist was absorbing and combining techniques, marrying the sense of those neon-coloured monkey heads she had seen glued to the second storey of buildings near the mosaics of Invader.

She surprised herself at taking such note of street art. Marjorie, who had long been enamoured of it, would be so surprised to hear her snobby mother was beginning to take it seriously.

Imogene straightened herself up and headed home, determined to reread the barricade sequence as her Hugo studies for that day. The man running the ten-euro fripshop nodded to her, as he had every day since she'd purchased her blue cardigan from him. Perhaps that was the way you enmeshed yourself into a neighbourhood, she mused, by bumping into people on the street or purchasing things from the local shops. Otherwise, you could live for years without knowing who lived near you. She thought about her apartment building back home. How many people could she greet by name, after having lived there almost two years? No more than two, which was the same as here, and within three weeks she had been out for drinks with one of these two, knew both their names, and had run into them elsewhere in the city. And western Canadians prided themselves on being such an open and friendly bunch. Of course, perhaps that was meant toward foreigners, not each other.

Once she was back up the stairs to her present apartment, the first thing was to make a pot of coffee. She washed her hands and set about her homely chore, smiling into the sunny warmth of the apartment. Raymonde had warned that it got very hot in the summer months, but in the spring it was perfect for Imogene, who ran a bit cold at the best of times.

She laid out the *pain au chocolat* on a small plate and prepared her coffee cup. The baguette was set aside for later and she popped the ready-made sandwich into the small fridge. The coffee bubbled and dripped and was soon ready. She took her breakfast to the table and sat with her back halfway to the window to avoid appearing to spy on her neighbours across the small road.

No wonder the barricades had gone up so quickly in these narrow streets. It wasn't as if you could reach across, quite, but it would be impossible for more than one vehicle to pass through. She was always impressed at how fluid the garbage trucks seemed to be as they drove along each morning, cleaning up the detritus of the previous evening's merrymaking.

From the corner of her eye, she could see the older gentleman coming to his window for his cigarette. She wondered if he did this out of custom, because she had never spotted anyone else in his rooms. Maybe his late wife had hated the smell of cigarette smoke in her curtains and upholstery, and he had compromised by leaning out the window. Or perhaps he had never married and took the time out during his tobacco break to engage in a bit of people watching. In the time-honoured tradition of living in tight quarters, he didn't acknowledge Imogene, or she him. This thin veil of respect allowed them both to pretend they couldn't see through into each other's lives. She hoped against hope that the glass curtains in her bedroom had left something to the imagination, and made a mental note to draw the full drapes the next time Marcel stayed over.

Breakfast finished, it was time to get back to work. Imogene flipped though the Marius section, smiling at the efforts Hugo had gone to in creating a character who could stand so firm in his convictions about his father's benefactor till proved wrong, and still maintain his love from afar for Cosette with no doubt. Perhaps that was Hugo's greatest vision of heroism, even more than the priest's ability to see the good in everyone—the capacity to change your mind. Perhaps that was why he had given Valjean so many different names throughout the book, and only that one constant prisoner number. Maybe it was Javert in opposition to Marius, rather than in opposition to Thénardier, who was the yardstick of man in Hugo's world. After all, Valjean himself might be the outlier, the *Übermensch*, whereas Marius and Javert were the ordinary men, finding their way to their destinies and trials.

God, he went into irritatingly dense political detail, did Hugo. Imogene read for a bit and then put the book down, shoving her ticket to the Sainte-Chapelle concert in as a bookmark. As she got up to get another cup of coffee, she heard a thud directly overhead. René must have dropped something quite heavy on the floor.

She wondered what exactly it was that he did. Some sort of illustrating or drafting work she gathered from seeing him at the art shop, but did one do that freelance at home? She wished she had her grandmother's more garrulous qualities. That woman could get a cashier's life history out of them in the time it took to bag her groceries. Imogene had inherited her gran's curiosity about people without her accompanying lack of boundaries.

There was another thud, not quite so loud but in the same part of the ceiling. Imogene sat still. Should she go up and see if he was all right? There was silence. Then suddenly she heard screeching, as if a heavy piece of furniture was being dragged. He must be okay. He was just redecorating and not being very careful about it. Imogene hoped he wasn't scuffing up parquet floors as pretty as the ones here in Raymonde's apartment. They looked the same age as the ones she had seen at Versailles, if not quite so intricate. She wondered if all the suites shared them. She should ask Toni if her apartment had the same sort of flooring.

It was odd; she had never seen beyond the door frame of Toni's home. But then again, she had never invited Toni upstairs to her place either. Perhaps it was like her friend Axel from grad school had once said about Germany, that one entertained out in restaurants, not by inviting people home to one's flat, unless they were immediate family, because housing was so small and so intimate that there were rarely rooms set aside just for company, like the formal dining rooms in North American homes or the parlours in British homes that were set up so that the "queen could come for tea." Would those parlours continue to be dusted and kept pristine now for the king, or was it the respect for Elizabeth as a person that had made people believe she might just pop by?

She could understand the concept of not having people

invade your personal space if you had only so much space at all. She supposed it didn't hold true for affairs of the heart, because there had been no compunction on Marcel's part to enter her suite when invited to do so. And if the clichéd tales of amorous Parisians were anything to go by, many doors opened wide for such occasions.

She wondered if Toni had a gentleman caller. She had never spoken of one, and Imogene had always felt it was as rude to ask if someone was seeing anyone as it was to ask if someone was pregnant. Was Toni at all shocked by Imogene's indulging in a relationship with Marcel? She didn't appear to be, just teasing her in the manner of all friends. If Toni did have a man, one would have expected to have heard someone on the stairs at any rate, which Imogene never had. Nor had she heard anyone walking up to René's apartment, but he seemed much more of a loner than Toni.

Loner young men were a worrisome thing. It used to be that one could just pity them and try to fix them up with one's dull cousin, but nowadays they were turning into radical misogynists and shooting up schools and churches and places of business. Imogene hoped René wasn't getting up to some destructive mischief. Perhaps he was writing a book or creating some continuous Rube Goldberg machine or forging paintings up there. She hoped it was something like that, and not a dirty bomb.

Imogene forced herself to get back to her own work and stop worrying about René's. She pulled the heavy tome toward her on the table. It was interesting that most people seemed to mistake the students' rebellion of 1832, which Hugo was highlighting in *Les Misérables*, for the French Revolution of 1790, or even the later Paris revolt. The student rebellion, the Friends of the ABC, was predicated on the death of a popular General Lamarque, who was the only Republican leader who appeared to have any care for the working and lower classes of Paris. His death during the cholera epidemic started a rumour that the royalists were poisoning the wells of Paris.

With cholera raging, it was interesting that Hugo had Valjean carrying Marius out through the sewers and not focusing on the dangers. Of course, Thénardier and Javert were of more danger to them than the disease, she supposed. Perhaps that was an aspect of verisimilitude that Hugo didn't map out. Valjean dies so soon after the wedding of Marius and Cosette. Could he have caught something dire in the sewers? Something that Marius, being younger and stronger, could shake off? Hugo made it appear that he died of no longer having someone to care for and love, but if that were the case, Imogene herself should probably start taking her vitamins.

You had to hand it to the French, they knew how to revolt. Imogene had watched the televised news of their reaction to their recent elections with fascination, where mostly young people took to the streets to make their feelings known that while they had to vote for the incumbent president to keep the fascist opponent out of office, they were not happy with the choice, and they wanted him to know it. The gendarmes had deftly herded the protesters through the narrower streets where damage could be done, into the larger Place de la République, which was huge and concrete and easier to patrol and close off at key entrances. The rebels yelled and the police stood calm with their Lucite shields held in front of them, and eventually all the smoke bombs were used up and the people went home, sated or deflated or whatever they needed to be.

It had been a bit different for Enjolras's bunch of the ABC/*abaissé* "abased" group who had created the barricades where Marius was wounded and Éponine was killed. They wanted attention and to bring the status quo to a halt long enough to make a difference. It didn't appear to have accomplished much in the way of political change, and, at least in Hugo's version of it, all the instigators were caught and executed.

Hugo's underlying sentiment seemed to be that people joined these sorts of groups for disparate reasons, but if you got enough people annoyed and they came together, they could create some major problems due to their sheer mass. He had Marius joining in with them, not out of political sentiment so much as despair that his love was disappearing, perhaps to enhance the idea of no clear rallying cry, but also perhaps just to keep him politically clean in the eyes of the reader, who wanted him to be heroically suitable for Cosette.

Imogene stood up to stretch, and walked over to the window. She could see the rue de la Grande Truanderie stretching only one short block before turning a sharp ell corner. If the blockade took place just beyond the corner, then no one could pass from Les Halles toward the rue Étienne-Marcel, or on towards the routes to the Place de la Republique. Supposedly, a final rout happened in the tiny Saint-Merri lane past the Pompidou Centre that Imogene took to get to the fripshops across rue du Renard in the Marais, but that one wasn't Hugo's concern. That was across the boulevard de Sébastopol, but, of course, the boulevard would not have been there yet. Imogene wondered just how many streets would have been removed in the creation of Haussmann's vision of Paris's grand boulevards. If they were all blocked off to provide no way in to the police or soldiers, how many people would be living inside the barricades?

Imogene riffled through one of the other Paris history books that Raymonde had set up on the hanging shelf in the living room. Apparently, while there were about twenty-two people per acre in the area around the Champs-Élysées during the time of the fictional Jean Valjean, whereas hereabouts a five square-metre room on the fourth floor of a building in the Châtelet, Les Halles, or Île de la Cité area could be housing more than twenty people. Imogene wondered how many people had been living in her apartment when it was first built, or even two hundred years later when Hugo had been walking these crowded, narrow streets.

While she realized it must have been horrible to be turned out of one's home when Haussmann's crew decided your building would be coming down, Imogene admired the boulevards and beautiful six-storey buildings created all over Paris. Along with his harsh solution to overcrowding, Haussmann pushed for more parks, wanting there to be one within ten minutes' walk of every Parisienne, and he was the impetus behind hiring the man who revolutionized the Paris sewers, turning them from the cramped tunnels that Valjean had to carry Marius through, into larger tunnels that fed into even larger collector tunnels with sidewalks and complementary signs to the streets above them. No wonder the tunnels took on such an air of mystery and beauty when Gaston Leroux wrote *The Phantom of the Opera*, whereas forty years earlier, the sewer scene in *Les Misérables* was the epitome of fear and horror. Cleaning the sewers and decongesting the city went a long way to clearing up the cholera epidemics, and in the long run likely pushed down the simmering urge to rebellion that had seemed endemic to the centre of the city.

Imogene had sunk into the sofa with the history books, caught up in the bygone times, which she could still see remnants of wherever she turned to look in this beautiful city. Haussmann may have made his imprint, but he hadn't gutted what was glorious about Paris, just enhanced it. She wished some of the city planners back home had the sense to understand that certain old and beautiful buildings should be left alone, instead of pulled down and started anew every forty years or so.

What Edmonton had tended to do when designating something worth saving was to move it down to the historic park instead of letting it remain in situ. Imogene liked the new thought of saving at least the street frontage of older buildings and reworking them into the fronts of the taller structures put in their place. Street fronts needed to be human sized, not canyon sized. Otherwise, people were intimidated by those blocks and would avoid them. And if people weren't walking a neighbourhood, no matter how many parking places you added to the site, the area wouldn't maintain vibrancy.

She looked at the time. It was almost two. No wonder her stomach was grumbling. She would eat her bakery-made sandwich and then get ready for meeting Toni to go to the movies. She hadn't even asked what was playing, not that it mattered. It was an excuse to get together, and that was all she needed.

Brie and relish and pickles stuffed into chewy crusty bread and a cup of tea was possibly the best meal ever. Imogene sighed in contentment and wiped the crumbs from her lips. She would shower and get ready now, and then she could read a bit more before Toni got back from work.

It was just as well she did because Toni texted her just after four. The plan would be to meet in the main level of the Pompidou at five and have a quick bite to eat in the café before seeing the movie, which would begin at 6:30. Toni would be coming directly from work so Imogene would make her own way to the Pompidou.

She decided to leave right away, and if she had time, she'd wander through the gift shop or bookstore there. The Pompidou Centre was completely wonderful as far as

Imogene was concerned, and she laughed wryly to herself, given the thoughts she'd been having earlier in the day about leaving the old well enough alone. She wondered which had been more horrifying to Parisians: the Pompidou Centre with its pipes and outdoor escalators and crazy colours, or the glass pyramids in front of the Louvre. Both had knitted their way into the firmament as far as she was concerned, but then again, she hadn't been around to mourn the passing of what had been.

She was noticing more and more of the mosaic graffiti as she got closer to the Pompidou. And since spotting her little rat near the barricades, she was getting a sense of differences in the mosaics. For instance, the Marilyn Monroe over by the bicycle racks didn't seem connected to video games at all, but then again, neither had the green dinosaur she had seen, which was evidently famously an Invader motif. There was a flat quality to Marilyn that the rathole surpassed. And now that she was aware that street art could be at foot level, she was checking more carefully as she went.

Aside from the beautiful boulevards, Haussmann's other gift to the city had been his edicts on keeping city walls clean and undefaced, at the risk of severe fines. She wondered if that had much to do with the lack of ugly graffiti in Paris. It seemed to her that only actual street art was tolerated by the citizenry. Tagging and scribbling were not what a city that took pride in itself would accept.

She was standing in the bookstore, admiring the art prints, when Toni walked up, looking as if she'd just stepped out of a magazine, not arriving after a day of turgid work. There was just something inherently chic about French women, Imogene decided. There was no use trying to compete. Just enjoy. She waved and set the Delauney print of the Eiffel Tower back.

"Toni! It's great to see you. So, what is it we are going to see?"

"Well, once a month they do previews of upcoming films in their *Séances spéciales*, what you would call "special sessions," I guess. And this month it's a Cate Blanchett film, the Australian actress?"

"Yes, I really like her."

"Oh, good, so do I. She is so iconoclastic, isn't she? Definitely choosing interesting and difficult projects."

"Do you go to the movies often?"

"Not as much as I would like to. They're getting more expensive to go to, and when I have the time I usually like to just stay home to watch them on a streaming network in my cozy clothes, you know?"

"I get that completely," Imogene agreed. "I am not sure I've seen more than four movies in the last two years. And that may sound like a lot, but I used to watch the Academy Awards after having seen every single nominee and then some." Imogene shrugged. "Some things fall away. I rarely put the radio on anymore. I don't go to films. It could be all those years of having to listen to students in lecture halls. I siphon the amount of sound I have to listen to these days."

"Oh! Should we have planned something else?"

"No, no! This will be an experience. I have never been to a film in a French cinema."

"Ah well, the Pompidou is the very best. Somehow, people are better about not tossing their garbage about in a cultural edifice, you know?"

Imogene and Toni laughed.

"First, though, let's pop up to the café for a bite to eat."

"My treat," insisted Imogene.

The women made their way to the extended escalators on the outside of the building, and soon were ensconced in the fifth-floor café, enjoying sweet potato soup and rock cakes.

"How was your work today?" Imogene asked.

"It was a lot of paperwork, really. All I can do is write up the findings of our investigation throughout the five hotels and leave it for when something else triggers the case alive again."

"Five hotels?"

"Yes, that was what we eventually determined, after poking into all the ice machines in Paris."

"That's a lot. You have to be a little bit impressed with the overall concept."

"When you put it that way, you sound like you admire this person."

Imogene was shocked. "Oh, not at all. It's just the scope of targeting so many places, and being so methodical, and having it all done before it was discovered."

"Do you think? Or did we interrupt his process?"

"That's a very good question. What's your take on it?"

"I have a feeling this was a set piece. The hotels were chosen with care, and were situated in places that would produce prime scandal had the items been discovered by tourists staying in the hotels. It's not like he just went down the road, one place after another. He chose middle to luxe hotels near the Champs-Élysées, the Saint-Germain arrondissement, near the Opéra Garnier, and by the Louvre. These are all especially frequented by American tourists because they are places they've heard of. They are safe hotels, with liveried doormen and security boxes. If tourists were to think they were just down the hallway from a murderer planting evidence of his crimes, the noises would be heard all the way to Versailles."

"That's a very interesting thing you've just said."

"What?" asked Toni.

"That the tourists would be repelled by the crimes."

"Do you think that has something to do with it?"

"I am not sure. After all, there are very few other places one might find an ice machine, right? Unless you have them by the gas stations here? You do have gas stations, don't you? I've not seen any, but, of course, I've not really been out of the centre of the city."

"We do have gas stations, but if they sell ice, it would be in small bags inside the shop, not in an ice machine like in the hotels."

"Aha. So, for the necessary effect, whatever it was, it had to be a hotel."

"True."

"Or, it could be specifically a hotel being targeted, and the ice machine was the easiest location to place the items for them not to be found piecemeal."

"By that you mean?"

"So they could be found all at once, once the first item was found. If they just left a bag in a hallway, the bomb squad would be called, if water dripping out or a smell didn't trigger some other reaction, right? It needed to be the ice machines."

"All right. I agree. There are two ways of determining the logic. One, the items were to be all discovered simultaneously, so they had to be on ice for a time, till they were all placed. Two, the items had to be discovered by tourists, hence they were placed in hotels, in places where they would mostly likely be discovered by guests rather than staff. So, there are two different agendas there. And if we follow them to their logical reasoning, we might understand why the items were being placed and therefore who might be placing them."

Imogene nodded enthusiastically.

Toni smiled but looked wan. "Much of this we have already tackled, Imogene. The psychologist attached to the Sûreté has given us a variety of personalities to review. The troublesome aspect is the fear that attacks will be perpetrated on residents in the hotels and that this is a precursor to those attacks. One concept is that this is a warning signal. Our psychologist emphasizes that most murderers wish to be captured and are constantly sending out signals to the police."

"Do you think that is true?"

Toni shook her head. "I can't believe that the purpose of brutal crime is to be captured. It would be much easier to shoplift, no? *Hélas*, we need to get downstairs. The film will be beginning soon."

They carried their trays to the counter and then took the elevator down to the main floor, where they slid into line just as the doors were opening.

The movie was subtitled in French, giving Imogene back a momentary feeling of linguistic competence, although she was pretty sure that most of the audience was fluent not only in English but in several other languages as well. North Americans, even bilingual Canadians or Spanish-speaking Americans, were so far behind the linguistic abilities of Europeans. The gall of English speakers to assume they'd be understood everywhere they went tended to diminish the colours of the world rather than unify it, in Imogene's opinion.

The movie centred on Blanchett's character's being a spy, masked by her outward celebrity and ability to move seamlessly from country to country. She played an opera singer whose Wagnerian stature had her travelling far and wide. After the film, Imogene and Toni discussed the believability of Blanchett as an opera singer. While she had capably manifested the sense of celebrity that she likely understood at an atomic level, there was something so slight and ethereal about her, stature-wise, and both women felt opera singers needed to take up more space in the world.

"Especially anyone singing Wagner," nodded Imogene. "You want to believe they could get down there and man the oars of the Viking ship when not offering up an aria, right?"

Toni agreed. "But I really bought the aspect of people not expecting someone so much in the public eye to be a secret agent. We tend to think of spies being anonymous and invisible, but how on earth would they get into important areas or cross borders and move about with impunity unless they were well known? Look at Mata Hari, after all. She was an entertainer. And wasn't Marlena Dietrich said to have been an Allied spy?"

"You're right. There were a lot more believable elements than problematic ones for me too. And truthfully, I could watch Cate Blanchett recite recipes for deworming cats. And now, shall we stop for a glass of wine?"

"I am afraid I cannot tonight, Imogene. I have to be back in the main office tomorrow morning by seven, and I have a load of laundry to do before I can think about sleeping tonight. But let's certainly plan to go out on Thursday after ballet, *non*?"

"Thursday it is! I think I will follow your lead and do some chores before I turn in. I have been getting quite a bit done the last couple of days on my manuscript, at least in terms of organizing principles. I should aim to get up early and get cracking while things are going well."

"Do you have a deadline to adhere to?"

"In a manner of speaking. I promised my editor that I would have something to her by the end of the summer, which means I will have to write my tail off once I get home again. I thought, though, if I could rough things out in terms of how the manuscript will proceed, then working from notes at home will be so much easier."

As they reached the main door to their apartments, Toni pulled her keys out. "After you, madame," she intoned like one of the doormen at the fancy hotels she'd been investigating, bowing her head and indicating the way to Imogene.

Imogene flounced through in her best interpretation of a grande dame and headed for the stairs. Even stopping to check her mailbox, Toni caught up with her before the fifth twist, just below the door to her apartment.

"Good night, Imogene. That was fun."

"Yes, thanks so much for suggesting it! Another Parisian activity I can add to my list."

"You are experiencing Paris like a citizen. That is a good thing, I think. Sleep well!" Toni waved at her as she pulled her key out of the door and went inside her apartment.

Imogene walked up the next flight of stairs, mentally checking for the loose tile on the half landing along the way but not finding it, and opened her own door. This really was a well-run building to have fixed that only days after she had noticed it.

She hadn't pulled the drapes before she had left and so not only could she see the lights of the restaurants down the street twinkling from her living room windows, she found the place a bit warm and stuffy, given how sunny the afternoon had been. She stepped to the window with the Juliet balcony and opened the French doors to let the air circulate. She hadn't turned on the lights, so she stood next to the drapes and looked out. Someone was hurrying away from their building; it was René. He was in a dark jacket, wearing a little dark toque, and he had a large satchel under his arm. Even at the best of times he was a bit odd, but she felt he looked particularly furtive now.

As if to prove her point he stopped suddenly and looked all around, even glancing up at the building he'd just left. Imogene was certain he couldn't see her, but she held her breath and stood very still, part of the shadowy curtains. Seemingly satisfied, René turned back the way he had been going and hurried along, darting around a rowdy group of people exiting one of the outdoor cafes along the street.

Imogene wondered what he was up to. It was something, all right. She really hoped he wasn't some sort of galvanized misogynist or bigot, off to do harm. But whatever it was, it wasn't her problem. She turned her back on the window and straightened her shoulders. Maybe she too should do a load of laundry before turning in.

# Echoes

Imogene was folding the laundry she had hung on the backs of her dining room chairs the night before when her phone buzzed with a message.

It was Marcel, suggesting they meet for lunch at the Musée d'Orsay. Imogene texted back her wholehearted agreement, wondering as she did if his choosing to meet at midday rather than the evening meant that her newly awakened sex life was coming to an end. She shrugged her best newfound Gallic shrug and said to the apartment at large, "Well, it was great while it lasted." As usual, talking out loud made her laugh at herself. Her father had used to say, when caught talking to himself, that he was "pleased to find a worthy conversationalist to bother with." She, on the other hand, always felt as if disturbing the air when she was alone was somehow too overt an action. She preferred to go through the world to an internal monologue rather than calling attention to herself, even if there were only dust motes to notice.

Since she hadn't yet been to the Musée d'Orsay, she wanted to get ready right away and head there with plenty of time to walk around before meeting Marcel in the restaurant. He had specified it would be the restaurant at the west end of the building with the "glimmery chairs" and not the one behind the clock, so Imogene was sure she would find her way.

She decided to walk to the museum, even though she knew she would be walking a great deal within the museum, which had once been a huge train station. Even if she didn't go home with a full first draft completed, perhaps she'd go home a size smaller. She strolled past the *bouquinistes* opening up their green stalls along the upper riverbank and crossed the river at the Pont des Arts.

She had read about the museum quickly in her apartment library of history books. During Hugo's time, the site would have housed the cavalry barracks and the Palais d'Orsay. She wondered if Javert's character would have gone to the cavalry for assistance there. Then in 1871, short years after L*es Misérables* was published, the Paris Commune riot burned the entire neighbourhood to the ground and the whole area sat in ashes until 1900 when the Beaux-Arts railway station and hotel were built for a rail line that took you to Orleans. Interestingly, there didn't seem to be a statue of Jeanne d'Arc here, seeing as how the train had run directly to her hometown, though Imogene had found three others of St. Joan in her wanderings about the city.

She lined up for a single ticket to the museum and was

soon blissfully wandering from room to room on the second floor. Imogene had long realized that, although she had appreciated many elements brought to her attention in her art history courses, her heart would always be with the Impressionists.

And here they were, in all their glory. Monet, Manet, Morisot, Renoir, Seurat, Degas, Toulouse-Lautrec. It was overwhelming. When she stood before the latter's small oil crayon of a woman flopped backward on her bed, called *Seule*, Imogene understood implicitly the utter overload the day had been for the woman. She decided to stroll through the Art Nouveau collection of furniture before turning to find the restaurant. She didn't want to keep Marcel waiting, but she also didn't want to arrive looking as gobsmacked as she felt after being in the presence of so many works she had previously seen only in art books or as posters.

Art Nouveau was her favourite of the classic lines of furniture, though she suspected it was a tad too fussy for her own daily enjoyment. She was a grandchild of some of the last settler-pioneers in the northern reaches of western Canada, and her grandfather's mission oak arts and crafts rocking chair was her family's version of splendid. It stood amidst her own IKEA furniture like a tolerant uncle; its split leather seat had been reupholstered the year Imogene had achieved tenure. Still, for sheer *joie de vivre*, Art Nouveau, with its undulating curves and flowers, was lovely to behold. Maybe an umbrella stand built like a stork for the grand hallway, Madame?

Imogene walked with purpose past the statuary in the central nave of the museum and then up the stairs at the west end near where she had begun her morning. It was obvious she could spend two or three more visits here and still not see everything. She turned where the sign said and found her way to the staircase leading to the long hall that was the Musée d'Orsay Restaurant. The window showed a ballroom, all gilt and chandeliered, with frescos on the walls and, just as Marcel had promised, glimmering chairs made of coloured resin. She saw him as soon as she stepped through the doors. The woman at the reception desk nodded pleasantly and motioned her through to wind among the tables to the window seat Marcel had snagged for them. He half stood as she arrived at the table, but she waved him back into his seat and hung her purse on the chairback, after touching its inviting texture. Then she slid out of her jacket and covered up the glimmer.

"Imogene, you look wonderful. Have you been into the museum already?" Marcel poured her some water from the bottle at their table.

"Yes, the one floor of paintings and the Art Nouveau furniture, nothing more. What an amazing place! And this room!" Imogene looked around at the gilt and painted panels of the warm yellow walls.

"I know, it is one of the loveliest rooms to sit in, I think, and the food is also very good." He handed her the menu, and she began to read the italicized English under each entrée. She was too hungry to try to work through the

French. It was just as well, because the waiter was there almost immediately.

She ordered the pork chop with anchovy sauce and fries and Marcel ordered a salmon bowl for himself, and a carafe of wine. Imogene knew she was going to have to dry out when she made it home, after enjoying so much wine at any old time of the day in Paris.

"I am so glad you could make it to meet me for lunch. My days have recently been so busy, I was worried you would forget me entirely," Marcel said.

Imogene laughed. "You'd be pretty difficult to forget, Marcel."

He nodded his head, smiling, to accept the compliment. "Then we are mutually admiring. I realize that you have an agenda of work that absorbs your time, but I am hoping to make the most of the time you have left in Paris. It is just that, along with the demands of my research, my father has become rather ill and I must take time to go out to him."

"Oh, I am sorry to hear that. Is it serious?"

"He is old, and everything becomes worn over time. But, yes, he had fallen earlier this year and the bone he broke has not healed well."

"That sounds awful."

"He is not what you would call a good patient, of course. The *médecin* told him not to put his full weight on his ankle for six weeks, but he refused to be seen using the *déambulateur*, what you would call a Zimmer frame?"

"That's more British than Canadian. We'd call it a walker."

Marcel nodded. "*Oui*, a walker. My father thinks they are for old men. Of course, at eighty-seven, he is a young pup and should be using only a cane."

"Isn't it funny what people determine is that line that must not be crossed? I have an aunt who dyed her hair well into her nineties, swearing she didn't have the complexion for grey hair. And a neighbour with gloriously gnarled hands once took umbrage with his son, a photographer, because he had shot an award-winning photo of those hands folded on the head of a cane. He was horrified that people would think he needed a cane."

They both laughed.

"Ah, who knows what I will do in his place but for now it behooves me to stay with my father at night to make sure he doesn't decide to get up and do something foolish in the dark."

"Does he live near you?"

"No, he doesn't live in Paris. It's a fifty-eight-kilometre train ride to a small city called Mantes-la-Jolie. I have a room in his house, and I leave my car in his garage, because it is too expensive to find parking anywhere near where I live in Paris. And really, it takes longer to drive almost anywhere in France than it does to take the train."

"You've been working in town every day and then commuting out and back to take care of your father? That's very commendable of you."

Marcel shrugged. "He needs to stay off that ankle for just another week or so. And then he should be back to normal."

"Another week or so is all the time I have here," sighed Imogene. "It felt like I was going to be here for such a long time and now the days are eating themselves."

"We will have to find some times to be together before you leave, *chérie*." Marcel touched her hand as the waiter arrived with their food. Unlike a North American, who would have pulled his hand away, almost embarrassed at being caught showing affection, Marcel squeezed her hand before straightening to allow the waiter to place their food. Imogene wondered what the server made of this late-middle-aged couple; could he sense the sparks emanating from them from just that connection of flesh?

She felt like a teenager. Marcel was letting her know as gently as possible that there were going to be very few chances for them to get together before she left for good to head home. And she had no illusions about this relationship straddling an ocean. She would think about Marcel with nostalgia and a little regret, but there wouldn't be any urge to move heaven and earth to be with him. However, the thought of not being able to enjoy themselves during the last days she would be in Paris seemed miserly, and she knew she was going to resent his hobbling father for quite some time.

Marcel smiled across the table at her. "I can see from your face that you feel the same way about my father at the moment as I do."

Imogene laughed. "I can't really mask my emotions, can I?"

"Yours is not a good face for a card player, no."

"I suppose all we can do is make the best of whatever time you can afford."

She took a bite of the pork chop with the sauce and moaned in appreciation of the taste.

" Save room for dessert, even if only a shared dessert. They are famous for their crème brûlée and their berry puddings."

"I don't know if I could. Maybe one bite of whatever you order."

"Very well, but I insist you will have espresso with me to finish off the meal."

"I wouldn't want to appear to be a barbarian."

Marcel summoned the waiter as if by telepathy and soon they were sipping espresso from attractive demitasse cups and spooning in decadent crème brûlée decorated with candied violets.

"How can anything be so perfect and beautiful and delicious at the same time?" Imogene asked.

"There is a great pride in making desserts beautiful here, I agree. This concept of making the entrée appear like a work of art with the sauce painted on the plate and the meats presented just so, that I think is a more contemporary phenomenon. But the desserts have always been a canvas for the chef. I knew a food critic who once told me that to really know the value of a restaurant, I should order an appetizer and a dessert, that those were the dishes into which the chefs would pour their hearts." Marcel smiled. "However, I am rarely that reserved. I have an appetite for more food than that."

"That does make a certain amount of sense, though. With

those plates, one can be more inventive than in a larger entrée." Imogene nodded thoughtfully. "Perhaps that's what I will try from now on. After all, you can't feel as guilty about ordering dessert if you have limited yourself to an appetizer, right?"

"Never feel guilty, Imogene. Life is too short! Be wild and free, and always have dessert."

Imogene laughed. "I should embroider that on a pillow."

"It's not a bad motto."

"It's the sort of motto that will eventually catch up with you, I think."

"Not if you outrun it, Imogene. You just need to keep on the move."

# Another Museum

As it turned out, Marcel wasn't trying to signal the end of lovemaking by suggesting they meet at noon. He had hailed a taxi to take them back to Imogene's apartment where they enjoyed post-luncheon amusements in her sunny bedroom. She was feeling as if she had wandered into a Jeanne Moreau film, but one of the later ones where she was crepey-skinned but still very sexy and full-tilt sensuous. Imogene pulled on her silk wrap and saw Marcel to the door, "in plenty of time to catch the train to Mantes."

Sated both physically and mentally, Imogene crawled back into her bed once he was gone and reached for the paperback *The Hunchback of Notre Dame* she had picked up earlier, after thinking about how the Île de la Cité would have looked in Hugo's time. She read and dozed and finally jolted awake in a dark bedroom, unsure of the time. It was quiet outside. She pulled the drapes over the glass curtains and went looking for her phone.

It was still in her purse, sitting on the kitchen counter. It said 2:04 a.m. She noticed she had messages and slid it unlocked.

Marcel had messaged twice, to thank her for a lovely afternoon and to ask if she would be free on the following Tuesday all day. Toni had left a joke message about fat ballerinas, and Daniel, her former colleague back home who was minding her plants and picking up her mail, had messaged to let her know that a package had been delivered and he'd left it on her kitchen table.

She texted Daniel back to thank him, and he immediately responded.

What are you doing awake?

> I had one of those stupid late-day naps and woke up just now.

Warm milk. Or scotch.

> LOL. Which sounds better?

So how is it going over there?

> Incredible. I am getting quite a bit done and really enjoying my time here. And I am told the weather is unusually warm and dry for this time of year, so I am appreciating that too.

Better than here. It snowed again yesterday morning, and the Pollyannas who had taken their winter tires off their cars ended up in fender benders all over the city. *can't wait for retirement*

> Argh, what a mess that must have been. Yes, there is a lot to be said for looking out the window and saying "no thank you, not today!"

When are you coming home and do you need picking up at the airport?

> On the 11th, and that would be wonderful if you're offering. I'll text you the flight and time when I am fully awake.

No problem at all. It will be great to see you, wearing a beret, I presume.

> But of course, and carrying a baguette!

Goodnight, Imogene.

> Goodnight, Daniel.

 She smiled at the phone screen. Daniel Worthington, her colleague in Comparative Literature who had had the office next to hers for eighteen years, had always been a pleasant coffee companion. It hadn't been till her divorce, though, that she realized what a staunch friend he was. It had been Daniel who had rented the U-Haul van to help her move, Daniel who had taken her for drinks on the day she had signed the finalized divorce papers a year after the split, and Daniel who had egged her on to take this leap of faith into writing another book after her retirement from teaching.

He was perhaps four or five years younger than she was, and had joined the department during the last big hire, after a couple of impressive post-doc placements and a well-received book on Scandinavian mystery writers. A few of the older professors had been a bit put out by his focus on popular culture studies, but Imogene had welcomed his fresh take on Comp Lit and his devilish sense of humour. He had been married and divorced before arriving in Alberta, and was a strong and steady ally for Imogene finding her feet again. Plus, he lived only four blocks from her in another high-rise apartment building, and was seemingly always available for a movie, concert, or drink out on a patio.

As much as she loved Paris, Imogene was feeling the urge to get home and back into her real-life routines and rhythms. She yawned and thought about heating up some milk, as Daniel had suggested. It seemed like too much trouble, so instead she padded back to the bedroom, plugged her phone into the charger with an alarm set to wake her at seven, slid into her T-shirt nightie, and crawled back into bed.

When the alarm rang she woke fresh, as if she had slept round the clock, which, she reflected, she nearly had. She indulged in a long shower, enough to cloud the mirror but bring herself clearly into focus, and she had soon dressed, made breakfast from yesterday's bread and some egg and cheese, and then set the apartment to rights.

Her books and laptop beckoned from the small desk between the living room windows. She had created a pattern for herself in the last few days, writing more than reading, although it was obvious from the Post-it notes emanating from her copy of *Les Misérables* that her reading had been intense.

The focus of her last book had been to show that reading a book in the same place as it was set offered a resonance to the plot and characters one didn't find when reading the same book in a distant land, or without a personal understanding of that area. She wondered if Hugo's prolific historical backgrounding and lengthy descriptions of situations were meant to make up for that lack of personal impression of Paris. Who was Hugo's audience, in his mind? Was he already seeing himself as an international voice for France, or was he more insular, trying to offer the next generations of French readers an insight into their shared past of complex political and societal upheavals? She needed to get a better sense of the man. Maybe what she needed was another visit to the Hugo House Museum.

Once she had thought of it, it was obvious she had to go. She kicked off her slippers and went to exchange her at-home clothes for more respectable trousers and a blouse. The weather looked mild, and Imogene figured she could manage with just a light cardigan, especially if she kept to the sunny side of the streets walking there.

Soon she was striding past the Pompidou Centre and down through the winding streets of le Marais to the Place des Vosges. Children were already out playing in the corner of the park fitted with jungle gyms and sandboxes. And young mothers and nannies were sitting along the edges, drinking coffee and chatting while keeping an eye on their charges. The Maison de Victor Hugo was in the far corner, and Imogene walked through the square park to get to it, rather than under the colonnades around the square. Supposedly this was the first park in Paris. While she was sure it must be quite lovely to live in this area, she herself would probably opt for one of those houses bordering the Parc Monceau if she were to live near Paris greenery.

She climbed the stairs, past the first floor that held an art gallery she'd already been through, to Hugo's rooms. The room with the *chinoiserie* that had been brought from his country house held a small bench that she contemplated sitting on, but she decided to head through to his standing desk to bask in whatever remnants of writing power might still be clinging to the wood. The handwritten manuscripts under glass were heartbreakingly human, making two hundred years collapse between his life and hers. Readers and writers. Europeans and North Americans, French and English speakers. What difference was there when it came to communication and creativity? What sparked an urge in one person to try to wrangle words into a clarity that transcended time for another mind to take in? What hubris or urge or desperation?

*Fyodor & Me in Russia* wasn't the only book Imogene had published over the years, but it was by far the most personal writing she had done since the songs and poetry she'd scribbled in notebooks in high school. It had been enormously freeing to step beyond the couched academic phrases steeped in citations and begin a paragraph with "it seemed to me."

She had presumed that this foray into reading *in situ* would be similar to her time with Dostoevsky in Saint Petersburg—the frisson of understanding when it came to seeing the bland face of the baker behind the counter, or the domes of the cathedral shining above the greyness of the streets.

And there had been some of that in Paris, especially when she had been walking in the rain after reading a passage where Fantine was wet and cold, or going past a table of young men and thinking of Enjolas and Marius and their crowd. But now it seemed to her as if Hugo was showing her the protesting heart of Paris. Choosing the June student revolution, one of the smaller and less satisfying protests of Parisian history, he somehow was demonstrating the underlying principle of protest. If Imogene were to think about conversations between herself and Toni, or herself and Marcel, she could discern the sparks of protest within them, as well. Toni's brother's dissertation on the height of stair risers. Toni's contempt for bus tour visitors. Marcel's adamant purchase of only French wines.

Hearing voices in the next room, Imogene roused herself and walked through Hugo's red bedroom featuring the bed he had died in, and went down the stairs to the cafeteria. There she purchased a croissant and a cup of café allongé and took them out into the secluded garden behind the house. It was already warm enough to sit in the shade with her back to the windows of the inner restaurant.

She pulled out the notebook that was always in her purse and began to sketch out a list of protests she had heard about or witnessed in the short weeks she had been there. The young people marching to denote their irritation at having to vote for their lesser of two evils. Toni's, or perhaps her brother's, opinion of architecture being for the people rather than the design. Marcel's pronouncement on certain foods and various ways to experience Paris. René and his idea of whether or not a non-artistic person belonged in an art supply store.

Just to amuse herself, she then began a list of her own bugbears, which included things like female genital mutilation, war, infidelity, and the stock market, all the way to people putting their feet on the seats of picnic benches, other people's children, taxes on books, and grocery clerks not bagging one's groceries. She snorted. She would never make a good revolutionary. While various things piqued her, she couldn't think of anything she could do to protest things she wanted to put a stop to.

She had once marched to the Legislature from campus when they raised tuition back in her undergrad days. And she had stood in solidarity with schoolteachers at some point while her own children held placards for their teachers out on strike. It wasn't that she wasn't capable of or willing to protest. It was just that she couldn't think of anything that roiled inside her till it could logically come out as an act of revolution.

Two women of a certain age, dressed beautifully, replete with scarves and earrings, entered the garden area and nodded to her graciously as they took a table near her. She nodded back, hoping she looked like a member of their group, the educated ladies who sought out cultural moments. She likely looked more like an aging academic on a last-dash sabbatical before retirement. She could hear an echo of Marcel in her head as she thought, ah, well, anything better than a run-of-the-mill tourist!

Marcel's antipathy towards tourists was really quite interesting. She wondered what it stemmed from. Her grandmother would have said, "Maybe a tourist scared his mother," which was an old wives' tale of how people came by irrational fears: their mothers were frightened by the source of the fear when carrying the child in utero. In other words, there was no explanation for it.

She stared at her notebook. There was nothing more she could think to write and, with her coffee finished, she felt reluctant to maintain the table as the time drew closer to the lunch hour. She folded things away into her purse and took her dirty plates inside, thanking the woman behind the counter again, unnecessarily.

Once outside the Place des Vosges, she strolled down the rue de Rivoli, thinking about Napoleon's desire for this street. She had seen a production of *Crazy Straight Lines,* David Hare's play about Robert Moses, the New York city planner who had created the train route to Long Island and various expressways. Rarely did she think about the power certain people had over the look of a city. In many cases, roads were built by chance, a track becoming a road becoming a thoroughfare. In Edmonton, however, the city was set on a grid, with numbered streets and avenues. Names were reserved for wiggly avenues along riverbanks and ravines, dotted with fancier houses and beautiful gardens. Eventually, the grid extended out to a point where the people who had grown up on numbered streets longing for named locations began to be in charge, and suddenly you needed a GPS guide to get you into some suburban addresses where streets with names all sounding relatively the same—like Maple Drive, Maple Wynd, Maple Lane—curled in and around each other.

Here in Paris, every good map and guidebook she owned listed every street and alley she had gone looking for. Perhaps it was just fine to name your streets as long as you had a guidebook or something like the London ABC. It was when people began renaming streets that things got problematic. But why shouldn't they? They were adapting to pulling down statues of men with problematic back stories. Renaming places commemorating such people could surely happen just as easily.

One of her colleagues in History had been moaning about the removal of problematic figures from history, during the removal of statues of some slave-owning generals in the Deep South and Sir John A. Macdonald in various parts of Canada. "Wouldn't it be better to set up plaques explaining how problematic these people were?" he asked a table at the Faculty Club one evening.

"Do you really think they're going to be forgotten, like Ozymandias? Who I hasten to say has not been forgotten," pointed out Daniel. "The trouble with statuary is that it has always had a connection and connotation to idols. And idols are made to be worshipped, not visited as problematic. Putting someone up on a plinth almost guarantees some sort of veneration, even if only by pigeons."

Imogene had agreed wholeheartedly with Daniel's argument. Secretly, though, she had a longing to visit the city in Russia where there was a whole park full of statues of Lenin that had been ignominiously removed from various public places around the country. It sounded like a very interesting sort of theme park.

She stopped at one of the intersections leading into a smaller road; she wanted to take a photo of another of the tiled Space Invaders high up on one of the walls of the nearest building. How could something like that go up with no one noticing? Wouldn't a person carrying a ladder and a bucket of glue and tiles be pretty obvious? Even if the art had been created at home and transported on a backing, so that the Invader person was only gluing up a pre-made work, it would still be self-evident that a man up a ladder in the middle of the night was not doing minor repairs.

What about in the middle of the day? Would anyone be paying any attention to one more workman in a high-viz vest and hard hat? Imogene stopped still. Could that be it? Did Invader just saunter along, operating within the daily grind with impunity? Maybe that was the trick to anything, just acting as if you had the right to do something, and no one would question your authority. Perhaps that is how the rat artist did it too, she thought, and they wouldn't even have to worry about a ladder. Especially if they were located by a drain and wearing a workman's vest would keep people from looking twice.

She should mention that to Toni. Maybe there was something about that audacity that would fit with her body parts case. Had they really questioned the fellow who had been dismantling the ice machines, for instance? Maybe he was there to have the situation brought to light and was just feigning shock.

And maybe there was some sort of audacity to the body parts in the first place. Maybe their perpetrator was a butcher who cut people up on the side. Or a surgical specialist who took his tools home with him.

That's if they were looking for an actual murderer. What if this were some sort of artistic statement, like the tile art, only in a sick dimension? The placement of the body parts was a message somehow, not just a means of getting rid of them. But who would have access to body parts? It wasn't like Invader, who didn't necessarily need to be a professional tiler but could buy his materials in DIY stores or art supply shops. A surgeon could maybe collect bits of people he or she had hacked off. Maybe the pieces found by Toni's team were diseased somehow; that could lead back to the surgical procedures. Imogene stopped to make a note in her phone to remind her to mention that avenue to Toni. While she had her phone out, she took a picture of the merry-go-round set up across the street, where the flea market had been the last time she'd been down this way.

Maybe the person leaving the body parts wasn't a surgeon but was someone involved with the removal of human waste in the hospital. What a hell of a job that must be. She made another note for Toni and then picked up her pace because she was getting into a more crowded area. She had learned to walk with purpose on the sidewalks of Paris when there were other people around. On the infrequent times she found herself dawdling, she could sense the seething annoyance of the people passing around her like a palpable wave of charged ions.

Who else would have access to human remains? Funeral directors would. And hadn't she read something about them having to cut metallic bits out of the deceased before they went into the crematoriums? So they'd have the tools and the knowhow. Forensic anthropologists were always cutting bodies up on crime shows, but surely they would be associated with the police and less likely to be spiriting away feet and elbows. Who else?

Coroners, of course. They dealt with every death, and did thorough and surgical examinations of any remotely unexplained death. Where did the coroners reside in the Sûreté? Another question for Toni. She pulled her phone out of her satchel once more.

"Imogene?"

She looked up, startled. It was her landlady, Raymonde, looking chic as ever in a belted silk dress and a short Chanel-type woven jacket that picked up the rose of the dress. Today, Raymonde had eschewed running shoes and instead was wearing beautiful rose leather pumps with a heel that made her almost as tall as Imogene.

"I have been meaning to call you and take you out for a drink or coffee. Do you have time now?"

"Well, yes, I do. I was just meandering home, and I'd love a coffee."

"There's a very nice restaurant just around the corner from here. I am sure they'd let us perch for a café; they won't be busy for lunch for at least another half an hour. Come!"

True enough, a quiet avenue tucked right behind the rue de Rivoli held two or three restaurants and some ritzy-looking boutiques, as well as a few doors to what Imogene figured must be very expensive apartments. Raymonde spoke with the maître d' who was standing at a dais in the garden layer of the restaurant, and soon they were sitting at a little table in the back of a very cute restaurant with Holstein-covered chairs and travel posters of the south of France.

"They are very well known for their beef dishes here and always busy, but since most people like the *jardin* effect for lunch, we can sit in here and relax, he says. Would you like anything more than a coffee? Perhaps share some *pommes frites?*"

"Oh, that sounds perfect!"

Raymonde turned her head slightly and a waiter was by her side. She requested two bowls of coffee and an order of fries, and then turned back to Imogene, fully focused on her. "*Eh bien,* you have been having a good time in Paris? I am supposing, since you have not been in touch, that there have been no troubles, am I correct?"

"No troubles at all. Your apartment is very well appointed and so convenient to everything I require. It's been such a blessing to be there."

"I am glad to hear that! Perhaps you will send me a letter extolling its virtues and I can put that on the website as a promotion."

The waiter arrived almost immediately with their huge bowls of café au lait and a tiny ginger biscuit sitting on each saucer.

"Your work is going well?" Raymonde asked.

"Yes, it really is. I will be able to write the bulk of what I need to when I get home, but I have the groundwork done. I think my publisher is going to be happy with me."

"Perhaps you will need to come back to Paris to check on things," teased Raymonde. "You just let me know."

"I will be sure to see if your apartment is available any time I come back to Paris. It is a wonderful place to stay." Imogene realized as she said this that she really would love to make visits to Paris a regular thing. She wondered what Marcel would think of that possibility.

"And it isn't too noisy for you?"

"You mean the restaurant crowds? Not really. I close the windows and pull the drapes and that muffles pretty much all the sounds till the garbage trucks roll through."

"Oh yes, no getting around that beep beep, not in the core of the city at any rate," Raymonde laughed. "Yes, you chose a good time to come. It gets hot in the summer months and then you absolutely need to keep the windows open, to catch any breeze you can find. I have that little air conditioner under the counter there, but it doesn't do much." Raymonde shook her head sadly, as if the inability to control the weather was a personal failing. "What I was really meaning was are you hearing anything from your upstairs neighbour?"

"René?"

"Ah, you've met!"

"Yes, I mean, yes, we've met. He's not that noisy. He wears his shoes indoors and has dropped something once or twice, but that is all."

"That is good to hear. The tenant two before you, one of the opera singers who likes to rent the place, was really put out by the noises. Lots of thumping and bumping and sometimes a mechanical whine, like a factory noise, she said. But then again, she was fussy about a lot of things."

"Oh no, nothing like that."

The fries came in a metal cone with a waxy paper twirled

into it, and Imogene and Raymonde began to pick at them, alternating dipping them into three pots containing some sort of dill mayonnaise, a homemade tomato ketchup, and an oil and vinegar concoction—all delicious.

"If fries came like this at home, I'd weigh three hundred pounds," sighed Imogene.

"I know. I tell myself that I can eat anything I want because I walk everywhere," Raymonde said, "and then, don't you know, I hop onto a bus the minute I make that sort of justification."

"You ride the bus?" Imogene couldn't help the sound of disbelief in her voice. "I sort of assumed you went places in limousines, you're so stylish."

Raymonde accepted the compliment with a twinkle. "Oh no, I am not so aristocratic as all that, Imogene. I take the bus, and sometimes a taxicab. But walking in Paris is so easy, don't you find?"

Imogene nodded. She agreed wholeheartedly with Raymonde. If there was one "place in the world a woman could walk," to crib from an old Grace Paley book of short stories, it was Paris.

The women chatted for another half an hour, and while Imogene found her charming, she realized that she had very little in common with Raymonde besides the fact that they were close in age. Where Imogene had opted for academe and kept her nose in a book, as her gran would have said, Raymonde appeared to have been a businesswoman from the moment she left school. The apartment she was renting to Imogene was one of seven she owned in Paris, and she apparently had several more in a city called Nîmes that catered to holidaying Parisiennes. Imogene had the sense that if they had met under any other circumstances, Raymonde wouldn't have given her the time of day. They just moved in different circles and valued different things.

Raymonde insisted on paying for coffee and offered Imogene the French both-cheeks kisses before they went their separate ways, with a promise to get in touch before Imogene left.

"And remember, just put the keys on the counter when you leave, with the windows closed. I'll be around later that day, no worries." And with that Raymonde was off, the silky skirt of her dress swirling dramatically.

Imogene decided to head home through the little streets of Le Marais, rather than back out to the main thoroughfare of the rue de Rivoli. She popped her head into the thrift shop where she'd found a lovely handkerchief cotton blouse for one euro in the bin at the back, but today the store was too crowded to be comfortable. She nodded to the man on the stool by the door and backed out the way she had come in. Across the street was the corner where one of the student barricades had been, apparently one where people had actually been killed. Imogene wondered if Hugo had sent Marius and Éponine to the Grande Truanderie barricade instead in order not to diminish the deaths of those at this barricade, or whether it was because that had been the barricade he had been caught near when walking home that night? Or perhaps there was another reason. Maybe the sewer entrance necessary to get to the exit near the Champs-Élysées had to be nearer to the Les Halles sewer. She began to look for manhole covers as she walked along.

How could Jean Valjean have been able to carry Marius down safely through a manhole or a grate? He'd have been a dead weight. And who but someone who had spent so many years incarcerated in hellish dungeons and prison ships would have considered the sewer a possible gate to safety?

How could Hugo have imagined such a scenario? Had he heard such a story? Was he thinking about the Catacombs and the people who found sanctuary deep below the city? Was there even talk, in his day, of the sewer project that would come to be?

Imogene's daughter had taken a tour of the sewers when she had visited Paris in her early twenties, but there was no way that Imogene could see herself going down into the bowels of the city. It wasn't being underground that bothered her so much as being in tight places with strangers where she couldn't see a clear exit. And mostly, if she was being honest with herself, it was the irrational fear of going feral in such a situation that bothered her. There was such a fine carapace that kept people civilized, living cheek by jowl in a city. Push them too close together, and Imogene feared to see what even she might become.

She could see no obvious entrances to the sewer, but just as she turned the corner to pass the old building that had been a public bath, she spotted another little mosaic rathole.

This one was orange and and yellow and green, picking up the colours of the Pompidou Centre across the plaza, but the little rat was the same and the intricacies making the tunnel appear to be three-dimensional were identical. She knelt down this time to take a proper photo. She wondered how many of these little rats there were and what the artist truly intended by them.

She dusted off the knees of her trousers and decided to cut across the plaza in front of the Pompidou Centre and go home by way of the small grocery shop that carried good marmalade, five-euro bottles of wine, and baguettes. There were no more baguettes to be had, so Imogene settled for a bottle of lemonade and a bottle of Côtes du Rhône, and bought another reusable bag from their pile, because she liked their message, "*ce petit sac bleu est vert.*" As well as being sturdy and useful, she thought they'd make nice souvenirs, so she popped three more onto the counter. She really should be thinking soon of presents to bring home. The young man behind the till smiled at her and bagged her bottles with an extra paper on one, either so they didn't break, or so they didn't clink and let the neighbours know. Imogene smiled in return.

She had bought a lot more liquor since her divorce than when she was married, she realized. It could also have been the pandemic coming when it did, but on the whole it was a mind-bending concept to realize she could drink alone without worrying about becoming an alcoholic. That had always been the line of demarcation when she was younger, but once everyone was forced to be home and she didn't have to worry about being a bad influence on anyone else, she was quite happy to have a bottle of wine in the fridge and some hard liquor set out on the sideboard for when she fancied a mixed drink. And here in France, it was unheard of not to have some wine with practically every meal. What a civilized country this was.

Home at last, Imogene kicked off her Skechers and padded into the kitchen area. She popped the lemonade into the mini-fridge and set the wine on the walled end of the counter for later in the evening, then hung her jacket on the wall hook by the door.

Had being in Victor Hugo's house brought her any insights? One of the things she was aware of was the comfortable living Hugo would have had while writing of the poor situations for his characters, especially the awful garret Marius was living in. How had Hugo come to know of those places? And where would they actually have been? Imogene couldn't imagine that the apartments surrounding her, with their handsome windows and high ceilings, could ever have been homes for the downtrodden. And yet supposedly, the centre of the city was always where the 'hood began, with the oldest buildings going downhill.

She had the sense that Marius's garret was somewhere in the Left Bank area, closer to the Jardin des Plantes, mainly because of his searching for Cosette off in the parkland beyond there, but for all she knew, he could have walked many kilometres each day to get there. She needed to look up an older map of Paris and superimpose it on her present-day map of the city. Still, reading the book and knowing that most of the cobbles she walked to get to her morning baguette were the same ones that Hugo would have trod to explore the places where he was setting his story had an effect on Imogene that she hoped she could translate to others in her own writing.

And perhaps, if she were brave enough to divulge it, she could also talk about how the scene where Marius sees Cosette and is immediately smitten might not be completely outrageous, that there was some quality of Paris that made one open to relationships on first glance. She doubted she would be that brave. After all, many of her former colleagues would supposedly be reading this book. What would they think of Dr. Imogene Durant, Emerita, suddenly becoming a round-heeled hussy? Ah, but then they would have to get a sense of Marcel, wouldn't they? His strong jaw, his twinkling eyes, his shoulders so broad, his hands so skilled. She sighed and shook herself. Thinking like this wasn't going to get any work done. She set herself down into her writing chair and opened her laptop.

A sparrow alit on the windowsill, distracting her for a minute. She looked further and could see someone's curtains billowing out through an open window across the street. This was such a crowded neighbourhood, even without twenty-two people per apartment. She could feel the humanity surrounding her in a way that didn't occur to her in her own apartment building back home.

Someone on the street laughed, and Imogene smiled at the sounds of joy in the air.

She wondered what Marcel was up to right now, and if he was thinking about her. And then she wondered if it was too early to open that bottle of wine.

# Second Thoughts

Maybe she'd had a weird dream she couldn't recall, or perhaps something had shifted in her brain as she slept, but Imogene woke up the next morning with an appalled sense of judgment for her recent behaviour.

How in the name of all that was holy had she decided it was fine to just fall into bed with a complete stranger? And how could she possibly believe he was altruistically in it for the mere pleasure of her company? What if he was some sort of fortune hunter, trying to seduce her out of her retirement nest egg, or a con man, trying to get hold of her credit card numbers?

She tried to think if he had ever been alone with her purse and of course he had. She had been asleep when he went out for breakfast that first time, and who knows when she had left him alone with all of her things any other time he'd been in the apartment. Her passport was locked in the little safe in her bedroom, but what about her credit card? What sort of measures should she take to secure things? Perhaps a quick call to her bank would be a good idea.

She had been on autopilot as she fretted, making coffee and pulling the drapes. Now, as she stood with a cup of coffee, looking out down the avenue, she paused. What possible indication would she have given to Marcel to make him think she was wealthy? She wasn't dressed ostentatiously; she wasn't tossing out great sums of money in front of him, although that cheese shop on the rue Montorguiel was on the pricey end of things.

And perhaps she was underplaying her looks a bit. She wasn't so long in the tooth that she didn't present as a fairly attractive woman still. She glanced to the mirror over the fireplace and took stock. Her hair was a mess, but it was still an attractive mess, curling and waving into a halo of auburn, with a tinge of grey starting near her right temple. Somehow, she hadn't yet developed many lines, thanks probably to a predilection for large sunglasses and a rigorous schedule of daily moisturizer. She could pass for ten to fifteen years younger than she was, and she knew it. So maybe it wasn't out of the realm of possibility that a discerning middle-aged man like Marcel Rocher might be intrigued by an adventurous sort of single woman such as herself.

It was so long since Imogene had considered herself to be on display that it was difficult to gauge. One of her friends from work had told her that she thought Daniel had been subtly flirting with her at their next-to-last staff meeting before Imogene retired, but Imogene couldn't quite fathom that. Daniel had been her work pal for ages. She didn't think her change in marital status would make a difference to their relationship.

But who knows, perhaps it did. Maybe Imogene was blind at home but somehow Paris had awakened her senses. She thought about the sequence in *Les Misérables* where Cosette came of age, suddenly realizing she was pretty, and then when she considered the attentions of the arrogant colonel walking past the gates each day until she heard from Marius and then found the handsome colonel, who was coincidentally Marius's cousin, to be repulsive. Hugo was sensitive and indulgent to the thoughts of youth, especially when it came to the minds of Marius and Cosette, and Fantine before them. He understood the aspects of self-doubt and the ways in which context provided different ideas.

What had it been that made her doubt Marcel and their dalliance? Was it a dream? She couldn't recollect many of her dreams and this morning was no different. No, it was something Raymonde had said, about her places in Nîmes being very relaxing, like "holidaying on Capri." And like words often did, "Capri" had bounced around in Imogene's head the rest of the afternoon, leading her to recall the comic Noel Coward song about Mrs. Wentworth-Brewster, a widow who made a display of herself on the island of Capri in "A Bar on the Piccola Marina" with various fishermen, much to her children's dismay.

That's what had provoked her doubts in herself. She laughed out loud, startling herself. She wasn't yet a pigeon-chested dowager. The mind was a strange and often mean-spirited thing.

"Finniculi, finnicula, finnick yourself," she warbled, à la Coward.

What she needed was more coffee and maybe some companionship. She looked at the time.

It was eight a.m. She had enough time to make herself a terrific breakfast and then head off to the Rodin Museum, which she had promised her good friend Larry she would visit, it being his favourite place in Paris. Rodin had always been a favourite of hers, as well, ever since she had visited the museum in San Francisco devoted to his work. And although Larry was a painter, not a sculptor, it made sense to listen to an artist's views of an art museum.

She would go to the Rodin Museum, find herself some lunch somewhere, and walk home via the *bouquinistes*. She had decided to purchase a print or two from the fellow who had sold her the Vogue postcards as additional decoration for the dressing corner of her bedroom. And then, when she got back to the apartment, it would be time to leave for ballet class with Toni. As days went, it sounded ideal.

The walk to the museum was slightly longer than she had thought it would be but interesting in its own right. The street one back from the Seine on the Left Bank, which wended along behind the mint and the Musée d'Orsay, held private galleries and decorating businesses, so the window displays were gorgeous. She also had to stop and take a photo of a nondescript house with a glorious green door, because a plaque told her that Edith Wharton had once lived there.

The Rodin Museum grounds and house were magnificent in and of themselves, even without all the amazing sculpture to be seen around them. The ticket seller suggested going through the museum itself first and then taking a walk around the grounds. Imogene purchased a small book that would give more information than the free brochure, which held the map, and took herself off to pay her respects to *The Thinker*, who sat pondering halfway between the ticket house and the entrance to the mansion. He was set in a circular garden, so that viewers could walk around him. Already, there were several people on the grounds, but, as the ticket seller had gaily assured her, "no school groups today!" Imogene offered to take a photo of two Dutch girls with the statue, and they responded in kind, snapping a rather good picture on her phone for her.

She ambled through the museum, marvelling at *The Kiss* and entranced by several other smaller statues she'd never before encountered in art books. She came to a room of some of Rodin's own art collection, which include a Monet and a van Gogh, and some interesting El Grecos.

It struck her, in this more biographical area, that Rodin had been alive and about the same age as Marius in the time delineated by Hugo in *Les Misérables*. Here he was, a youth with idealized ideas of mankind, wanting to bring a naturalness to the form of sculpture and to celebrate the regular people, not just the gloriously beautiful or godlike.

From all accounts, while his family knew of his talent, he wasn't making it as a prodigy in school. Who's to say he wasn't feeling a bit of malcontent and joining into a student revolution or two? Twenty was such an age for dissatisfaction. Imogene could recall her own early twenties as a time she wouldn't want to relive, but she could also recognize the truth of it from all the students she had taught over the years. Her introductory-level courses were filled with young people who were, if not starry-eyed, at least still capable of wonder and enchantment. By the time they got into her third-year and fourth-year seminar classes, they were much more likely to be jaded or filled with angst. She wasn't sure when the ennui or cynicism ironed itself out of them: maybe after their first child or work bonus or layoff. With her, it had been her first book published, which had been her dissertation beefed up with a snappier intro. Shortly after that, she had married, netted her tenure-track job, and had two children, and her life rolled out before her like the yellow brick road in the land of Oz.

Is that why Hugo put twenty-year-olds under the microscope by examining the students' rebellion? Was it an inevitable growing pain towards a republic? Or, as he intimated, an unfortunate occurrence because of the results of the Battle of Waterloo?

After a good hour in the mansion, Imogene wandered over to the *Burghers of Calais* in the grounds of the museum. In a way, she had appreciated it even more as viewed from the road in, through the windows in the wall. *The Gates of*

*Hell* were more impressive. All that work for a cathedral that never got built. That was art for you. At least he had been paid, she hoped. And, of course, it was splendid to see it here.

She strolled past the statues and into the garden area, where she sat for a while on a bench in the sunshine and read through some of the booklet she'd just purchased. As nice as the booklet was, she had a feeling it was going to end up as part of Raymonde's shelf library. She had to mind how much weight she'd be bringing home.

Several other people were sitting about in the garden. If she lived here, she might be tempted to buy an annual membership, just to be able to come and sit here in the sunshine, among the peonies. She closed her eyes and let the spring sunshine beat down on her face. It might be a good idea to buy some sun cream, if the weather was going to continue this pleasant. On the other hand, she had SPF 15 in her moisturizer and only ten more days in Paris. She'd risk it.

She really needed to leave, if she was going to walk home with time to shop for prints and some time to flake out a bit before meeting Toni for ballet. Plus, a quick shower wouldn't go amiss. All the walking had made her sweat, and sitting in the warm sun hadn't done anything to cool her down. She was looking forward to the relative cool of walking home by the river, but it wouldn't make her any less pongy.

She checked that she had everything tucked into her purse, then heaved herself off the bench and walked back along the pathway next to several different varieties of peony. She walked past the little outdoor café, which made her even more sure she'd buy a membership if she lived there, and headed back to the street, saying one last goodbye to *Baudelaire* and *The Thinker*.

She walked along the Left Bank for a while, crossed at the Concorde bridge, and then hugged the Right Bank, down past the Tuileries and the Louvre. As she got closer to the *bouquinistes*, the sidewalk traffic began to increase, and she held her purse a little closer to her side as she wound through groups congregated on corners and in front of vendors.

There were two places in particular she wanted to look through, the one that had the boxes of vintage postcards and another that seemed to focus on prints and old magazine covers. Her idea was still hazy, but she thought a larger print next to the grouping of her Vogue postcards would make a fun and unique remembrance of her time in Paris. Why the concept of a collection of wafer-thin mini-skirted Vogue models might bring back Proustian memories for her, housed as she was in a body that had definitely been eating madeleines, she wasn't sure. It had to be the air here. Somehow, her time here, connected as it was to the youthful Toni and the virile Marcel, had her thinking of herself as she once had been, before the ennui of a repetitive career, a disappointing marriage, and the humbling of middle age had had its way with her. She knew there was more vigour in her attitude; whether it was the lack of everyday stressors or the joy of discovery and adventure, she couldn't be sure. Perhaps it was both. Or maybe it was just Paris.

The magazine covers weren't speaking to her. They were

either too yellowed or too expensive for what she wanted to do with them. She moved on, after smiling at the taciturn man on his stool, and found the vendor with the long boxes of postcards.

He also had a manger filled with prints sheathed in plastic. Flipping through them, she discovered a view of the Eiffel Tower painted from what had to be the Pont des Arts, at nighttime, with the lights of the tower shimmering and reflected in the waters of the Seine. It would accentuate the cards she had previously bought and remind her of that evening with Marcel. She paid the vendor, who nodded approvingly of her choice and rolled the print tightly and slid it into a small cardboard tube for her.

She looked at her watch as she entered her apartment and discovered she was half an hour earlier than she'd assumed it would take her to get home. Maybe she was getting more fit. She had time for a shower and even a brief lie-down before she needed to think about making a bite to eat.

The water pressure in the apartment was a glorious thing, she thought, as she always did as she stepped under the shower head. Imogene stood, letting the water sluice over her shoulders with her head bent forward, for longer than she normally allowed herself at home.

How on earth could Hugo have imagined the sewer sequence? Had he ever seen the sewers himself? Was he a fastidious person and tried to think of the very opposite element that would disgust and horrify people? He seemed to plunge Valjean so often into hideous elements: the mud under the cart he raised with his shoulders; the deep, cold waters he dove into from the prison ship; and now the running streams of shit in the dark underground of what was a cholera-infested dirty city to begin with.

Just the thought of it made Imogene soap herself twice.

Finally, she got out of the shower and buffed herself dry with one of the fluffy white towels. She drew her silky kimono around her and wrapped another towel around her hair, and went into the bedroom, ostensibly to pull out some underwear and get dressed. The sun through the glass curtains felt warm, and the walking of the day had tired her, so she decided to stretch out on top of the coverlet, just to relax a bit.

The next thing she heard was a rapping at the apartment door. Groggy, she rolled off the bed and went to peer through the peephole.

It was Toni, hair in a bun, with her ballet bag over her shoulder.

"Imogene? Are you there?"

"Oh, good lord! What time is it?"

"Don't worry, I'm early. I was going to see if you wanted to stop for a bowl of noodles on the way, down at the Chinese restaurant."

"I can be ready in five minutes. Why don't you head there and order for us, and I'll catch you up?"

"Sounds good! How spicy do you want to go?"

"Mild, mild!"

Toni laughed. "Coward!"

She clattered down the stairs and Imogene ran back to

the bathroom to undo the towel and see how impossible her hair might be. It was still damp, and Madame was not going to be impressed. Imogene whipped it into a ponytail and twisted it into a semblance of a bun, screwing four curly pins in to hold her springy hair in place. Then she raced into the bedroom, yanked on her tights and leotard, and pulled her navy jumper dress over her head. She grabbed a scarf, her jacket, her bag with her ballet slippers and a towel already packed, and dumped her purse into the bag. Soon, she too was clattering down the stairs.

Toni had snagged one of the three tables outside the Chinese restaurant, which, no matter what time of day, always appeared to be crowded. She was watching the cooks through the window, filling bowls that had various clothespins attached to them indicating what meat and what level of hot sauce had been requested. It seemed to be a very good system and made for efficient timing, because soon steaming bowls were set before each of them.

"So, you were working?" Toni asked.

"I was sleeping. I think I wore myself out in the sun today." Between spoonfuls and hums of pleasure at the taste of her food, Imogene told Toni about her visit to the Rodin Museum.

"Maybe you should start riding the Metro more," Toni laughed.

"Ah, but with all the walking I am doing, I can afford to eat bowls full of noodles and drink plentiful amounts of wine, without returning to Canada unrecognizable."

Toni saluted her with her water glass. "I think that calls for wine after ballet, then!"

"I think that sounds like a splendid idea! So how was your day? Obviously, you weren't spending it napping."

"No, it was full of paperwork, and I would have welcomed a nap."

"I was thinking of some things yesterday about your case, and it led me down two opposite directions, both of them having to do with dissection."

Toni looked interested, and Imogene leaned in a bit so she could speak quietly. She laid out her theories of who had access to the tools and the means to do the things that had been done without anyone necessarily questioning them.

"So, if they really are the murderer, they would have to be in those professions. But if they are in those professions with just having access to body parts, you have a whole line of different motivations to try to ascertain."

"And can you think of any motives that would go along with what we found?" asked Toni.

"Someone might have wanted to ruin the owner of the ice machines?"

"Or protest the making of ice in general? Some sort of waste of energy in our climate situation?"

"Does the same company own all the hotels in question?" Imogene asked. "Maybe the perpetrator has a vendetta against the hotelier?"

Toni shook her head. "No, two are owned by an international chain and one by a French chain. One is a family-owned hotel that has been a local institution for three generations. And another is owned by a Saudi investment group. We had thought of that too."

Imogene sighed. "Of course you had. I am sorry. I don't mean to be suggesting that you haven't done all there is to do with this. It is just so puzzling, and when you set a professional reader onto a puzzle, she cannot help herself."

Toni said, "I appreciate any and all insights you might have, Imogene. I especially like the idea of the anatomy lecturers or students in a class. I think, though, that cadavers prepared for an anatomy class would have been injected with formalin or formaldehyde, for preservation. None of the body parts we found had any formalin in them. So, unless they were taken before they were prepared for the class, that is not likely to be our answer."

"Would a body be prepared with formaldehyde before a cremation?" Imogene asked.

"Only if there was going to be a viewing prior to the cremation, which does not often take place. More likely, the body would be on ice prior, and not even dressed if the service was held at the crematorium. In many situations, though, the body is removed by the mortuary, cremated, and then provided in whatever urn has been chosen, for the ceremony."

"Yes, my mother's urn, a photo of her, and a small tree were at the front of the church at her funeral. We later planted the tree, in her honour," Imogene reflected.

"That sounds like a lovely idea," Toni smiled. "My

grandparents were both buried in the graveyard in their village, and my mother wants to be cremated and inurned on top of her own mother's grave. I am not certain the church will allow that because it sounds a little bit, shall we say, too economical?" She signalled the waiter, who brought their bill. Imogene handed her fifteen euros and Toni went inside to pay.

Imogene sighed. It felt strange to talk about burial rites on the same day that she had been considering herself so reinvented. All her thoughts of vigour had ended up with her needing a nap, though, so perhaps she wasn't all that newly fit after all.

Toni re-emerged, and took on what people were now calling a superhero pose, legs slightly spread, fists on hips.

"*Alors*, are we ready to hit the barre, Imogene?"

"First the barre, and then the bar!"

They hoisted their ballet bags over their shoulders and headed off down the lane toward the dance studio.

# What You Don't Know

Madame had been mildly complimentary to Imogene about her turnout in her demi-pliés, and so Imogene bought them a full bottle of wine to celebrate.

"I've only got one more class to make her break down and actually say '*Bon!*' so I am taking this as a win." Imogene poured them each a generous glass once the waiter had left the table.

"You are doing well. I can see the difference in your shoulders and you don't groan as much when we're changing our shoes after class either." Toni saluted her with her wineglass, grinning.

"What I would like is to have arms that don't embarrass me in sundresses," Imogene sighed. "There are certain ways your body just humbles you as you age."

"It shouldn't be that way, but that is what Samuel Beckett said about Descartes in his essay. That he was setting us up for disappointment when he declared that God had created each animal including man into a perfectly functioning organism."

"And that man's body degenerates in an equal rate to his brain developing and his mind acquiring wisdom," Imogene recalled.

Toni nodded. "And that the only way that Cartesian man could exist in reality would be if man were on a bicycle."

"No wonder the Tour de France is so popular," joked Imogene, and they clinked glasses, pleased with themselves and their shared recollection of philosophy classes of long ago. Probably not so long ago for Toni. Heck, thought Imogene, perhaps she read philosophy for nighttime relaxation. She really didn't know everything there was to know about Toni. Once again, she was the lesser curious of the pairing. Maybe it was a failing she had always had but just hadn't recognized till now.

As if she was reading her mind (how did she do that?), Toni asked her if she had found out anything more about where Marcel worked.

"Not really. I was going to ask, and we got caught up in other things." Imogene must have blushed a bit, because Toni started to giggle.

"I don't want to make this sound strange, Imogene, but you are my hero. I want to be just as sensual as you are when I get to be your age."

"You are French. Of course, you will be."

They toasted each other once more.

"I mean it, though," Toni continued. "I admire your

ability to come away on your own and to be open to all the experiences that come your way."

"My children would probably be horrified if they knew what I was getting up to."

"I think they'd be proud to be of your line."

"From your mouth to their thoughts." Imogene looked quizzically at Toni. "Are your parents not particularly amorous?"

Toni shrugged. "What can one tell about one's own parents? They seem happy together, and I think my father is content with the way things are, but I know my mother always wanted to do more with her life. She has an adventurous spirit, but they married young and my brother came along quite quickly, so she was a wife and mother and then eventually she went to work running the office for the local dairy because the hours were the same as the school day. As a result, she never went backpacking through the Himalayas, or whatever it was she was dreaming of."

"That is sad, but don't you think she still has time to do those sorts of things if she wanted to?"

"I think it could be possible. She is still fit, I mean, but her dreams may have been packed away. And I don't know if she has the energy to haul them out and dust them off. And what would she do with my father? I can't see him even climbing on a tour bus. He's happy in his own backyard."

"Like Candide."

Toni nodded. "Exactly."

"You could be right. Even though I have felt as if I've been set free to roam, what with the divorce and the retirement, it's not as if I am having to breathe life into a dream deferred, and I can understand how much energy that would take, or seem to take, if you were contemplating it. I've always managed to get travel in, what with conferences and winter getaways and some decently located old friends from grad school it is always good to connect with. As a Comp Lit prof, you can chalk it up to research and upgrading to get out and about, although I certainly didn't manage much when the kids were younger."

"But you could have shrivelled up with two blows happening one after the other, and instead you blossomed," Toni raised her glass. "To you, Imogene Durant. My hero of coming of age."

Imogene found herself tearing up for a second. Toni's use of the phrase, whether she realized its meaning in English or not, was something Imogene had been mulling for the past year or two. There was something in the zeitgeist about discussing menopause and the general ignorance or disinterest the world had for this monumental time in a woman's life. Imogene had been considering it as a topic for study, which of course was how she tackled most aspects of the world, but aside from reading some Doris Lessing novels and Annie Ernaux, she could find very little in literature that focused on the radical changes women faced as they aged out of fertility and into what could well be the second half of their lifespan. To be appreciated for weathering the storm and surviving the journey in a positive manner was so touching.

Because, as she looked back on it, Imogene knew it had been a storm, just one that had so few words to describe it beyond jokes about hot flashes and night sweats and sighs about drops in libido. Imogene felt that there should be public service announcements for middle-aged women, much like the ones funded by the LGBTQ community for teens, to say, "It gets better." Maybe that could have an equally positive and preventative effect on the several marriages she had seen founder, including her own, and the suicides of a variety of older women, including one academic whose writing she had greatly admired.

She blinked a couple of times and came back to the conversation they had been having. "He did tell me something about his personal life, though."

"Marcel?"

"Yes. He has been having to go out of town to see his sick father the past week or so. His father broke his ankle and it's not healing quickly enough for the old man's patience and he keeps trying to walk on it."

"He lives on his own, then? How old would he be?"

Imogene shrugged. "Late eighties, I seem to recall."

"And where is out of town?"

"Someplace called Mantes something."

"Mantes-la-Ville?"

"Erm, I am not sure."

"Mantes-la-Jolie?"

"Yes, that was it. Nice name for a place. I wonder what makes it so pretty."

"I've been there a couple of times. A friend from school

was from there." Toni took a sip of wine and looked thoughtful. "There are a few nice churches and a rather famous basilica, but mostly just tidy homes. It's almost a suburb of Paris by now. I believe a lot of people commute."

"That is what we would call a 'bedroom community,'" said Imogene.

Toni nodded. "Yes, although I think people are tending to retire out to places like this more now, rather than begin there. There was something else I heard about Mantes-la-Jolie, rather recently, but it's not coming to me. So, Marcel is staying out there, minding his father's recuperation?"

"Yes, which was his reason for not being quite so available these past few days. I have honestly been so caught up in my research and writing, I'd not entirely noticed that there had been a lapse."

"I wonder if he grew up in Mantes. Maybe my friend's family would know his family."

"That sounds a bit creepy, checking up on him."

Toni laughed. "You have no idea how fully some young man would be scrutinized by the girl's family if he began to show an interest in their daughter. Wanting to know a bit about his family background would be the least of it. I am sure there are *mamans* who demand DNA tests to check for madness in the family genes these days."

"And there I was, just admiring my husband-to-be's lovely straight teeth," giggled Imogene.

"Teeth? That's how you gauge horses, not husbands, Imogene!"

"Well, I know that, now!"

Both women broke into laughter loud enough to turn heads at a few other tables.

"Seriously, Imogene, I am happy to ask my friend if she knows of a Marcel Rocher from around there."

"Just as long as the poor man doesn't think I am checking his teeth!"

"No, nothing like that. I can be very discreet."

"You are the police, Toni. Does discreet ever enter into it?"

# TGIF

The next morning, Imogene felt a slight residual hangover from the wine she and Toni had consumed the night before. Either there were more tannins than usual in that vintage or it had been an exceptionally large bottle, or maybe it was due to their not having eaten anything with the wine, since they had noshed on noodles before their ballet class. Imogene filled the electric kettle with water and readied the teapot, dropping two tea bags in instead of her usual one. A couple of acetaminophens wouldn't go amiss either, to fend off the headache, so she added them to her morning pile of pills. She looked at the dosettes she had filled before coming on her trip. She should be able to manage with the weight load of her souvenirs heading home, since she wouldn't be hauling half a medicine cabinet back with her.

This really was the ignominy of aging. Where she had spent most of her life taking one multivitamin in the morning, with calcium added when she'd been pregnant, now she had pills to manage her thyroid, another three to assuage incipient arthritis pains, two for digestion issues, and a vitamin D to make up for the fact that she no longer worshipped the sun by baring much more than her forearms.

The tea made, she took a cup, along with a small bowl of granola, over to the kitchen table. She portioned out her pills into piles of two, one big, one little, each to be taken with a swallow of tea once it had cooled a bit. She drew her phone toward her to check for any messages that might have come in the night from Canada.

Sure enough, there was one from Marjorie, her younger child who still lived in Edmonton, letting her know that she and the boyfriend had been to her apartment to check on her plants and have a swim. "All is well."

It was good to hear things were fine without her presence, including her adult children. As much as she delighted in the company of either of her children, she was proud to see how independent and resourceful they each were. She remembered a friend saying to her, way back, that she had thought Imogene would suffer extreme empty nest syndrome, since she had been so wrapped up in her children. Imogene had been somewhat surprised herself in how easy it was to watch them fledge and fly. But her job was done. She no longer had to be a watchdog; she could now just enjoy her children as the people they had grown into being. And she was fine with that chapter of her life being done.

Chapters really were a good way to look at one's life. It was a long-spooling story, fed out to you chapter by chapter, without a clear opening blurb on the flyleaf of the cover. You went into the story blind, not even knowing if it was a bestseller. And you got caught up in each section, but it wasn't something you could stop and go back to and change direction, like one of those children's choose-your-own-adventure books. It was a three-volume novel and it moved ever forward.

It was easier to explain abrupt endings, like divorce and retirement, when one considered the variety of chapter endings that one witnessed over time. There were cliff hangers, the sorts of endings that kept you turning pages long into the night, unable to put the bookmark into the first page of the new chapter. There were chapters that contained italicized prefaces, à la Henry Fielding, offering a small summary of what lay ahead, so that you knew when the chapter would be coming to a close. And there were endings with lines drawn under them so thick that, as a reader, you knew there would be no going back along that trajectory. Abandon hope, all ye who turn this page.

Victor Hugo went one further than separating his story into chapters; he also had it separated into five sections. Like Dickens, he had published the book in instalments, and it was publicized widely ahead of time, so the build-up for readers was intense. "Fantine," the first section, went immediately into reprint.

It was so thrilling, even today, to think of the excitement a book could cause. Was that why we put pen to paper, Imogene wondered, to create that sort of a thrill between writer and reader? To meet, neuron to neuron, the distillation of words on the page moving from their placement by the author to their readers' minds, rebuilding the vision for themselves.

Imogene had once heard it said that fiction aimed at the head where images were disseminated and created, and poetry was to be read by the heart, where emotions were replicated in another. Transmitting images would be more than enough for her, if she could find a way to explain how walking the same cobblestones that Hugo must have strode along made the visions he provided in his books so much clearer than they had been when she had read them as a teenager in western Canada.

Could she impart her awe and do him justice? So many more people would have had the chance to see Paris than Saint Petersburg. Perhaps her earlier success had been due to the greater sense of exoticism and not her insights.

Maybe this was the hangover talking.

Imogene hoisted herself up from the breakfast table and ferried her dishes over to the sink. A shower would clear her head and get her away from gloom thinking.

Sure enough, clean and dressed with her hair pulled back into a ponytail, her bed made, and a load of laundry stuck in the washing machine, Imogene was feeling much more herself. She washed her dishes, swept crumbs off the table with the dishcloth, and opened the curtains wide to the bustling day beyond. It was just turning nine a.m., and while some of the stores weren't open yet, people were streaming steadily out of the entrance to the Metro under the shopping mall down the street. Imogene brought a second cup of tea to her desk and flipped open her laptop. Only one of her three online newspapers had been delivered to her email as yet, but the crossword puzzle for the day was already posted, so she did that and then turned to the file containing her manuscript and Hugo notes.

Even though she would edit it severely, she was also keeping notes on her discussions of Toni's body parts case as part of her section on Toni. She wouldn't write about the case itself, but if she could, she would include some of the elements of Toni's questioning and need for answers. It was essential to show how humane and thoughtful Toni was in comparison with her fictional counterpart, Javert.

And if Toni stood for Javert, she supposed Marcel stood in for Marius, the lover. So did that make her Cosette? Imogene didn't think so. She was starting to admit that she was equating herself with Jean Valjean. After all, readers were meant to align themselves with the hero of the piece. She just didn't want to discover she had a Thénardier in her own Paris adventure. So far, she had been very lucky, she knew, because the people she had dealt with had all been unfailingly gracious.

But who would ever want to be the bad guy, anyhow? She remembered her cousin always trying to make her be the robber or the fox or the German in any of his games. The only time she got to be a law-abiding good guy was when they were playing pirates, in which case Will was all swashbuckler all the time.

Imogene settled in to write about her ideas of the criminal in Toni's case, and all the reasonings she could recall that Toni had given for her theories not to be accurate. She had to look up formalin and discovered it was formaldehyde watered down. So the cadavers for anatomy classes were soaked in a solution, rather than having it pumped through their deblooded veins. It would account for cadavers looking a bit more leathered, she supposed. She wondered what had been pumped into those bodies she had seen in the display that had toured the world, showing the inner workings of the human body. Plastic of some sort, to keep them clear and lifelike.

The donation of bodies to science was a noble thing. She had read about people donating their bodies to the FBI's body farm to help forensic scientists learn more about the natural elements of decomposition, and bug and animal interaction with bodies in the wild or in shallow graves. She didn't think she would be able to do that, not because she thought her body was so special it should be exalted or burned on a pyre. It was because she thought she might feel shamed in some way, that someone would be looking at the striations of fat along her liver, or at her thighs and tutting at her excesses. They might laugh at her scraped kneecaps or the little finger broken in a volleyball game and never properly healed— laugh mostly to shield themselves from the very human fear of death and bodily harm—and somehow that would feel as bad as having to walk past groupings of teenaged boys egging each other on to say something snide or workmen leering from beyond the scaffolding. Sometimes you had to put yourself in the way of the jeering, just to get on with your day. You didn't have to offer your vulnerable, dead self up on a silver platter for it.

Imogene had long ago signed an organ donor line on her driver's licence and designated in her will that she wished to be cremated once everything useful had been taken. That would be enough for her.

Her phone buzzed, indicating a message had come through. It was Daniel, who was up early, she thought. She looked at her watch to match up with the time noted on his message, and realized she had been working for two and a half hours. While it was early in Edmonton, it wasn't wee hours early.

> Greetings! I wanted to say, please send me your flight details, and I can arrange to pick you up at the airport.

Imogene was touched. He really was such a nice man.

> I am coming home May 11, on Air Canada to Calgary and then the hop to the capital. If only Air Canada would get their minds wrapped around that and provide a direct flight. Right now, it says I get in at 5:45 pm.

> Gotcha. I will keep an eye on that flight's ETA, and I will be there.

> That's so kind.

I've really been missing you. No one to bitch about marking with.

> Retirement is the answer.

You're making it look so inviting.

> LOL

Seriously, I am not sure I have more than one term left in me.

> Would that give you your full measure?

I am checking with the admin. I think it would, if I paid into my half sabbatical from three years ago.

> Ooh, that's exciting!

Yes. So how are things going?

> Good. Productive. But almost ready to start packing.

Really? Thought we might have to lure you back with promises of accordion music and riverboat cruises.

> Haha. Is the riverboat going yet?

The ice isn't completely off the river yet, but the trees are in bud, so hope of spring springs eternal.

> I'll be glad to get home. I think five weeks anywhere away is my limit. This six-week length is just a tad too long, but that was the way the apartment lease worked.

Aha. Well, you will have had spring and can come back to another.

> Yes, two springs for the price of three.

LOL

> Well, I should get back to it. Thanks again. XO

XO

She stared down at her phone for a moment. Had she and Daniel ever signed off with a kiss and a hug before? This Gallic physicality was obviously seeping over into her relationships with everyone.

It would be nice to see Daniel, of all her colleagues and friends. He, more than anyone, knew the path she was on, both in divorce and coming to the end of a career. And they had been through so much together, workwise. She wondered idly if there might be any romantic possibilities with Daniel in the future. There it was again, the Paris influence on her thinking.

Imogene pushed herself back from her desk. She needed to get out of the apartment for a while. She looked out the window to check the weather and noticed that for once there didn't appear to be a line formed down below at the popular restaurant across the way. She had been so curious about it. Why not take herself out for lunch?

She checked her teeth and hair in the bathroom mirror, pulled on her jacket and shoes, and grabbed her keys and purse. At the last minute, she dodged back into the bedroom for her e-reader.

Le Petit Bouillon Pharamond was a beautiful little jewel-box of a restaurant on two or three levels with outdoor seating, as well. It had been featured in the film *The Sun Also Rises,* and was famous for having been a mainstay of the area since 1879. The décor, according to the small history on the website Imogene had scanned, trying to figure out the place's popularity, was retained from when they decked themselves out as the Normandy Pavilion during the World Exposition of 1898. A waiter, dressed in white shirt, black pants, and burgundy apron, greeted her and seated her with pomp at a small table inside the restaurant.

Imogene scanned the menu and decided on steak tartare and a carafe of red wine. The waiter approved her choice and brought her the wine immediately, pouring a third of it into her glass. She looked around. Not many empty tables at all. She had just been lucky in beating the rush, which, from what she could tell, was almost non-stop all day long. She admired the tiled floors and the painted walls and beams. It seemed that every surface was gilt or floral, enhanced by judiciously placed mirrors. Families, couples, and one or two other single people were all enjoying the atmosphere. A circular staircase halfway down the room led to more tables on the next floor, and apparently yet another floor, and Imogene enjoyed watching the waiters climbing it briskly with a loaded tray in one hand.

When her own meal came, it was a thick patty of raw beef and a scramble of fries curved around it. Some dried onions and chopped parsley decorated the top of the meat. She sliced a French fry in half and cut and spread some of the steak onto the potato. She found herself nearly groaning out loud in delight at the seasoning. All her paltry North American worries about salmonella and E. coli were tossed aside, and she made her way industriously through her meal. Her waiter paused to pour more of her carafe into her wineglass and smile at her before rushing on his way down the aisle to the kitchen.

No wonder there was always a line-up to get in this place. Maybe she would treat Marcel to dinner here some evening before she left. Or Toni. Time was growing short. She had barely a week to wrap things up and head home. She did want to wander down to Esmeralda's, the café behind Notre Dame, to get a feel for Hugo's vision in his *Hunchback of Notre Dame* even though she couldn't imagine anyone wanting to follow her down the rabbit hole of discussing a huge tome like *Les Misérables* and then find themselves adding on a book or two. It was just the sense of voice she wanted to absorb, to see if his huge sociological and historical sequences were particular only to Jean Valjean's story, or whether he wrapped sermons and dissertations up in entertainment all the time.

She felt a little sad as she slid the last morsel of steak into her mouth and held it there, just to burnish it in her memory bank. If this were a madeleine moment, what would it bring back to her? Maybe the beautiful realization that she was respected as a woman alone, dining. She had not been placed at a table behind an archway, or near the toilets, or close to the kitchen, to minimize her. No, they had sat her in the centre of the main floor of their very busy restaurant, and maintained service to her throughout her *déjeuner*. Paris might be for lovers, but it was considerate and demonstrative to *une femme d'un certain âge* and Imogene was grateful for it. She thought it likely that the sensibility of being of worth, recognized and valued and even flirted with, would hold her through the continuing humbling that was the aging process.

Back home, people spoke of women becoming invisible as they grew older. While it hadn't happened to her yet, she had no doubt that it happened. She had read Carolyn Heilbrun's sad take on aging, which was one of the reasons she had continued to dye her roots and maintain an eye on fashion. At the same time as she felt judged for being a tad fanciful by some of her more rigorously feminist colleagues, she was herself feminist enough to feel that all paths could lead to equity. Of course, she wondered if she'd be feeling this way if she hadn't been having amorous relations with a handsome man and texting pleasantly with another one back home. It couldn't just be attentive waiters honing her consciousness, could it?

She pulled herself out of her reverie and signalled for the bill. It was very reasonable, which might be another reason the lines were always so long to get in. She pulled out her credit card, and soon was ready to head home again. She looked around. Now the restaurant was filled and the line had formed. She had been just lucky to have found that miraculous break in which to come and taste the magic.

Home again, she kicked her shoes off and dropped her keys on the counter. Her phone, tucked into its designated pocket in her purse, began to buzz, now that she was once more in the location of the apartment's wifi. It sounded like someone wanted to get hold of her.

There were five or six texts piled up on the notification area of her phone's opening screen. Four of them were from Toni, and two from Marcel. His, which she opened first, were suggesting an evening cruise on a *Bateau-Mouche* to see the sights from the river. He was free the day after next; was she?

She sent him back a thumbs-up emoji with a note saying how pleasant that sounded, and that, yes, she was free.

Toni's messages were a bit more cryptic, but the gist was

she wanted to see Imogene as soon as possible and was she available; where was she; could she get back to her asap; was she okay?

Imogene texted back saying, "Sorry, I was out of wifi reach for a bit, having lunch next door. Fantastic lunch. Can I be of some help?"

Toni phoned her through the messaging program almost as soon as Imogene had pressed SEND. "Imogene! There you are. It is imperative that I see you. Are you available this afternoon?"

"Sure. Where are you? Would you like me to come to you? Or are you at home?"

"No, I am at the office. Would you mind coming down? I can meet you at the doors closest to Notre Dame. It shouldn't take you more than fifteen minutes to get here, *non*?"

"I still have my jacket on. I won't be long."

This was turning into a very interesting day, all-round.

# La Sûreté

It ended up taking a few more minutes than intended, because Imogene went across the wrong bridge, the Pont Notre Dame, ironically bringing her to the Sainte-Chapelle end of the Préfecture de Police rather than the Notre Dame end, instead of the Pont D'Arcole, which she usually took to get to the flower market. She eventually walked the entire circumference of the Préfecture before finding Toni standing on the sidewalk looking the other way for her approach.

"There you are, Imogene," Toni smiled and kissed her on each cheek. "Do come with me, and you will see where I work." She held the door open for Imogene and waved them both past the officer at the desk. They went up a set of stairs and down a corridor to a large room containing several desks. Toni led them through the desks to a series of narrow offices with frosted glass windows set into the top third of each door. Hers was the third from the end, and Imogene wondered if that signified anything in terms of seniority.

Inside was a medium-sized metal desk, about two thirds of the size of Imogene's back at the University of Alberta, a desk chair, guest chair, bookcase, and bulletin board. There were also three hooks behind the door on which hung Toni's overcoat, an umbrella, and a dress uniform encased in dry cleaner's cling wrap. Imogene sat in the chair Toni gestured her toward and waited expectantly to find out why her friend had asked her to come down to the actual police station. As far as Imogene was aware, Toni wasn't letting anyone know that she had been discussing her ongoing case with her upstairs neighbour, an old lady from Canada.

Toni sat carefully in her own chair and pulled herself up to the edge of the desk. "Thank you for coming down to see me. There is something I have to tell you and I don't want you to feel as if I have overstepped our friendship in any way."

Imogene laughed, a bit nervously. "As long as friendship is involved and you're not arresting me for anything, I think we're okay."

"Ah well, we shall see."

Toni looked miserable and worried, and Imogene felt for the young detective. Whatever she wanted to talk about, it wasn't going to be pleasant.

"Why don't you just spill whatever you have to say," she said. "I promise not to go crazy about whatever it is."

"Okay." Toni placed both hands on her desk in front of her, and stared at her own fingernails before pulling her eyes up to meet Imogene's. "Do you recall how I asked you if you had checked on where Marcel worked?"

"Yes," Imogene said, "and I still haven't. You know how there is a point where it becomes sort of embarrassing to ask, because you haven't already asked? It's like admitting I've been a narcissist when we've talked about things, and well …"

Toni nodded. "Yes, I see what you mean. Well, I just thought, since I care about you and this has been so relatively sudden, that when you said he came from Mantes-la-Jolie, that I would check to see if my friend knew of his family. As one does?"

"You checked up on him?"

"Just to make sure he was not trying to set you up or dupe you in some sort of confidence scheme."

Suddenly, Imogene felt very tired.

"Because you thought that a handsome man making a romantic play for your middle-aged neighbour was so unbelievable that you figured you should check up on him before he took the old dear for everything she had?"

"No, it wasn't like that, and I don't want you to ever think that would have been my reasoning." Toni looked tortured. Imogene thought that had been her exact reasoning and felt herself blush, starting behind her ears.

She had thought a solid friendship had developed between her and this young woman, but maybe their connection was just Toni's benevolence, her good deed for the month of April. It was a Catholic country still; maybe she was Toni's Lenten project.

"So, I take it you have discovered something about Marcel

that I should be aware of. Do you think he has stolen my credit card number? Because I have been checking pretty regularly, and no odd payments have appeared."

"It is nothing like that, and, truly, I believe that it is entirely coincidental to your connection with him, but yes, there is something about Marcel that needs to be examined and I wanted you to know about it before my team goes forward. Because you are my friend."

Imogene looked directly at Toni as she spoke, and searched her face for pity, but all she could see was concern. She shook off the irritation and annoyance she had been feeling and tried to focus on what Toni was actually saying.

"Marcel is a criminal?"

"I didn't say that."

"But you want to investigate him. What for?"

"As I said, I was talking to my friend from Mantes, and she told me something that triggered some alarm bells for me."

"And what was that?"

"You told me his last name was Rocher. According to Juliette, my friend, the only Rochers in Mantes-la-Jolie are the undertakers. The family has owned a funeral home in town for three or more generations. They buried her uncle and her *grand-mère*."

"And?"

"And they also have a crematorium attached to their funeral parlour. Which means they fit into the grouping of people who have access to body parts."

"You think Marcel has something to do with your body parts case?"

Toni nodded, her face serious.

Imogene felt lightheaded and was thankful she was sitting down. Toni, with her eye on her, was perhaps wise to this sort of reaction in regular citizens. She reached to the side of her desk for a carafe of water and poured Imogene a glass. Imogene took it gratefully and took a long swig. She was adjusting, marginally, to her world being turned ninety degrees on edge. Everything she thought she knew was somehow now being seen from a different perspective, and it was giving her mental vertigo.

"What makes them so suspicious, more than any other undertakers in France?"

"For one thing, we have investigated all the funeral parlours in Paris. It's a backburner project, but to find a funeral parlour owner with a son who is going back and forth from Paris taking care of him offers us a link to an outlying place."

"Okay, I can see that, sort of. But what would make Marcel more of a target than anyone else, even his father? Why Marcel?"

"You said his father broke his ankle and cannot get around very well."

"Yes."

"So he's not likely to be visiting hotels around Paris."

"Granted."

"It is more likely, given our possible scenario, that Marcel could be the one secreting body parts around the capitol.

And therefore, I would like to question you about your knowledge of Marcel Rocher."

"Is this a formal questioning?"

"If you like, it can be. That would be my preference, so that if anything were to come of it, we would have clear lines of documentation."

Imogene shrugged, an action she was learning to do with precision from even such a short time in Paris. "Why not?"

Toni nodded. She pulled out her phone and set it on record.

"*Je parle avec Imogene Durant, une Canadienne anglaise. Alors, cette enquête sera en anglais.* It is May 3, at 11:30 a.m. Imogene Durant has been so kind as to come to the Préfecture for an interview about her knowledge of one Marcel Rocher, of Paris and Mantes-la-Jolie." She looked directly at Imogene and began the interview.

"Imogene, how long have you known Marcel Rocher?"

"About three and a half weeks. We met while shopping in the rue Montorgueil. He chatted me up in a cheese shop and we went for coffee."

"And you have since been on several dates with this man?"

"Yes."

"And can you tell me what you have spoken about with Marcel Rocher?"

"He's been interested in my research about Victor Hugo, and we have talked about Paris and things to see and do."

"Such as tourist stops?"

Imogene squinted, as if that would help her recall their conversations.

"More things that weren't necessarily on tourist maps. He wanted me to get the 'true sense' of Paris, he would say. I don't think he cares much for tourists."

"What makes you say that?"

"He said something once about disliking the groups getting off buses and following someone holding up a little flag."

"Disliking how?"

"I think it was just that they crowded the sidewalks and made it hard to go about one's normal day."

"Do you think he was targeting you in any way?"

"You mean, as a tourist?"

"In any way, at all."

"I was flattered that he took an interest in me, but we quickly found we had things in common—a background in research, an interest in books, as well as a very strong attraction to each other."

"And your relationship, it is sexual in nature?"

"Is that important to this?"

"It gives us an understanding of your possible connection to this man."

"Okay, yes, it is. I don't think it's serious in nature, though, if you understand my nuance."

"Yes, Madame, I do indeed."

"There was a point where he complimented me for wanting to do things more typically Parisian than just lining up to visit the Louvre, like taking a ballet class. And I got the sense that his distaste for tourists was that they were satisfied with a very superficial understanding of the places they were visiting and that somehow I was distinct from that grouping."

Imogene paused.

"Yes, go on?" Toni prodded.

"I am not sure, though, that he was being sincere. I mean, I think he was enjoying my company and happy to know that I was finding interesting things to do during my stay here, but I am not so sure he was making a real distinction between me and other visitors. It was probably just his way of flattering me. And I am not sure how I can tell that, but it may have been just something in the intonation or his laughing as he said it."

"But you always felt safe with him?"

"Oh yes. I am not normally so quick to bring defenses down, but it all felt very natural getting to know Marcel."

"That, I am afraid, is often the way with a very good con man."

Imogene winced. "Yes, I suppose you are right. And there was a moment where I wondered if he was setting me up for something, but I couldn't possibly think what it would be and there was no sign of any bad transactions on my credit card, so I put it out of my mind and decided to just enjoy what seemed like a shipboard romance."

"Did he ever mention hotels to you?"

"Not that I can recall."

"And he never asked about your relationship with the Sûreté? I am wondering if he somehow knew that you and I were friends, as criminals sometimes try to get close to the investigation of their crimes."

"No, I don't think I ever spoke about you being a police officer. I mentioned you as my neighbour I took a dance exercise class with, or my neighbour who had a brother who was an architect, because I think I discussed the stair levels with him, but not anything to do with your job or your investigation."

Imogene wondered if Marcel had seen any of her notes for Toni, at times when she would have been in the shower. Could he have got into her computer? If he was some sort of Napoleon of crime, she supposed he could do anything.

"Thank you, Ms. Durant. I am now stopping the tape, at 11:55 a.m." Toni pressed the button on her phone, and fiddled with the file while explaining she was emailing it to the secure file on the case.

"We'll be looking into more of Marcel's activities, so don't be surprised if you find he is less available soon. He may get wind of us."

"We have a date to ride a *Bateau-Mouche* the day after tomorrow."

"That sounds very nice, and also very touristy."

Imogene smiled sadly. "Yes, he suggested it, I think, because I mentioned how romantic they looked once, and because I am leaving soon. I think we are in the process of tying things up and putting them aside to think about on a rainy day in our respective dotages."

"*Dotages* means?"

"Old age. This will have been just a lovely vignette, not even a chapter."

"I am sorry, Imogene, to tarnish this vignette in any way. But can I ask that you not discuss this with Marcel when you see him next?"

"You think I should keep the date?"

"Oh yes, please do nothing to alert him to our suspicions. It all may be nothing, and then life can go on as normal. And I am sure you will be safe on the Seine."

"But nothing will feel normal after this; you have to know that."

"I do, and I apologize." Toni did look sad, and Imogene felt bad for doubting her motives earlier. For all her professional integrity, Toni was a good friend, and Imogene felt sure that they'd be connecting by text or email for years to come.

To make up for bringing her in for an interview, Toni gave Imogene a mini tour of the Préfecture and led her out the fancier doors Imogene had initially tried to get in. Imogene walked down the street toward the clock corner but decided to perk herself up with a wander through the flower market.

In one of the stalls spilling over with flowers of all sorts, she spied long spindly stalks with bulbous buds on the ends. The man who owned the stall saw her and smiled.

"*Les pivoines!*"

"Peonies?" she responded and he obligingly shifted into English.

"*Oui, peonies de Bretagne*. Brittany? They change colour, and will turn yellow."

Imogene eyed the red bulbs, suspicious that she was somehow missing something in translation.

"They are very thirsty. All the time, thirsty."

"All right, I would take some, please."

They were pricy but worth it for her last week in the apartment. He wrapped up her purchase and introduced her to his pampered chihuahua lying on a pillow.

"She is *Monsieur Marguerite*. Mister Daisy!"

Imogene laughed for what felt like the first time in forever and waved to the man and his dog as she walked home, through the flowers, across the bridge and through the crowded streets of Les Halles.

It made her feel so connected to Paris to buy cut flowers, because hotels wouldn't be the place to find empty vases. Only citizens buy flowers, she thought, knowing she was fooling herself and not caring in the least. For now, she was a citizen and Paris was her home.

# The Art of Artifice

The closer it got to her date with Marcel, the more nervous Imogene became. As Marcel himself had noted, she should never to try to play poker, because her face reflected every single thing she was thinking, and she was afraid that somehow she was going to signal to him that he was being suspected of being at the worst a serial killer and at the least a terrorist of some sort.

She tried to quell her anxiety with work, and found herself easily able to be enmeshed in rereading sections of *Les Misérables*. Having delved into Graham Robb's riveting biography of Victor Hugo, she wasn't sure she would have liked Hugo the man, but she very much admired Hugo the social critic and Hugo the romance writer. There were so many segues and side streets that he took the reader on in his huge novel, and sometimes he came back to the minor character the reader had noted as a delicate miniature in passing, and other times he skewered a character onto the reader's retina in one line and moved on, leaving them in the wake of the story.

She had been trying so hard to map the rebellion that her book fell open there, but she flipped a few pages back to read his treatise on slang, which arose out of his denoting the thieves who used it and petit Gavroche, who tried to instill it into his younger brothers.

"Slang is the word made convict." What a brilliant way of capsulizing his treatise that once a word has been demoted into the usage of a singular group, it is reduced to their usage and lost to the annals of time once they had moved on. She thought about the words that teens and young partymakers had conscripted into their vernacular. Some of the words bounced back, some lost their original meaning altogether, and some drifted in the grey area of not being used for fear of misunderstanding. Why was it that the young always seemed to be those who played with and manipulated the language? Was it a form of rebellion, or of wrestling with their culture to find their own way in? Maybe she and Marcel should think up a neologism or two, just to strike a note for the middle-aged. Of course, if he was indeed a criminal, perhaps he had access to a whole different vernacular. And in another language entirely. Could one ever understand another person in translation? Wasn't that the eternal question underlying Comparative Literature, anyhow?

She glanced up to see the time and noticed her peonies, open fully for the past couple of days, and in a full vase, because she was happy to pay attention to their "thirstiness."

To underpin her previous thoughts about translation, they were bright pink, and Imogene figured she must have misunderstood something about them "turning yellow." Maybe that they would wither quickly? But didn't all flowers? She was going to be here only one more week. It wouldn't matter to her.

One week. All the planning that had gone into this trip had made it seem as if it would be an eternity. People had looked slightly horrified when she told them she'd be away for six weeks. Well, not her work colleagues so much, who were used to heading off somewhere for a sabbatical trip for six months every so often. But her friends and neighbours and children had been a bit disconcerted.

And here it was, almost over. She wondered what she would do with herself at home during the evenings in the time she had earlier perused apartments for rent. She had been so lucky to find Raymonde. Was she wasting the moments left here, thinking of her adventure being over? Or was she projecting herself ahead to when she'd be back in Alberta and not part of this problematic issue of potentially dating a criminal?

Just then her phone buzzed a text from Toni through.

How are you?

Feeling a bit worried about giving it all away with the wrong look.

> Don't worry. We are working on things at my end. You may not have to worry at all by the time you see him.

> We're meeting at six this evening.

> Just look at him and think about that thing he does with his tongue. ;)

> How did you know? ...

> He's a Frenchman. They all know how. I think they take them out of the classroom and teach them, right about the time we are getting the menstrual lecture.

> LOL

> Be happy, Imogene. And enjoy your cruise on the river. X

Imogene laughed out loud as she reread Toni's messages. Maybe she could get through this evening just thinking about herself in her own romantic comedy. Not that she would be dressed in a billowy dress on the river at night. It was chilly enough along the banks if there was even a slight breeze.

What was she going to wear?

When she had packed, it had been with the assumption that she was not going to really see anyone twice, so it wouldn't matter if she wore the same outfits five or six times. Even with judicious mixing and matching, she only had about seven looks and Marcel had seen five of them. He'd also seen her in the altogether, so it wasn't as if she was dressing to seduce him. Mission already accomplished. But she was dressing to give him something to remember whenever he thought of her and the springtime they had shared. Because this was definitely going to be the last time they saw each other, unless Toni could give him a clean bill of innocence.

And how could she do that? The best she would manage would be to find incriminating evidence to prove it was him they were looking for. Not finding anything wouldn't mean he wasn't their suspect; it would only mean he was very clever at hiding his tracks.

And Imogene already knew he was a very clever man. How on earth would she be attracted to him if he weren't?

Her phone buzzed again. Speaking of clever men, it was Daniel.

> Good morning! Or should I say good afternoon?

> I'll take afternoon. And good morning to you! How goes the war?

> Offering to teach this spring course to get out of a final course in winter term was a monumentally stupid idea. Why didn't you talk me out of it?

> You kept saying something about retiring and heading straight to the beaches of Mexico.

Right. They're sounding awfully expensive now.

> They're making up for their downtime during early COVID, I guess.

That's probably it. Maybe I'll just tag along with you. Where are you reading next?

> ☺ That would be fun. I am not sure yet. Got to see if the publisher likes this one first.

How's it going?

> Really great. So many connections. Nothing like turning one's ankle on the same cobblestones as Hugo to bring a text alive for a reader.

Don't break a leg. I need you back here to keep me sane through undergraduate scenes from Peer Gynt.

> Haha. I'll be there on the 11th. The haggard one not having slept on the airplane, waving a fridge magnet at you.

> I'll make a rude sign to welcome you.

> OMG, of course you will.

> have a good evening! XO

> have a good day! XO

They were definitely flirting. How was she going to look Marcel in the eye, after flirting with Daniel?

She stopped. Perhaps that would be her get-out-of-jail-free card. If he suspected her of anything, she could admit to having a fellow back home who had been rekindling things. Marcel didn't have to know that the kindling was just beginning. And honestly, for all Imogene knew, Daniel had been setting this campfire for months without her realizing it. He had been very kind while she was reeling from the divorce, after all. Perhaps he had just been biding his time till she was in a frame of mind to consider his advances.

And what a gallant gesture that was, if so.

Was it Paris that had reignited her passions, she wondered? Or was it a natural progression out of the tunnel of menopause back into a sense of self? Women were given too little information about this time of their lives. Imogene recalled asking her own mother when her own menopause had begun and her mother responding very bemusedly, not recalling for certain, but knowing that she had suffered very few of the recorded symptoms such as headaches, hot flashes, or weight gain. Since she had been a widow and living a very simple, single life during that time, there was no mention of a shift in libido.

Imogene wasn't sure whether her passage through menopause was completely over, but she had come through it relatively unscathed, if you didn't count the divorce. Water under the bridge, Imogene thought, and that phrase brought her back to the moment. Water and bridges. What was she going to wear that evening for the *Bateau-Mouche* cruise?

She had heard some of the boats offered music and dancing while others were just a sitting cruise with an announcer mentioning things to look for on either bank. She wondered what Marcel had in mind for them. She also wondered if Marcel was thinking of this as their last hurrah too. If they intended to continue the hurrah back here in the apartment, she'd better tidy away anything that might make him suspicious of her talk with Toni.

Could he possibly have known that Toni was the officer in charge and targeted Imogene as her friend, to get close to the investigation? It seemed unlikely, but then everything about Toni's body parts case seemed so bizarre. Imogene laid out a set of black leggings on the bed and matched them to a long black turtleneck and the teal green jacket she'd purchased along the boulevard de Sébastopol. She wouldn't need a scarf, and the jacket brought out a slightly different green to her eyes. With her black flats that she was wearing only for shorter jaunts, she'd manage a '50s Sophia Loren or Audrey Hepburn homage. She could tuck her phone and some euros into one pocket and her keys in another, and make do without a bag. There, sorted.

She spent the rest of the afternoon tidying the apartment and then reading more Hugo. Whenever the thought of Marcel accusing her of ratting him out to the police flitted through her mind, she tried to bat it away with considerations of Valjean carrying Marius through the sewers. Would he have bumped his head or bruised himself, being hauled along, unconscious? She could imagine the original readers' groans of disbelief when Marius was horrified by Valjean's past and refused to see him, without knowing he had saved his life. Hugo toyed with his readers so much throughout the book, it was a wonder people stayed with him for the journey.

But how couldn't they? It was a sweeping, glorious story, and while it could have done with a few musketeers, especially of the BBC's most recent variety, it was a gripping story from start to finish.

It was a good thing she hadn't bought too much in the way of souvenirs because the books she had purchased were really going to weigh her down. She wondered whether Raymonde would mind if she left the Simenon novels behind for the next tenant to read. Even so, the Hugo tomes and the biography and Sylvia Beach's chatty memoir were all coming home with her.

At about four, she closed her books and powered down

her laptop, and went to get ready. She had a quick shower and then got dressed. She moisturized her face, and applied a light touch of mascara and a gleaming bronze lipstick, which she blotted with a tissue, creating a kiss that reminded her of a Barbara Gowdy novel. Her hair would be good down around her shoulders, with her gold earrings shining out from behind her auburn curls from time to time. She decided against a necklace. The colour of the jacket was enough. Looking herself over in the full-length mirror in the bedroom, she nodded. This was the perfect outfit for a night on the Seine. She checked the bedroom for neatness, fluffed the pillows to make them stand at attention, and went in to the living room to find her phone. It wasn't yet five, and she was to meet Marcel on the rue de Rivoli by her favourite Café Benjamin at quarter to six.

He had texted to say he had made dinner reservations, so she assumed they weren't doing the dinner on the boat cruise. She hoped her outfit would pass muster wherever he had planned. Since he hadn't made a point of telling her to dress chic, she assumed that whatever level of clothing she'd presented in the past was suitable.

She plunked herself down on the sofa and stared out the window at the street life. People were heading home, and the crowds that converged outside Les Halles were dissipating, making way for the commuters going down into the bowels of the mall to the train level. Windows were opening up along the street, and the funny little restaurant across the way that was so rarely open seemed to be getting ready for the evening crowd.

She had put an average of 14,000 steps on the pedometer app of her phone each day she'd been here, and yet it would be these moments of looking out the window onto the everyday actions of Paris that she thought she might recall the best. She felt embedded into the city, rather than visiting it, and as much as she knew that she'd barely scratched the surface, she would take home with her a sense of truly having lived in Paris.

Maybe that was what Marcel meant when he spoke admiringly of her choices. Paris wasn't a box to be checked off or a pilgrim badge to be achieved. It was a world to be experienced as fully as possible, a life unlike anywhere else, and to do it justice, you had to dive in wholeheartedly and become as close to a citizen as you could get. It would never be the same, looking out from a hotel window. For one thing, they might not even open, and chances were you'd be looking directly into another hotel window.

And you'd never be able to buy flowers, she thought, turning to look at her peonies, which from this angle were by god beginning to turn yellow, just along the tips of the petals. They weren't fading, they were as full and lush as they had been pink, but the colour was leaching out into a warm butter yellow. She hadn't misheard the florist, he had been clear all along, with his little dog, Monsieur Marguerite. She snapped a picture of the yellowing peonies, knowing no one would believe her otherwise.

She considered having a glass of wine to settle her nerves but decided she might be better off with her wits fully about her. There would be wine at dinner, after all, and she didn't want to lose track of being on her guard.

Another trip to the lavatory. Another application of lipstick. Finally, it was time to head out. She grabbed her keys, took inventory of her pockets, and at the last minute slipped a hair elastic onto her wrist, in case the wind whipped up on the Seine.

She was locking her door when she heard someone coming up the stairs. It was her upstairs neighbour, René.

"*Bonsoir,* René," she smiled, waiting for him to pass her on the narrow landing. He looked pleased with himself, and much more pleasant than usual.

"*Bonsoir,* Madame," he replied, nodding his head toward her.

He passed to continue up and Imogene took hold of the banister, thinking of Toni's discussions of how old the staircase was. She wondered how many generations of people had slid their hands along this wood. Perhaps someone heading down to join the student barricades of 1832 had gripped the banister with conviction and headed out to do what they thought was their Republican duty.

She wound down past the half-open window that looked out into the back of the Japanese restaurant, which she knew was Japanese only because there was an old wok hanging in the open space beyond the window. When she got to the small foyer, she noticed that someone had pulled the garbage bins out from their home under the staircase and set them in the doorway. She had no idea who did this, but Raymonde hadn't intimated that she should bother with anything so plebeian, so she had just allowed the weekly cleaner to handle her refuse.

Everything was standing in brighter relief, now that she was down to being here less than a week, much like it had when she had first arrived. She stepped over the rivulet of water running from the restaurant across the way, where they'd hosed down the outdoor patio area to prepare for the evening.

Several shops were still open, but the card shop was closing as she passed. Toward the arches, the second-hand bookshop with its outdoor bins was doing a brisk business. Thank god people were still reading books, she thought, with all the effort she was going through to get this book done.

There were already people gathered at tables on the rue des Halles that became the rue Saint-Honoré further on, and Imogene looked both ways before crossing, even though it was a one-way, because she'd nearly been hit by a scooter going the wrong direction a week earlier. According to plaques, a king had been assassinated near here, in bad traffic. It wouldn't do not to heed that sort of warning.

As she came down the street toward the rue de Rivoli, she could see Marcel already waiting outside the Café Benjamin. He was so handsome, even from here he gave her pause. She waited at the light, and smiled and waved when he caught sight of her. He offered her the requisite two cheek kisses and squeezed her shoulders when she arrived at his side.

"You look *magnifique*, Imogene. It is so good to see you.

And you are spot on time. I have a bus ticket for you, because we are going to catch the bus to our destination this evening. It's walkable, but why bother?"

Imogene laughed and took the token. She hadn't realized this was a bus stop, but sure enough, a bus appeared and Marcel ushered her on ahead of him. She presented her ticket to the driver, who pointed to the slot, so she inserted her ticket, which got stamped, and then moved on down the aisle to the first empty seat for two. Marcel was right behind her and even before the last people were seated, the bus was on its way.

"This driver is a bit abrupt. He may be running a bit late," Marcel mused. "They are usually very kind, especially to the older ladies getting on with their shopping bags."

They rode down the rue de Rivoli, past the Louvre and the Tuileries Gardens, turning at the Place de la Concorde, which was busier than Imogene had seen it, with cars moving seemingly in every direction. The bus headed along the outer edge of the huge square, and turned right down a long green road past the Petit Palais and what seemed like an inordinate number of parks. The traffic stopped from time to time, but it wasn't long before Marcel was indicating that they wanted the next stop and they got up and stood by the back door of the bus.

"Now it is just a few minutes' walk from here, to a place I hope you will enjoy."

"I have enjoyed every place you've shown me, Marcel. I am sure I will."

"This, I think, is my salute to the romantic indulgence that is Paris, veering very close to the tourist concept, but more, I hope, the vision projected by the films."

They walked down the rue New York, which began at a replica of the Statue of Liberty's torch, and arrived at a restaurant called 6 New York, where Marcel presented himself to the maître d' and they were ushered to a table inside, but with a magnificent window view of the Eiffel Tower. After they were seated and given menus, Imogene turned and smiled at Marcel.

"This is spectacular!"

"Yes, all the view, with none of the pickpockets," laughed Marcel. "This is a very fine restaurant, with a strong Normandy background to the foods. I can tell you that anything you choose will be a good choice. However, allow me to pick the wine, *non*?"

Imogene acquiesced immediately. "I know so little about wines, I am happy to take your recommendations there. It's only as I have grown older that I have even begun to enjoy red wines, but now that is pretty much all I drink. Aside from the occasional Aperol spritz or gin and tonic."

"To everything a season, and red wine is for the more refined palate, I believe."

"Maybe. I know that when I was younger, I chose white wines because they wouldn't stain the carpet of a rental apartment. Now, I am either less afraid of spilling or better equipped at stain removal. Or I can afford to lose the damage deposit."

Marcel laughed. "Well, there is a very nice Côtes du Rhône on the menu, so I suggest we go with that. It will enhance either seafood or pork, and they do both of those dishes very well here."

"I was noticing the lobster pot-au-feu," Imogene admitted.

Marcel took his time with the menu. He suggested they share an appetizer of shelled crab, and then ordered the veal. Imogene stuck to the half-lobster pot-au-feu. The wine came and was wonderful.

"Let me take your photograph, Imogene, here with a glass of wine and the *Tour* behind you. You look exquisite."

Imogene blushed, but handed Marcel her phone, open to her camera.

"Watch you only give me one chin," she teased.

"You look *très belle*," he assured her.

The waiter arrived at the table and offered to take a picture of the two of them. Marcel handed him the camera and slid himself into the chair next to Imogene, smiling.

After the waiter had gone and Imogene looked at her photos, she realized that this was probably the only photo of the two of them together. She had a few shots of Marcel when they were out and about, but none of them together. Maybe that spoke more to the ephemeral nature of their liaison than anything else. She smiled, a little sadly.

"Allow me to see?" asked Marcel. She held the camera toward him, and he nodded. "Yes, *un souvenir d'une belle affaire*." He laughed at the look on her face. "Do not look concerned. I don't think it means the same thing as in English. I am not cheating on anyone, Imogene. Are you?"

"No, I am not, although there is a man at home who might become someone close."

"That would be a good thing. You deserve to be showered with loving attention, Imogene Durant. You are a beautiful and fascinating woman."

"And you are a charming Frenchman, so I can believe only a third of what you say," responded Imogene.

Marcel laughed, and touched his wineglass to hers. "Aha, you are learning the deeper levels of the French culture, I see."

The meal was amazing, and the sun sank slowly, offering a movie lens view of the Eiffel Tower, rising across the Seine, with the light green foliage of spring trees masking any other lesser sights between them and the iconic metal structure. In fact, the whole evening was like a movie, not one Imogene had actually seen, but the perfection of the moment seemed slightly too constructed, making her doubt everything and yet enjoy it all.

Marcel suggested dessert, but Imogene demurred, feeling both perfectly sated and not wanting to mar the memory of the lovely lobster dish. When they finished their wine, Marcel insisted on getting the bill.

"I don't think I am pulling my fair share when we go out," Imogene said.

"Your company is so delightful, that is all you need to bring to the table," said Marcel, as he pulled her chair back so she could rise.

She laughed and shook her head at him. "That is not the way modern dating works, Marcel. At least let me purchase the tickets for the *Bateau-Mouche*."

He smiled and acquiesced.

The departure site for the tour boats was just across the road from where they were, but the traffic was busy and they waited obediently at the lights before crossing.

"It won't be so busy on the river," Marcel said.

"Are there actual river buses, that people take to commute?" Imogene asked.

"There is a boat that makes stops at various places, but it is mostly utilized by tourists, I believe. The *Bateau-Mouche*, however, goes down the Seine past Notre-Dame and comes back on the other side of the river. We will want to sit on the left side if we can, because they will be focusing on the bank closest when they describe things."

"Left side, got it."

They climbed down the steps to the pier, and Imogene purchased tickets for the next launch. They were just in time to line up to board, and near the front of the line. Imogene was more excited than she had thought she'd be; it hadn't really occurred to her till now that this event was indeed one she'd associated with romantic Paris.

The crewman opened the gate on the gangplank and the line began to move. Marcel held her hand as she stepped onto the boat and then led them up the stairs to the front, where they secured seats near the side on the left.

"Is it all right with you if we stay outside?" he asked. "We will achieve the best views from here, but you must tell me if you begin to feel a chill, and we can go below into the closed-in lounge. There are windows all around there, so you wouldn't miss too much."

"No, this is fine. And if I get chilly, I'll snuggle." Imogene laughed.

The announcer spoke in French, English, and German when delivering the information about each important site they were gliding past. Having wandered the city for the last few weeks, Imogene found the information about the bridges they were going under to be the most interesting tidbits, and the aspect of seeing underneath them and coming at them sideways instead of going over them was a new vista.

Marcel was a wonderful companion, adding interesting bits of information to the loudspeaker's commentary and pointing out places that Hugo had written about, which Imogene appreciated. She took a load of photos, including several slightly windswept selfies of Marcel and her, seated on the plastic chairs bolted to the front upper deck.

It was a pity she wouldn't get in to see Notre-Dame, still under construction after the fire, but, as Marcel said, it was a very good excuse to come back to Paris another time. The boat turned, and as it did, Imogene realized the sun had set completely and the Eiffel Tower was lit up with its golden lights, because she could see the beacon wavering above. Soon they were back along the river within eyesight of the tower, then going past it to turn beyond the Pont d'Iéna, and offering some stellar photo opportunities from the other side of the Eiffel Tower.

Imogene posed for Marcel, and then took pictures of him. Most of the people on the boat were moving about, taking photos, and the loudspeaker was playing "La Vie en Rose."

Marcel opened his hands in the universal sign of "shall we dance?" and Imogene walked into his arms. It might have been the most clichéd of all romantic moves, but it felt perfect and complete in the moment. They were the first and the only, and this moment would last forever, and would have to, because it would be the last. Forever.

Marcel leaned in and they kissed, with the sound of the engines pulling and braking into the port.

"This was wonderful, Marcel, thank you so much for thinking of it."

"You will be gone soon, and I wanted you to have only the best of thoughts from your time here. After all, you are transmitting those thoughts in your own book to others, who will be tempted to become true temporary citizens of the City of Lights."

Imogene looked around her as they climbed up out of the docking area. It truly was the city of lights. Besides the tower lit up, the street lights twinkled up to the Pont de la Concorde far ahead, which was beautifully lit in the evening.

Marcel asked her if she wanted to take a cab, but she felt like walking and he was happy to do so. They ambled along, discussing the relative size of Paris at various points in history, holding hands. As they walked, they passed several other couples, both on the sidewalk and on the lower walk in the park lining the riverbank. It was a very lively city at all times, everywhere, Imogene decided, not just under her bedroom window. It was decidedly quieter here, though, other than the general thrum of the traffic beside them. The huge trees they walked under did their best to muffle and eat the noise.

By mutual silent agreement, they left the Seine at the Place de la Concorde and walked back along the Rivoli side of the Tuileries, which had just closed for the night. In some portions of the sidewalk, they had to walk single file around groups of people, and Imogene, looking for it, could feel Marcel's irritation.

"They think like sheep and act like sheep," he muttered.

She squeezed his hand in solidarity and they kept on walking quietly, up and over past the Bourse and down the rue Rambuteau, past the Pied de Cochon, the twenty-four-hour restaurant.

The beggar in front of Saint-Eustache had gone home for the night, and the street was quiet until they turned onto rue Pierre Lescot. Then the merriment of the restaurants assailed them, bringing them out of their shared reverie.

"Would you like to come up for a glass of wine?" Imogene asked euphemistically.

Marcel smiled at her. "That would be *merveilleux*," he answered.

She pulled her keys out of her jacket pocket and sidled past the garbage bins to the door, pushing it open as she touched the fob to the pad.

She turned on the timed light switch that would probably get them up to her place, though she always pushed the one past Toni's door as well, just in case. The foyer was different somehow, and she realized it was because the door to the small room under the stairs was closed. She hadn't even realized there was a door there; usually the bins were visible, pushed up against the wall. Someone must have decided there was a draft, she supposed.

Up they went, and she pushed the switch halfway. Marcel noticed and teased her. "You think we are so old we cannot make it on one push?" he said.

"I am only commenting on my own limitations," she laughed. "But we probably could have made it."

They stood on the small landing by her door, and Imogene fumbled with her keys, once more slightly nervous, thinking about their intended actions. Marcel put his hand on the small of her back, and it steadied her at the same time as sending a pulse through her spine.

"There we are," she said, sliding the key into the lock.

Everything after that seemed to happen all at once.

The stairway light went off.

A clattering of boots on the stairs seemed to come from above and below. The lights went on again and suddenly there were police officers in combat gear all over the staircase. Marcel pushed them into the opened doorway, only to find Detective Antoinette Lamothe, in full uniform, standing in Imogene's foyer.

"Marcel Rocher, I am arresting you on suspicion of

terrorism. You have the right to silence. You may contact an attorney. You may be held in *garde à vue* for a maximum of six days, depending on the severity of the crimes for which you are suspected. Please come with me."

Marcel, looking like a cornered marten, turned on Imogene. "Did you do this?" he cried.

"No!" she wailed.

He turned to check the stairwell, full of gendarmes.

Just then, the stairwell lights went out again.

# Mayhem

Imogene felt herself being shoved aside, and banged her head into the coatrack in her foyer. Toni was there, too, yelling something in French to the crew out in the stairwell, and the lights came on as she began to hear someone shouting upstairs.

It was René, it had to be, shouting something like "*les flics, les flics!*" Imogene couldn't tell from the tenor of his voice whether he was calling for help or in outrage.

What she could tell was that Marcel was no longer beside her. She couldn't see him anywhere around her. Toni was looking startled and annoyed in equal measure.

"Get into your bedroom and close the door and stay there," she said to Imogene.

Imogene moved obediently to the doorway of her bedroom, and turned on the light. There was no chance that Marcel was in there, since her closet doors were slid open and the bed was on a solid plinth. She sat on the edge of the bed, smoothing the material of her leggings over her knees in some childhood recollection of calming herself.

What were the police doing in her apartment? How did they know it was him they were looking for? Toni must have come up with some solid evidence to bring out so many officers. And why had Marcel disappeared? It seemed to indicate he really was the person they were looking for, a terrorist of some sort.

And why was René still yelling? Imogene wished Toni hadn't been so adamant that she close the door to her bedroom. She would be able to hear a lot better with it just a bit ajar. Of course, understanding all she heard would be a different matter. Her bedroom window was just above the door to the apartments, though. Perhaps she could hear something from that angle. She moved quietly around the bed and reached through the curtains for the lock on the window. Trying not to make any squeaking noises, she raised the sash slowly and looked down through a slit in the glass curtains.

There were two officers standing by the garbage bins.

The door to the bins! The police must have been hiding in there, waiting for her to come home with Marcel. What would have happened if she hadn't invited him in? Toni must have been pretty secure in her knowledge of Imogene's libido.

There was a knock on her bedroom door.

"Yes?"

"Imogene, it is me." Toni turned the knob and entered.

"Well, hello."

"I am so sorry to have put you in the middle of all of this, and I am afraid you are not out of the woods yet. Marcel has escaped. We think he went up and out the hatch to the roof."

"There's a hatch to the roof?"

"Yes, there are hatches and doors to all the roofs of Paris, and while it isn't quite the James Bond sort of chase I know you are picturing, it is possible to get quite a ways from roof to roof till you find another open passway and head down a different staircase. I have two officers making their way along the rooftops and another set at our doorway, in case he doubles back. My guess is that he will come out somewhere on rue du Cygne, but if he's athletic enough to jump, he could be strolling down Étienne-Marcel by now."

"And we are sure it is Marcel? The person with the body parts on ice?"

"Yes, I am fairly certain. We will need to question him for the rationale of his actions, but his access to the human remains is verified, and that they were frozen. It was the process his father maintained to lead to cremation if there was a delay in the service. He would also put any deceased with acknowledged artificial joints into cold storage to make it easier to cut the joint out." Toni shuddered a bit as she mentioned it.

"You talked to his father?"

"Yes, and he doesn't appear to have a bad ankle, for what that is worth."

Imogene crumpled a bit. "That was a lie. While one

swallow does not a summer make, one lie usually indicates a whole swarm."

Toni nodded. "Like rats. If you see one, you can be sure there are many nearby."

"Oh lord, I am glad you didn't mention that tidbit sooner in my stay. I saw a rat out on the street the first night I was here."

Toni shrugged.

"No, you don't understand, I come from Alberta. We are rat-free. It's one of the things we can be justifiably proud of as a province."

"Well, anyway, we have enough to arrest your Marcel and keep him for questioning."

"Let's not call him my Marcel anymore, okay?"

"I am sorry, Imogene."

"I just want to know one thing. Well, I want to know ALL the things, like why he did what he did and how he did what he did and when he did it and all that. But really, I need to know whether he targeted me to find out about the investigation."

"Did he ever ask you about your neighbours?"

"No, not that I recall."

"And you never talked about me and my work?"

"I mentioned that I did a ballet class with my neighbour, that's about it."

"I think this was just a very stunning coincidence, Imogene. I wouldn't worry that whatever you and Marcel shared was authentic."

Imogene smiled sadly at her friend, who knew exactly the right thing to say.

"So, I think there will be an officer in the stairwell tonight, just to be sure of your safety, but my advice is to deadbolt your door and not open it to anyone except perhaps me, tonight." Toni made to move out to the hallway.

Imogene realized she had another question for Toni before she left.

"Can you tell me, what was that shouting from upstairs? Did the police officers startle René? Or did Marcel hurt him as he fled?"

Toni cracked her first real smile of the evening.

"That's a story for a full bottle of wine!"

# Cemetery thoughts

It was another two days before Toni and Imogene had a chance to meet and discuss the events of the evening Imogene felt would rival scenes from the movie *Charade* for her.

She had spent the previous day washing clothes and working on a preliminary packing of her suitcase. There was a small pile of clothing folded and set aside, which she decided she would take down to the fripshop rather than risk having to pay an overweight charge on her luggage at check-in. The books and various pieces of clothing she had purchased in Paris needed the cargo space.

On the whole, it had been a successful trip. She had narrowed her targets for reading and had it approved by her editor; she had managed to develop an outline and good drafts of the first three chapters. She had made a solid friend. She had indulged in a dalliance. And she had helped to solve a major crime.

So why did she feel so melancholy? She had been raring to go home just three or four days ago, but now, as she looked out on the streets of the 1st arrondissement, she felt herself longing for a way to remain, part of the scene, part of the firmament.

She pushed down on the lid of her suitcase and, satisfied that it would close, gave up on the exercise for the moment. She still had two days in the city by which she would judge all other places in her lifetime. She had to be judicious in what she chose to do.

Her friend Lynn, who had worked down the hall from her for years in the French department, had extolled the virtues of Montparnasse, and Imogene hadn't ventured that far into the Left Bank. That should be her area of exploration before she left, or she would never hear the end of it. Besides, she wanted to pay tribute to Samuel Beckett in the cemetery there. She had already wandered the Père Lachaise Cemetery and been touched to see the resting places of so many of her cultural heroes—Oscar Wilde, Gertrude Stein, Edith Piaf, Marcel Marceau, Rosa Bonheur. It was fitting she should pay respects to Beckett and Simone de Beauvoir and Jean-Paul Sartre before she left.

She briefly considered taking the metro to the Catacombs stop but decided instead to walk. Since coming to Paris, she had averaged about 14,000 steps a day on her phone pedometer and she wasn't about to stop now.

She pulled out her handy book of maps of the *arrondissements*. If she were to head due south down the boulevard

Saint-Michel, past the lovely restaurant Marcel had taken her to, she would be able to veer off toward the cemetery once she made it to the boulevard du Montparnasse. Her friend Sighle had once spoken of staying in a hotel on that boulevard, as she recalled, and had liked the area.

She loved to walk in cemeteries and yet had no desire to descend into the bowels of the earth to visit the ossuaries in the Catacombs. For one thing, her claustrophobia would kick in, and for another, the concept of so many anonymous bones was not something she wished to contemplate. Death and memento mori were very personal to Imogene. It was the time to reflect on the person who had once inhabited the bones and the space, not the bones themselves, that she cherished.

It was a concept that had come slowly to her. As a young woman, she cared nothing for graveyards, and even when her parents had died, she had no sentimentality about where their ashes were to end up. Her mother had explicitly wished to be inurned in the northern part of the province where she had been born, in the plot next to her own father, mother, grandmother, and infant sister. So that is what Imogene had done. Her friend, a United Church minister, had quietly suggested they inter a cupful of her mother's ashes in the memory garden of an Edmonton church, so that, should she wish, she'd have someplace convenient to visit. At the time, she had bowed to his suggestion mostly to be pleasant. After all, he had been in the business of joy and grief a lot longer than she, but she didn't think it would be an issue.

However, on the tenth anniversary of her mother's death

she found herself suddenly inconsolable, and ended up taking flowers to the memory garden, glad that she didn't have to make a six-hour drive to make the gesture. He had been right. Sometimes having a place to connect with the memory of lost loved ones was essential.

The graveyards of Paris were more for pilgrimages than grief, it seemed, with maps to the stars available. In fact, it occurred to Imogene to download the layout of the Montparnasse Cemetery before she left her apartment, to be able to find Beckett easily. And then, having made up her mind to visit the cemetery, Imogene spent no more time in getting ready to go. She was combed and washed and about to head out the door when her phone pinged in her purse.

She checked her message in case she needed to reply while she still was connected to wifi. It was Toni, at last. Imogene had been leery of trying to contact her, since she knew she'd be up to her ears in the criminal proceedings against Marcel. But she had been so curious.

Bon jour, Imogene!

Hello!

Things have been so hectic, but I want us to get together. Tomorrow is my day off and I know it is your last full day here. Can we do something together? I have an idea.

> Of course!

> Great. I think you would like it. A little cruise up the canal Saint-Martin to the Parc de la Villette and then a stroll back. I think it will give you a sense of your Valjean without the discomfort.

> Sounds intriguing! I am in.

> À demain, mon amie!

> XO

Yes, she had made a solid friend.

The walk along the boulevard Saint-Michel was pleasant, and Imogene enjoyed the people-watching as much as anything. Students from the Sorbonne nearby filled the coffee-shop tables, and various shop windows looked enticing.

She reached the intersection where she'd need to veer off for the Montparnasse Cemetery but decided to walk farther down and enter the cemetery from its southern access point. She passed a large statue of a lion in the middle of the road, close to the signs leading to the Catacombs. She realized, in reading the plaque, that this was the *Place d'Enfer,* or Place of Hell, that Hugo referred to when talking about Gavroche's little lost brothers. No wonder they had been exhausted when he walked them all the way to the elephant statue near the Bastille. She was pretty tired from her own walk and that was barely half the distance the fictional children had walked.

She strolled toward the entry to the cemetery, and noted a café on the corner across the street. Since she was on no one's timeline except her own, she popped over and ordered a café crème and a croissant, and sat at one of the small tables out front, entertained by several delivery trucks stopping to provide groceries to the café.

Revived, Imogene paid up and thanked the proprietor, and made her way across the street and into the graveyard. It was large but somehow more manageable than the Père Lachaise cemetery, possibly because it was obviously flat. She walked in her first entrance on the left and soon found herself in front of the grave of Samuel Beckett, who had entranced her with his cryptic wit and mordant vision when she was an impressionable undergraduate.

She had been considering a focus on Beckett for her master's thesis, when she read somewhere that more had been written on Samuel Beckett than anyone else, barring the possibility of "Jesus Christ, Napoleon and Wagner." Still, he remained a favourite and she had enjoyed teaching his play *Endgame* in her modern drama class, because it had been written first in French, even though it had been translated by Beckett himself, and therefore could be classified as a work in translation.

There was a bench across from his grave, but Imogene had just been sitting at the café and didn't particularly feel the need to tarry. She saluted her literary lion and moved along, noting the grave of Baudelaire, replete with lipstick kisses, and Susan Sontag's, and finally, near the northern gates, the shared gravestone of Jean-Paul Sartre and Simone de Beauvoir. Their grave was littered with small stones holding down metro tickets, the meaning of which wasn't clear to Imogene, but she took a photo, to remember to do a bit of research. People had also left them on the grave of Serge Gainsbourg, the singer, but not as many and not pinned down with stones. On his grave she had also seen a bottle and a pack of cigarettes, as well as flowers.

How did acolytes know what to leave and how to commemorate their heroes? What would she be persuaded to leave, and for whom? There was a psychology thesis waiting to happen, Imogene decided as she left the graveyard. Her thinking was that she could continue in a north-easterly direction and find her way into the Luxembourg Gardens, and wend her way through them back home. Sure enough, having wandered down a street filled with tantalizing toy shops, making her wish she was shopping for a grandchild, and passing a crowd of schoolchildren in uniform milling about, released from their studies, she crossed a small street and entered the gardens through huge gates. This was a corner of the park she hadn't explored, and she saw a set-off group of beehives, delighting her. She had read about these urban beekeepers.

Strolling through the gardens, noting people sitting on benches and metal chairs, children sailing rented boats in the pond, and lovers walking hand in hand, she wondered what was the ratio of tourist to citizen she was witnessing. Parisians seemed to be devoted to an active appreciation of their city, as she had noticed when walking in other parks around lunchtime and seeing young professionals exercising and eating their boxed lunches in the green spaces.

Maybe Marcel had been right. You needed the time to sit a while in the various corners of the city to truly appreciate it. You couldn't engage with Paris from a seat in a tour bus.

What was she doing even giving Marcel and his arguments time and credibility? For all she knew, he was a serial killer. She hoped tomorrow's conversation with Toni would give her some answers and even some closure, a term she despised for its overuse.

Just then, she came upon a white marble statue of a strong-looking woman, her arms crossed with a scroll of a letter in one hand. She had long hair, some of it hanging in two plaits reaching almost to her knees. Her gaze was serene, almost benevolent. Imogene went closer to read the plaque beneath her feet on the plinth. It said *Sainte Geneviève, Patronne de Paris, 423–512*.

Imogene blinked back spontaneous tears. Geneviève had been her mother's name. It felt like another sign that she belonged to this city in some small way.

# René and the Walls of Paris

Toni had left another text to indicate how early in the morning Imogene should be ready, and so she had dutifully set an alarm on her phone, something she had got out of the habit of doing, and was showered, dressed, and fed in time to meet Toni on the stairwell at nine a.m. sharp.

"Imogene! I am so pleased we could do this."

"Me too. I was scared you were going to be too busy to have time for me before I left."

"Never. Are you all packed?"

"Pretty much. I will have some food left over that I will give to you when we get home. And I thought we could drop off this bag of clothing on our way to the Bastille?"

"*Parfait*. Of course. *Hélas*, are you giving away that lovely blouse? Give me that bag. I will go through it first and then take it to the frips." Toni turned back to her apartment door, unlocked it and tossed the bag Imogene had been holding into her hall. Locking up again, she turned and said, "Okay, *allons-y!*"

The canal they were going to cruise began below the Bastille and went all the way north to beyond one of the original city toll gates. Toni had never been on one of the cruise boats that went through the locks of the canal but had always wanted to go, and Imogene was up for anything.

"You are going to tell me what happened with Marcel and René, right?"

"Everything I can, *ne vous inquiétez pas.*"

The two women walked through Le Marais, past the Place des Vosges and into the Bastille area. The southern end of the plaza where the original prison had stood was commemorated by a huge column, which Toni said was the July Column. Imogene wondered where Gavroche's elephant would have been and again marvelled at Hugo's orphans trudging all the way from Montparnasse to this area. She would have paced it off to get another perspective, but the plaza was quite huge and Toni was eager for them to head toward the canal. Toni pointed to their destination, the Port de l'Arsenal, and, after taking a few photos of the July Column and the modern opera house beyond, Imogene followed.

They purchased their tickets and lined up for the little cruiser. There were few passengers, possibly due to the early timing, and Imogene congratulated Toni on her idea.

"Yes, the tour up the canal takes over an hour, and then we will want to wander back along the canal on foot and find a place to lunch, so I thought the earlier a start, the better."

They decided on seats inside the glassed-in area of the boat, up at the front.

"This way we will see the workings of the locks first-hand," said Toni.

"I've never been in a lock before," Imogene said, "though I have watched the Rideau Canal lock in Ottawa, from the street."

"Yes, it's a fascinating concept, isn't it? I think some of the oldest inventions of mankind are still the most magnificent in their scope."

As the boat's engine began to rev, Toni leaned toward Imogene. "We will be going underground for a bit of the journey, but I am told it is not a frightening aspect. There are skylights and the canal is wide enough for two boats to pass. You will be all right with this?"

"A bit late now, if I weren't," laughed Imogene. "Yes, I think I will be okay."

And she was. The portion of the canal that ran directly under the Place de Bastille and up toward the Place de la Republique was eerily beautiful, the green water lit by skylights above and the stonework arched ceiling high and airy. There were sidewalks on either side of the canal, and every so often there was a street sign that the guide pointed out and said corresponded to the street above, so that if a worker was ever in trouble in the canal, and likewise in the sewers, these signs would enable them to locate themselves when calling for help.

If the sewers of Paris had been anything like this, Imogene would have been able to read the section about Valjean carrying Marius with less shuddering horror. She knew from her history books, though, that they had been nothing like this civilized passage through the bowels of the city in the time frame of *Les Misérables*.

In about thirty minutes, they were out of the underground portion of the canal and approaching the first lock. The gates closed behind them, and the water began to churn, lifting them up to match the level of the next part of the canal.

Imogene pointed to a rat running along the top of the gate. Toni shrugged.

The canal was charming and soothing. Imogene felt herself unwinding from the tensions of dealing with Marcel and his escape, and the sadness at having to head home. This canal had been here since Napoleonic times. That sort of time span gave her hope that she herself could return to Paris.

Toni looked over to the right and grinned at Imogene, pointing out the sad little rundown building that was the Hôtel du Nord.

"Atmosphere! Atmosphere!" they chanted at each other, to the tour guide's delight and the other passengers' bemusement. Imogene had never felt more Parisienne.

The boat went all the way to the Parc de la Villette, and turned, showing the artsy side of the park along the eastern bank and the science park on the other side of the water. Then it chugged back to the beginning of the Bassin de la Villette, where the guide mentioned they could catch the Metro back to the Bastille or walk along the canal back.

"Walking was my intention," Toni said, and she steered Imogene to the west side of the canal and along the towpath.

"There is a very charming small café down along here that I think you will enjoy."

"Fine. But can we talk now?"

Toni laughed. "Yes, we can. I don't think anyone will be overhearing us as we walk, unless those old men playing boules have extrasensory abilities with their hearing aids."

"So?"

"So, the most important thing to let you know is that Marcel Rocher has been found and detained."

"You got him!"

"*Oui*, he apparently spent the night plastered to the side of the roof by the rue du Cygne, just opposite the optical illusions place? I guess he was hoping to wait us out, but someone from the building opposite spotted him and called it in, so we had him down and off to the Préfecture by breakfast time."

"And? Have you charged him?"

"Yes, with terrorism."

"Terrorism? How did you come up with that?"

"From what we could ascertain from his father, Marcel had access to body parts. It was my belief that he was planting those body parts to frighten tourists and cause a general boycotting of Paris from visitors. Since that was a means of causing fear in a populace, the charge of terrorism fit. And it meant we could hold him for six days, which is four days more than the limit on other charges. As such, we would have time to build a case if he wasn't cooperative. And of course, if that doesn't fly with the lawyers, we can aim for desecration of bodies. Or public littering."

"And have you managed to make him cooperate?"

"Once I mentioned that we had spoken with his father, he was more than cooperative. In fact, I think he was happy to talk. It all came spilling out of him like a manifesto."

"You were right, then? It was to scare away tourists?"

"Yes, there is a deeply imbedded resentment of visitors to Paris in that man. I am not sure whether it stems from his having to work so hard to get himself out of the suburbs and into the city himself, or whether he had been inconvenienced one too many times when walking past the Louvre, but Marcel Rocher does not like the average visitor to Paris, of that I am certain."

"It's a wonder he bothered to talk to me at all," mused Imogene. "I was dithering about buying cheese when we first met."

Toni laughed. "He mentioned that. But he used you as an example of how visitors to a city should behave. You were there, before him, looking to try local cheese, to sample the *vrai Paris*. And you were beautiful."

Imogene blushed.

"The other thing to mention was that he was assured that you had nothing to do with his arrest. I felt that was important for him to know."

Imogene shook her head. "That doesn't matter. I think we had already said our goodbyes."

"*Vraiment?* Ah well, I hope you will have only good memories of the tryst."

"I think so."

"Here we are! Chez Prune!"

It was a lovely little restaurant with a few tables out front on a sharp corner and more along the side of the other street. Imogene and Toni chose to sit out front, and a waiter was almost immediately at their table. He and Toni conversed very quickly in French and she turned to Imogene and asked if she liked smoked salmon.

"Like lox? Yes, very much."

"Shall I order for us, then?"

"Please do, I am off the clock when it comes to decision making."

Pretty soon the waiter returned with two frothy big bowls of café au lait, and then again with plates loaded with shaved lox with two folded crepes and some creamy sauce in a little glass bowl on them.

Imogene followed Toni's lead and used the crepes in the way she'd use a bagel at home, smearing some of the creamy sauce, which was very dill and garlic forward, on the crepe, and then spearing a layer or two of the salmon on top.

"Oh, this is delicious!" Imogene moaned.

Toni smiled and nodded. "One of my favourite places, and one of my favourite dishes."

After a few minutes of silent eating, denoting to Imogene just how hungry she had been, she sat back in her chair and sighed. "I am going to miss all of these wonderful experiences, and I am really going to miss you, Toni."

"Me, too, Imogene. It has been a delight to get to know you."

"Yes, Raymonde should advertise what *gentils* neighbours her apartment has, and she would beat out all the rest of the landlords. Speaking of neighbours, you were going to tell me about René. What was all that about?"

Toni laughed again, and then looked around her before leaning in. "René thought we were there to arrest him for defacing the buildings of Paris!"

"What?"

"Yes, he has been following in the footsteps of Invader, the street artist who puts up all the tiled video game characters?"

"Yes, I've heard about Invader."

"Well, that is René's hero. He has been concocting tiled masterpieces himself, up in his apartment above your head, and has managed to erect two or three of them already, I believe, though he wouldn't admit to that. When he began to shout, one of my men went through his door, thinking Marcel might have gone that way or was holding him hostage, so we had a valid reason to enter his apartment. Instead, we found his workshop laid all over his poor dead mother's good oak table and sideboards and him trying to squeeze himself into a hideyhole through his bedroom closet. His little *ratons* are rather sweet, but since it is technically a crime to deface the buildings of Paris, he has been fined and his materials confiscated."

"*Ratons?* Rats? Made of mosaics? I think I've seen them! They reminded me of the mouse exhibit in La Bourse, I even have photos of them. He put them close to where the barricades from the student rebellion were, the barricades in *Les Misérables!*"

"If you can find the photos, please, send them to me. Victor Hugo once again comes to the rescue," laughed Toni.

"Oh, poor gloomy little René!"

"I know," Toni said. "It makes me sad to think he has lost his *raison d'être*, but I have slid a brochure about teaching art to young people up at the Parc de la Villette into his mailbox. Maybe he can use his mosaic abilities for good?"

Imogene laughed. "I do hope so. Oh, do you think it was he who fixed the tile on the landing?"

"Very likely. I think he was very worried about being approached in his apartment and took a lot of care to be invisible. That tile might have necessitated a workman, and workmen might have had to be let into his apartment. Maybe that's why he was allied with me in maintaining the staircase as it was. Who knows?"

Imogene attempted to pay the tab, but Toni was adamant that this was her day to treat her friend. She settled up and they soon sloped away from the canal and down through the Place de la République and onto the rue de Turbigo that would take them almost directly to their door. Imogene marvelled again at what a walkable city Paris was.

"Thanks to Haussmann, whom so many love to hate," agreed Toni. "But without him, we wouldn't have these lovely sidewalks where we don't have to line up single file whenever we approach other pedestrians."

"True, but I adore the little streets around Le Marais and Les Halles. It feels like such a celebration of humanity to be able to touch a wall that generation after generation of people have touched before you. It's grounding you to the planet, like the fossil index. We have been here more than a thousand years. We walk where Victor Hugo walked, and see the skylines Napoleon knew. We drink our coffees where Sartre sat. We stroll in the gardens of Catherine of Medici. And you go to work each day, in a modern office, in the middle of all this history, and the echoes of every age resound."

Toni turned to Imogene, close to where they had originally bumped into each other, and hugged her tightly. Then, pulling back, and holding onto her by the shoulders, she smiled at the retired Canadian scholar who had come six weeks earlier, and found a friend, helped catch a criminal or two, and fallen in love with Paris.

Imogene looked at her clever young friend who was certainly going to rise in the ranks of the Sûreté, and grinned back at her.

Toni kissed her on each cheek, almost ceremonially.

"You have been romanced by our city, Imogene. I won't have to say *adieu* to you, my friend. I will say *au revoir*."

"*Oui, Antoinette, mon amie. À la prochaine!*"

# Acknowledgments

Please forgive me if I miss a name or two here. Books take such a long time to get off the ground and this ends up being the final task before the work finally goes to print. I am so grateful to everyone who helped get me back on my feet (literally and literarily) and into this grand adventure.

Thank you to my children, Madeleine and Jocelyn, who championed my plan to head to Paris alone, and then bounded over to play with me there for a few days. Thanks to Andrew for body part advice, and for tips on what to order in Paris ... and what to avoid. Blessings on Gina, who shared the name of the agency she'd once used to rent a place, and also on Raymond, my landlord, who was a wonderful host. Thanks to Lynn, once my French prof, forever my friend, for providing all sorts of advice on things to see, and the same to Larry, my chosen brother. Thanks also to Marya, who drove me to the airport. And thanks to Rita, who understands every step of this process so well, and who assisted with comparative lit phraseology. Massive thanks to Katherine who took me in for a rest after my Parisian adventure and who is the best fellow pilgrim on our highly idiosyncratic jaunts.

Thank you to the *bouquiniste* at the far eastern end of the line along the Seine who told me, on my first morning's explore, that my smile lit up his day. Thank you to the daffy Gobelin people moving the big teddy bears all over the city for my amusement. Thank you to the florist at the market who wrapped my little tulips up as if they were roses and to Monsieur Marguerite's owner who sold me magical peonies. Thank you to the jeweller on the Île de la Cité who chose the most glorious pearl earrings for me to purchase.

Steve, my utterly amusing muse, what can I say? Thank you for making the Eiffel Tower twinkle just for us.

And most of all, thank you, Paris, for being everything I dreamed of all my life: beautiful and regal, kind and wise, warm and welcoming, the most magical city on earth.

My fabulous friends Marianne, Kelly, Cheryl and Kate each listened patiently to my babbling once I realized that what I was writing was another mystery series. Ann and her wonderful family made it possible for me to get away and finish a draft, while piquing ideas for the next book. I so appreciate the generosity of all my friends online who shared in my pictures of Paris with warmth and delight, making me feel as if I was discovering it for all of us.

Turnstone/Ravenstone Press make lovely books and I am so pleased to be part of their stable of writers. Thanks to all the lovely people who read early copies of this to find all my typos and spelling errors (in two languages!). And thank you, Reader, for picking this book up, out of all the others, to while away some time with. I hope Imogene becomes your favourite travel companion.